D1489929

HOT ICE

HOT ICE

GREGG LOOMIS

MYSTERIOUSPRESS.COM

OPEN ROAD
INTEGRATED MEDIA
NEW YORK

ALSO BY GREGG LOOMIS

The Pegasus Secret

The Julian Secret

The Coptic Secret

The Bonaparte Secret

The Sinai Secret

Gates of Hades

For Suzanne

Science is built up with facts, as a house is with stones. But a collection of facts is no more science than a pile of stones is a house.

Jules Henri Poincaré (1854–1912),
French mathematician, theoretical physicist,
and philosopher of science

1

Sub-Saharan Africa
June of the Present Year

The white man wore a clerical collar and clergy black shirt. His bicycle left a narrow trail of red dust as it swerved between open sewers and around mounds of festering garbage in front of tin-roofed huts. Snarling, skeleton-like dogs, trying to scavenge anything humans had not already taken, growled but gave way. There weren't many of them left, the dogs. Cats had disappeared years ago. Most white priests had too, if for different reasons.

A few Anglicans had remained, made near mad by the African sun, feverish with dengue or malaria, or clinging to demonstrably false hopes that they could improve the lives of those who lived here. Things had, as they say, gone from bad to worse under President-for-Life Amer Bugunda.

As had happened so frequently in this part of the world, the freedom fighter in the heady days of collapsing empires had become today's tyrant; his rule had become as oppressive as any colonial power.

The problems of the country were only tangentially the reason the man was here.

Ahead, two militiamen lounged under the shade of a towering mahogany tree. In the last two days, these arbitrary posts had proliferated like mushrooms during the rainy season. The man was well aware of the reason and thankful he had been warned such roadblocks were likely.

As the priest pedaled the bike toward them, he used one hand to remove a tattered straw hat and wiped his brow with his forearm. His streaked blond hair, long for a priest, spoke of time spent in the sun, as did his tan skin. He had hoped to reach his destination before the worst of the day's soggy heat, which had already become a living monster, sucking the life from all it touched.

Dismounting, he submitted to a rough body search as well as an inspection of the small knapsack tied to the handlebars. They would find nothing of interest unless they looked closely at his feet. He was wearing not the cheap shoes common to clergy in the area but steel-toed, ankle-high waterproof boots, the sort issued to elite military units.

The boots might have raised suspicion among more alert or better-trained military, as would the man himself. Most priests here had spent the better part of their lives ministering to the needs of just one or two tribal villages. This one was young and muscular, with the physique of a man both well fed and free of the intestinal parasites endemic to the region. That meant he was a recent arrival, which, in turn, was unusual. Not even the most dedicated to God were eager to practice their ministry here these days.

Fortunately for the man in the clerical collar, these troops were neither well trained nor alert.

He simply smiled at the insults in broken English. He kept the expression in place when one of the men in uniform snatched the hat from his head and tossed it into the stinking sewer that ran parallel to the road.

"Colonial pig!" the soldier growled, using the epithet that included all white people here.

More eager to return to the shade than further torment or insults, the two militiamen waved him past. He toyed with the idea of retrieving the hat, considered the water in which it floated, and remounted.

Half a mile later, the road, no more than a trail, really, had narrowed to a point where he could have simultaneously have touched the dense bamboo groves on either side. He was well out of sight of the soldiers. He stopped, glancing around. It took him only a second to see it beside the path: a small flat rock on top of a larger one.

He dismounted again and lifted the bicycle off the dirt road and into what appeared to be a tangle of bamboo connected by impenetrable vines of strangler fig and the occasional hardwood that had spread its limbs to the sun before light-stealing bamboo had begun to sprout.

Off the road, he pushed the bike. By this point he could see a narrow path perpendicular to the road he had been traveling. He stooped to cover the bicycle with dead leaves. The rest of the trip would be on foot. If there were patrols, he only hoped he saw them first.

A few more paces brought him to a dead baobab tree across the track. He examined the ground carefully. Few insects or reptiles here did not bite or sting. He knelt, reaching inside a hole in the trunk. He produced two objects: One was a large package wrapped in waterproof canvas. The second was an oblong steel box about three feet in length.

He opened the larger one first. Inside was a camouflage shirt, pants, body-armor vest, and a smaller package that contained a compass; steel mirror; greasepaint in brown, green, and black; and a pre-programmed, handheld global positioning indicator of the type used by hikers. Propping the mirror against the log, he quickly applied the paint to his face until it resembled the mélange of colors around him. Standing, he stripped to his underwear, pulling on the clothing from the package. In the pants pockets he found a pair of cloth gloves, which he put aside for a moment while he opened the metal box.

Inside was a disassembled Heckler & Koch PSG1 rifle with scope.

He would have preferred the larger, more accurate Walther WA 2000, but the WA was intolerant of the rough treatment the H&K had likely received on its way here. Plus, ammo for the Walther was not always available. Still, the H&K 7.62 mm with its 815 mps muzzle velocity would do quite well. The 25-inch barrel and 8.1 kg weight were bulky, but the blowback mechanism was more reliable than the WA's recoil if he needed a second shot.

Most important, the Heckler & Koch was used by armies all over the world. It was untraceable to any particular country.

He assembled the weapon and checked the five-round magazine, then carefully put the scope in a pocket to be mounted later. Slipping through heavy growth presented too much of a risk of it being knocked askew or, worse, scratching the lens.

Reaching into the larger parcel, he withdrew a large, fine mesh net. Most of it was already filled with paper and plastic flora, copies of that common to the area. He would complete his sniper's blanket when he reached his destination.

One item was missing. He found it under the camouflage blanket: a knife. The hilt was a replica of a cavalry saber, with protective steel around the grip. The blade was ten inches long, no more than half an inch wide, with finely honed cutting edges on both sides. It was a weapon he had designed himself, its thin double edge perfect for stabbing or slashing without the risk of getting entangled in bone or entrails. He pulled it halfway out of its scabbard, satisfied himself the edge was razor sharp, and returned it to its case, which he stuck in his belt.

Finally, he stuffed the vest into the hollow log. Too heavy and too hot. Besides, if he was in a situation where body armor would help, he would be dead soon anyway.

Although the bamboo gave some protection from the sun, it also cut off any breath of breeze. Moving deliberately, stopping every few feet to listen, he might as well have been hiking through a sauna. Thirst had replaced heat as the enemy of the moment. He had a military canteen almost full, filled with presumably nontoxic water that morning; but he had a long day ahead. Reaching in a pocket, he pulled out a hand full of salt tablets, dry swallowed two and continued on.

An hour later, he came upon a line of termite mounds, some higher than his head. Using these as cover, he moved from one to the next, pausing under a jackalberry growing from one of the towers of dried soil. The tree's ample girth, perhaps sixteen or more feet, gave welcome shade where he paused long enough to make certain he was still alone and to check the GPS again. He glanced up at the white flowers above his head before putting the instrument away and moving on, careful to make as small a ripple in the sea of grass as possible.

When he reached a few ragged rows of sun-browned maize, he stopped. Beyond was a field waist-high weeds shared with stubby sprigs of millet, the source of the bitter beer that was the main beverage of the area. He listened to a symphony of insect buzzes, birdcalls, and sounds he could not identify before he heard it: human voices. They were both male and female, young and old, and didn't seem to move—the sounds of a village. At the same time, the faint breeze shifted, bringing him a whiff of charcoal and sweat with the faint undertone of untreated sewage, the smell of human habitation.

A few more steps and he heard women's voices approaching. He flattened himself among the spindly stalks of millet just as two statuesque women balancing water jars on their heads gracefully stepped across what would have been his extended path. Each wore bright prints and was bedecked in beads and necklaces of small bones. Their heads were shaved except for a single queue.

He waited, listening as their voices faded. Then, he stood and unrolled the loose mesh that was his sniper's blanket. Picking grass here, weeds there, the few empty spaces in its mesh were soon filled. Cradling the rifle in one arm, he pulled the material over him. Instantly, the heat blurred his vision. Ignoring his discomfort, he began to crawl.

After about fifteen minutes, he stopped and peered through the gaps in the foliage of his cover. Twenty or so mud-and-thatch huts formed a semicircle around a dirt square. In the middle of the open space, workmen were completing a platform. The men wore loincloths, along with necklaces, anklets, and armbands of bone and fur. A few wore headdresses of ostrich feathers, had painted faces, and carried long spears. Few Africans dressed in native costume in their day-to-day lives. Today was a special occasion where the normal cheap, imported blue jeans, mail-order dresses, and flip-flops had been temporarily put aside.

This was President-for-Life Bugunda's tribal village. He preferred its humble backdrop, which emphasized his native Shana heritage to the palatial presidential palace in the capital when making a speech he knew would be filmed or perhaps televised to the rest of the world.

The president was, by his own account, a humble man, was he not? A humble man who had removed the chain from his people's throat and set them free from the foot of the oppressor.

Perhaps.

He was undeniably fond of metaphors. And today's would be a momentous speech indeed, if not the way the president intended.

For an instant, the sniper almost pitied whoever was in charge of the man's security detail. A building can be secured as tight as needed. But facing acres of open space with head-high grass?

The sniper rolled onto his back, affixed the scope, and returned to his stomach before he checked the scope's stability in its mount.

Ordinarily, the ravings of African dictators were ignored by Western civilization, the brutality of an Amin or Mugabe the source of amusing headlines somewhere in the inside pages of newspapers. Genocide? No threat to national security. Famine and plague? Quarantined by oceans.

Except where national security was involved.

Months ago, Bugunda had startled the world, or at least the world's intelligence communities. ECHELON had picked up a series of telephone transmissions between Bugunda and eastern Pakistan. Thinly coded, they had been quickly deciphered. Bugunda would shortly be hosting Al Mohammed Moustaph, al-Qaida's number-three man.

Although Bugunda was no threat outside his own borders, Moustaph was one of the world's most wanted men. Suspected of engineering train and subway bombings in Europe, an attempt to blow an international flight out of the air, and a mass shooting at a beach resort in Australia, the various rewards offered exceeded the gross national product of most third-world countries.

That was where the sniper became involved.

2

Ischia Ponte, Isola d'Ischia
Bay of Naples
Five Days Earlier

Brush in hand, Jason Peters stood in his villa's loggia before the easel, not quite content with the seascape he thought he'd finished. The jagged rocks of the coast were right; he could almost feel the spray. There was something not quite right with the color of the sea, though. Of course, that color changed hourly as the sun moved. A dark, almost black morning ocean became cerulean by noon, electric by sunset.

Perhaps the fishing boat needed to be painted out.

Perhaps acrylic was not the proper medium.

He bobbed his head as the mathematics of a Mozart concerto danced through the villa. Then he put down his brush and simply admired the same view he had enjoyed for the last three years. Half a mile away, the medieval Cathedral of the Assunta crowned a hill that dropped into the sea. He could also see the fifteenth-century causeway that joined the tiny hamlet to the larger island, a rugged bit of rock that jutted out of the water like some legendary sea monster about to devour a ship and its crew.

His view was not entirely for aesthetic purposes. With the high, rocky coast, the only approach to his villa was by that path and the single road that came up the hill to his front gate. There had been a time when he had first come here that security was more important than scenery.

A loud snore was audible over the music, disrupting his artistic thought. Turning, he saw the large dog sprawled across the tiles of the floor. It was difficult to even look at Pangloss without smiling. Part German shepherd, part collie, part whatever had been available to a promiscuous kinsman, the animal personified the description "mutt." He also had been the only friend Jason had had for a very long time, a time from the death of his wife until Maria . . .

The dog awoke suddenly, lifting his head, and whined softly.

"Yeah, I miss her too," Jason said, kneeling to take the big furry head in both hands. "But she had to go to Hawaii to observe the eruption of that volcano. You understand?"

A long tongue polished a black button nose before the animal gave a sound that could have been a sneeze or a snort. With Pangloss, one was never quite certain what was going on.

"I'll take that as a 'yes.'"

Having assented, the dog stretched, extending shaggy legs in a move that, had it been made by a woman, might have been sexy. Well, maybe not exactly sexy, Jason thought, but it did somehow remind him of Maria waking from the afternoon nap indigenous to the island and all of Italy.

Maria. God, but he missed her.

Whenever she was not actively pursuing her profession as a volcanologist, she had shared Jason's villa and the dog's affection. An eruption somewhere on the globe—Indonesia, the Italian mainland, or northwestern America—meant days of absence. Worse, boredom.

Jason had gotten used to living alone before she came into his life. He had actually enjoyed having only Pangloss's company for days on end. The peaceful serenity of obscure islands had appealed to him since his life had undergone a violent change over a decade ago. He could paint without interruption and had no social obligations to waste his time. He also could keep fully apprised of who came and went, an unfortunate necessity of his former employment.

Maria had changed all that. It was well and fine that he lived what most would consider a dull life while she was in it. But when she was gone . . . ?

He sighed, turning back to the easel and reaching to pick up the brush. She was all the excitement he needed when she was there. When she was gone, memories of past adventures seemed sweet indeed. He had lived up to his promise of retirement, but that pledge might be hard to keep if the opportunity arose, the chance . . .

His BlackBerry beeped and he frowned, hands on hips.

There were no phones in the house, no landlines, anyway. Jason detested them. Always ringing at inconvenient times, bringing news he either didn't want to hear or didn't care about. There was no need on the island anyway. It wasn't as if he had to call ahead for a dinner reservation at either of the two trattoria. If he showed up, they were glad to see him. If he needed to speak to his housekeeper or one of her cousins, grandchildren, or in-laws who comprised his staff when they were off duty, he got on a bicycle and rode to their nearby house.

Since Maria's arrival and subsequent business trips, he had agreed to the BlackBerry. She was the only one who had his e-mail address. Her infrequent messages lessened the burden of her absences.

No doubt it was Maria e-mailing. What the hell time was it in Hawaii, anyway?

Jason stepped into the relative cool of the villa's interior, where the sunlight would not make the tiny screen difficult to read.

At first, he thought he was not seeing what was clearly printed: COME TO MOMMA. NAPLES A'PT 0800 TOMORROW.

Jason glanced over his shoulder as though he suspected someone might be watching the fulfillment of what might have been a wish. Mephistopheles never sleeps. His first reaction was to return text something short and obscene. That didn't work. UNABLE TO TRANSMIT appeared on the screen just as he knew it would.

"Fuckers!" he snorted.

Pangloss opened one eye.

How the hell had they known how to contact him? Why now?

He went to a seventeenth-century buffet deux corps, fussed with the iron latch, and opened the bottom doors. Removing a half-full bottle of Antinori Solaia 2006, he fumbled with the recorking mechanism and poured himself a generous glass before crossing the room to sprawl onto a couch.

The heavy Tuscan red would have gone well with the mustard flavor of a lamb dish or the garlic of roasted pork loin, two of Jason's favorites once winter's chill replaced the heat of summer. To hell with the seasons. At the moment, he wanted something thick, almost viscous.

Pangloss got up, stretched again, and came over to sit in front of him, brown eyes looking into Jason's from a cocked head.

"So, what are your thoughts on the matter?"

If he had any, Pangloss kept them to himself.

Jason took a healthy swallow of wine, the hearty red sticking to the back of his tongue for a moment. Almost instantly, his anger faded along with the lingering taste. Drinking during the day usually put him to sleep or at least made him drowsy. He wasn't thinking about that. He had been angry that the wall of privacy, if not secrecy, he had taken so much trouble to erect had been breached.

But, his logical mind interrupted: *You were just thinking about the good old days and how bored you are.*

"Maybe so," Jason said aloud, "but I don't think they've perfected mind-reading. At least, not yet."

"*Mi dispiace?*"

Gianna, his housekeeper, was standing in the doorway, a plate in her hand. From what he could see, his lunch would consist of *frutti di mare freddo*: octopus thinly sliced and tender, prawns, clams, and squid, all served cold. Sometimes it included a half *l'aragosta*—small warm-water lobster. The dish was one of his favorites.

"*Prego.*"

The Italian word that means everything from "quickly" to "pardon me" to "you're welcome."

He pointed to a long oak table, a piece he had rescued from the refectory of a Umbrian monastery. Gianna lifted an eyebrow as she noted the red wine. Jason rarely had alcohol with lunch. Even on the occasions he did, he invariably had a single beer or a glass of a Gaja, a buttery Piemonte white.

Jason managed a smile as he took the plate from her and pointedly said, *"Grazie."*

He waited until she left the room before he sat down. He was immediately joined by a ball of orange fur that plopped down on the table from nowhere. Robespierre, the cat. Robbie, as he was known, never slunk into a room with the hauteur common to felines. He dropped from something, pounced, dashed, or exploded like a missile.

"Never see you till there's food on the table," Jason observed, moving the plate away. "Fine friend you are."

Robbie licked a paw, pretending not to care. Jason knew that trick: the minute his attention was distracted a good part of his seafood lunch would disappear.

The cat had simply appeared in Jason's villa, origins and return address unknown. The only thing clear was that the animal had come in a very distant last in some feline dispute. Half an ear was missing, as was a good bit of fur and skin. The creature was so pitiful that Jason, not a cat lover, felt compelled to take him to the local undertaker who, in absence of a medical doctor, served as the community's physician and veterinarian. After their first encounter, Pangloss and Robespierre had reached a tenuous truce if not a friendship. The association involved no effort on Jason's part other than vigilance at the dining table. Besides, since no one really owns a cat, how do you get rid of one?

His logical mind returned to the text message. *So*, it persisted, *you were feeling deserted, bored, and generally sorry for yourself. Then, like a genie in a bottle, along they come and you get pissed off because your precious privacy has been violated. Jeez, give me break!*

Jason methodically peeled a prawn and began to chew. Robespierre still feigned indifference.

So?

So, I promised Maria I was through with them. No more killing, no more violence.

That's not exactly what you promised.

Oh?

She left you after that episode in Sicily when you fed that terrorist to a feral hog. . . .

Actually, it was in Sardinia.

OK, Sardinia. She left you because she couldn't stand violence. If she's not here, she won't be exposed to anything that's distasteful to her. What you promised was that if she stayed with you, you'd give up working for them and you did. Now she's not here.

I doubt she'll see it that way.

I doubt she'll see it at all. If you can do a job and be back here before she is . . .

Jason started on the cold slices of octopus, took a bite, and put his fork down. Mozart was starting over. He stood, moved Robbie to the floor, crossed the room, and changed CDs, switching to a Mendelssohn. Son of a German philosopher, the composer's sonatas had a logical cadence helpful in resolving moral dilemmas.

He finished his meal without further intrusion.

True, with Maria gone, he was bored. Also true, she could be gone for a month or more. He hadn't been off this rock in . . . He couldn't remember. What was the harm in catching the early hydrofoil, meeting someone at the Naples airport? He could always walk away, spend the day at Italy's finest archaeological museum and be back by dinnertime.

He would not have liked to explain why he put his paints away and began to search the villa for a suitcase.

As the cab from the next morning's ferry climbed above the harbor that is Naples's front door, the twin humps of Vesuvius marred the western horizon like a malignant wart. Jason remembered the observation station on the slopes of the volcano, now largely a museum, where Maria had worked and where the last part of what he recalled as the "Hades matter" had begun.

Maria.

The thought had returned that morning as he regarded his face in the shaving mirror. What kind of a guy promises the woman he loves to abandon his previous life and then goes back on his word as soon as she's gone?

I'm not going back on anything; I'm just going to the airport, he argued with himself. To say "no." After all, I'm rich because of that organization, well-off for the rest of my life. I owe them the courtesy of a face-to-face reply.

His reflection had grimaced back at him. *Yeah? Then why the packed suitcase?*

Answer: shave faster.

The taxi exited the four-lane, passed the rental-car lots, and turned into the mass confusion that surrounds the Naples airport. Fat buses farted clouds of diesel fumes as they went through the useless ritual of honking at cars blocking the entrance. Tiny Fiats discharged entire families like circus acts. Men pushed carts stacked above their heads with plastic luggage while their wives restrained small children and dogs the size of rats.

Jason climbed out of the cab while the driver was still yelling at the stopped car in front and making those obscene gestures that are part of every Italian male's vocabulary. He looked at the meter, retrieved his single bag, the one he wasn't going to need, from the trunk, and peeled off several euros. He checked his watch as he walked toward the single-story structure that was the terminal building.

07:58. Right on time.

He looked around. His guess was that he would be contacted before he entered the chaos inside that made the disorder outside look like a military drill by comparison. Italians tend to all speak at once. When several hundred are confined in a single large room, all clamoring for tickets, flight information, or simply directions to the nearest restroom (always out of order at the Naples airport in Jason's experience), the decibel level becomes ear-shattering.

He was almost to the entrance when a man in a *Polizia* uniform detached himself from a group of his fellows whose sole function appeared to be the inspection and critique of the dimensions of female passengers, a favorite pastime if not the national sport.

"*Signore* Peters?"

Jason nodded, instantly alert. He was searching the shifting mob for anyone who might show interest in the encounter.

"This way, please."

Jason followed the man to a small white Alfa Romeo with the blue markings common to Italian police cars. Before he tossed his bag into the backseat and climbed into the front, he gave the crowd a final look. If there were an observer, it would be pure luck if he spotted him in the mass of seething humanity.

The Alfa drove around the edge of the terminal and out onto the tarmac. Ahead, on a deserted concrete slab, was a Gulfstream G4, There was no corporate logo, nothing to distinguish it from other private aircraft other than the United States N-number and the fact its clamshell door was slowly swinging open. The car stopped at the bottom of the stairs built into the door. Jason got out and grabbed his bag. Before he could say anything to his driver, the police car was gone.

He looked up at the plane. He could hear the whine of its engines at low rpm, and the distortion of its exhaust rippled the air behind it. Clearly the occupants intended to keep the aircraft's systems functioning.

At the top of the stairs, he blinked, waiting for his eyes to adjust from the blinding sunlight to the dim interior.

"Hullo, Jason. Come give Momma a hug."

He didn't have a chance. Before he could respond, he was smothered between breasts that would make a silicone-enhanced Hollywood starlet look anemic while being crushed by arms the girth of telephone poles. He smelled the familiar odors of flowers, charcoal, and sweat, the odors of the woman's native Haiti.

When she finally pushed him away to look at him, he saw a huge black woman, perhaps three hundred or more pounds, swaddled in a flowing caftan with a bright African print. She was the president and sole shareholder of Narcom, Inc.

She shook a gigantic head wrapped in a turban that matched the other print. "My, my! Ain't seen you in forever! You ain' 'zactly stayed in touch with Momma. How you doin'?"

Jason suspected she showed the same affection for all of her "boys," although he couldn't be sure. By the nature of its business, Narcom was strictly compartmentalized. Other than this woman he knew only as Momma and a few of the permanent staff in Chevy Chase just outside Washington, he had met few of the company's "contractors," as they were euphemistically called. He was aware that Momma had fled her native land with the fall of the Duvalier regime and the subsequent abolition of the Tonton Macoute, Haiti's secret police, whose brutality would have shocked Stalin's NKVD. Momma had been the second in command.

Peering around her, Jason saw an office setup: desk and two chairs. He eased into one of them.

"I've been OK." He arched an eyebrow. "Retirement agrees with me."
She waved a dismissive hand the size of a football. "I figure you bored."
He started to disagree, tell her he simply was no longer available.
He didn't. Hell, he *was* bored.

How had she known? He wasn't willing to even consider the
supernatural possibilities of the voodoo she claimed as a religion.
More likely he'd been under surveillance before her call. Professional
surveillance, or he would have noticed. He found the thought both
annoying and mildly intriguing.

He shrugged nonchalantly. "What makes you think that?"

The Gulfstream's door whispered shut and Jason became aware
that there were no windows. No Plexiglas panes to vibrate with voices
to be picked up by long-range listening devices.

"That gal o' yours, she been gone awhile."

He had never mentioned Maria. Annoyance at having his privacy
invaded was quickly overcoming curiosity. "She'll be back when she's
finished what she's doing."

"But while she's gone . . ." Momma sat at the desk, the chair groan-
ing with her weight. "Mebbe you want to look at these."

She handed him three black-and-white photographs. The grainy
quality told Jason they had been shot at a distance and the subject was
probably unaware they had been taken. As he studied the face, he felt
as though he had magically been transported to the Arctic. The chill
made him wince and his hand shook with pure rage.

"Al Mohammed Moustaph! Where did you find him?"

Momma shrugged. "We didn'; CIA did."

"So, why didn't they . . . ?"

Momma reached out a massive hand to take the pictures back.
"Time they had someone in place, he gone."

Jason's voice had become nearly a growl. "You didn't bring me here
to tell me the son of a bitch escaped."

Momma waved a hand as though to calm a small child. "They
didn't get him, no. But they know where he'll be in five days."

Jason stood, making no effort to conceal his eagerness. "Where?
I'll take that bastard out for free."

Momma leaned back in her chair. "Knowin' the special feelin's you got for him, I thought of you the minute the business came our way, figured you'd be interested. But ain' nobody gonna kill him, least not yet."

"But . . ."

Again, the wave of the hand. She smiled, her teeth a crescent of white. "Jason, you always impatient. Just sit 'n' listen to Momma a minute. Job pay a flat million, your share th' reward, put in the same Liechtenstein bank. 'Course, you want to stay retired . . ."

Since its fees were paid by the US government, Narcom's only customer, freedom from taxes had always been part of the bargain. As administrations changed, however, promises were sometimes forgotten, and the jobs too risky or too dirty for official action by Washington could stir periodic outrage by the increasing number of voters who believed America could prevail against Muslim fanatics with rules more applicable to the playground than the real world. Narcom gave the government the shield of plausible deniability and numbered bank accounts were a bulwark against climates that changed, the quicksand of public opinion, politicians who routinely reneged, and the IRS who was . . . well, the IRS.

Jason forced himself to be calm. "OK. What's the catch? Even the most bleeding-heart American can see the need to get rid of Moustaph. Why can't the government do the job itself?"

Momma handed Jason another photograph, this one of a black man in a coat and tie and obviously posed. "Because this is the man you take out."

Jason recognized the face. "Bugunda? I admit few people would mourn his passing, but, far as I know, the US has no interest in his country other than wringing its diplomatic hands like everyone else over what he's done to the poor bastards living under his regime."

Momma leaned forward, a shift of so much weight so suddenly that Jason imagined he could feel the floor quiver. "Five days from now Moustaph will be visiting Bugunda, who's supposed to give a speech welcoming his fellow opponent of Western tyranny, oppression, et cetera. The United States can't afford to be caught meddling in African politics; enough people hate us there already. So, we get the job. We got men in place, Bugunda's guard, ready to snatch Moustaph. What we need is a diversion. You the best marksman I got."

"*Used* to got," Jason corrected.

Momma shrugged and Jason thought of Vesuvius shifting its axis.

"We don' get the confusion, we don't get Moustaph."

"Why not just shoot him instead of Bugunda?"

"Bugunda's got no information we want."

Jason was silent for a moment. Despite the current political sympathy for terrorists, if Moustaph were taken prisoner, it was unlikely he would be brought to the United States and questioned politely in an air-conditioned room and served coffee and doughnuts with his court-appointed lawyer present to frustrate the investigation.

In the hands of Narcom, the Muslim terrorist would be taken someplace where human rights were of little concern. They might not kill him, but after a couple of days in the company of Narcom interrogators, Moustaph would wish he were dead. And not just because of the number of virgins allotted in paradise to such brave martyrs with the blood of children, women, and innocents on their hands.

Amnesty International, the ACLU, the World Court, and others that were not charged with fighting terrorism or that were simply closed-minded might decry torture as a means of retrieving information from an uncooperative subject. Their mantra assures the civilized world that inducing pain rarely produces the desired result. Jason's experience pointed to the contrary. Every person has a breaking point, a state in which the information withheld is no longer worth the agony of physical abuse, lack of sleep, or sensory deprivation. The mind and body can take only so much before the strongest will break. Some take longer than others but, in the end, all talk. Or die in the process.

The thought of Moustaph's less-than-bright future made Jason smile. There was no torture, no agony, that would adequately repay the debt the Arab owed him.

And a million dollars wasn't exactly chump change either.

"OK, Momma, you got yourself a shooter."

3

Africa

A trickle of hot sweat burned Jason's right eye. Blinking was the only movement he allowed himself. He tried to concentrate on the activity in the center of the village.

Peering through the rifle's scope, he estimated the distance to the platform under construction. It would have been helpful if he'd had the opportunity to visit the earthen square, mark the precise location with the GPS, and compare it with his present position. There were as many armed soldiers milling around the project as there were workers. A rough calculation would have to do.

Besides, the distance was, what, only two and a half football fields? Almost a gimme in his trade.

Slowly, he moved his head to make sure someone had not wandered into his area. Certain he was alone, he adjusted the scope to 250 yards. Now he was thankful for the suffocating stillness around him. The slightest breeze could cause a millimeter or so of deviation, which, at this distance, could turn a kill into a miss.

He tried not to fret about the ammunition. Ordinarily, he loaded his own, weighing both projectile and powder carefully to ensure uniformity with practice rounds and to be careful the brass casing was perfectly crimped. The tiniest of cracks in the seal around the lead could diminish muzzle velocity and arbitrarily increase the parabola that is the path of all bullets. There had been no time for self-loading or practice.

He almost succeeded in comforting himself that for once a kill was not imperative.

But why shoot Bugunda at all?

Though certainly villainous, he posed no threat to Jason or the United States. Jason had been trained on the basic level of all military—a step-by-step suspension of morality inculcated since birth: Kill the other guy before he kills you, the basic credo of the combat soldier. From there it was a short transition to kill before your opponent *has the chance* to kill you. Not exactly a major step. Next came the leap of killing the enemy simply because he *is* the enemy, not because he poses an immediate threat, the moral justification of the long-range killers, artillery, bombs, missiles, the snipers. Anyone who kills at a range beyond his sight. Then the final abrogation of civilized society's normal mores: letting others' decisions determine who is, in fact, the enemy and therefore subject to extermination. Once that process is complete, the soul's aversion to the slaughter of one's fellow human beings is suspended and those who make a profession of it feel a high, a sense of Olympus-dwelling superiority that dwarfs mere drugs.

That is why killing can become addictive.

Jason had realized all of this but his retirement from the military had been motivated not by a sense of what might or might not be moral but by the opportunity to spend his time in other pursuits, time with Laurin, painting. But 9/11 had changed all that. The rage he had felt at the loss of his wife, followed within days of contact by Momma and her shadowy organization, had been a perfect channel for his feeling of impotence to protect the woman he had loved. The chance for some measure of revenge too sweet to bypass. The money—lots of money—was a distant second in motivation. Once he had participated in the assassination or capture of half a dozen Islamic terrorists, the line between them and their allies blurred. You were either against the extreme Muslim world or part of it. Had Maria and her aversion to any form of violence not come into his life, he supposed he would have been a Narcom "contractor" until his palsied hands could no longer hold a rifle steady.

Before he could linger on the thought, a van pulled into the square scattering children and raising a cloud of dust. The dish on top signaled its purpose as a TV truck. He watched a crew of four unload equipment and set up cameras and klieg lights as finishing touches were applied to the platform.

He was so intent on observing the television crew, he almost missed it: a light impact with the ground nearby, felt more than heard.

Jason froze, reducing his breathing to short, shallow gulps of the humid air. He was thankful he had taken the time to complete filling in the sniper's blanket, his only defense. With it over him, he was indistinguishable from the ground around him.

Then he heard a voice—a grunting, guttural language he did not understand. And he didn't need to. Someone was scouting the area to make sure it was secure. The fact he had spoken indicated more than one, probably a patrol.

As though to confirm the guess, a boot planted itself less than a foot from Jason's face. He did not dare look up. The light reflecting from his eyes could give him away. Instead, Jason slowed his breathing even more and suppressed the sudden urge to urinate. There was another voice, this one to his right. For whatever reason, the patrol had stopped literally right next to him.

He heard a familiar scratch and smelled a whiff of tobacco smoke. A metal canteen opened behind him and he could hear the sound of rapid, greedy gulps.

Swell. These guys were going to take a break right here.

Well, if he were lucky.

If not, they were going to form a perimeter around the village until after Bugunda and Moustaph left.

No plan is without unanticipated contingencies. This one, at best, could blow the mission. At worst, it could get Jason killed. Without knowing the number and location of the militiamen, there was no chance Jason could neutralize all of them. His best bet was to remain still and hope no one stepped on him.

There was a splash of liquid that splattered Jason's face. Christ, someone was taking a leak inches from his nose! Worse, the thought increased his own urge.

There was a cry and then another from the village, a swelling of voices that blended into a single wavering ululation and handclapping that Jason guessed was a traditional tribal greeting. Above it, he heard the sound of engines.

Footsteps crashed around him and retreated toward the sound.

Jason counted slowly to sixty before he dared look up. Six armed men were between him and the village, running to where a cavalcade of vehicles was charging down the narrow space between huts. A World War II vintage jeep with a mounted fifty-caliber machine gun led two Mercedes limousines followed by another armed jeep. All halted in swirling dust in front of the platform.

Forgetting his bladder's protests, Jason trained the scope on first one and then the other Mercedes as their passengers emerged. Although he had never seen the man in person, he recognized Moustaph immediately. He wore the traditional white headdress and flowing robes of his Bedouin ancestors. Carefully placing the scope's crosshairs between the Arab's eyes, Jason breathed deeply and felt his finger tighten on the trigger.

It took an act of monumental willpower to relax it.

Instead of the dark, bearded face, Jason was seeing the tiny office, more a cubicle, really, at the Pentagon on a bright late-summer day. Captain Peters, J. had already handed in his resignation from Delta Force, the Army's super-elite commandos. His last month would be spent shuffling paper in Washington instead of crawling through or jumping into some of the world's least hospitable places. He was looking forward to the day he would exchange his uniform for faded jeans and paint-splattered T-shirts. His pictures were selling well and he would soon have enough for half of the down payment on that house on the beach in the British West Indies he and Laurin were going to buy. Her real-estate investments, the ones she had inherited from her mother, would easily have covered the sum, but Jason insisted he put his money into the home too.

They had seen their last cold, drab DC winter.

Laurin, his wife of three years and a junior partner in one of Washington's premier law firms, had surprised him that morning by walking into the cubicle. Like most DC law firms, public relations—or more plainly, lobbying—was a major source of business.

Lobbyists, the people we hire to protect us from the people we elect.

One of her firm's major clients was the United States Army, which, like any large business, had its special needs that required congressional attention (or, at times, a specific lack thereof).

On this particular morning, she had finished her appointment early and dropped by to offer to fetch Jason a cup of coffee from the officers' mess two floors below. His mouth sour from the brand that came out of the Mr. Coffee in his office, he had readily assented.

In the confusion that ensued almost immediately, the one thing he remembered clearly was glancing at his desk calendar: September 11, 2001.

They never found her amid the charred wreckage. Oddly, the one thing that survived was the simple gold wedding band, identified by the engraving inside: their initials, the date of the wedding, and *per aevum*—for eternity. He still wore the ring on a chain around his neck. He needed nothing to remind him of her. She was in his thoughts always, a fact Maria not only accepted, but also found endearing. But in places like this, the pressure of the ring against his chest reminded him he was not just doing a job; he was on a crusade. Money was not the point. He had more than he would ever spend, but he would never fully enjoy it until those responsible for Laurin's death had paid in full.

It had quickly become apparent that 9/11 was not going to be avenged anytime soon and the so-called War on Terror would be the typical political football. Instead of simply nuking the country that had hosted the perpetrators of the outrage back into the stone age along with any who protested the action, forces were sent to overthrow the Taliban and rid the world of al-Qaida, an enterprise Jason found as useless as trying to find a specific ant in a series of anthills.

The only difference was that this particular ant had been identified before 9/11 and ignored by a president more concerned with the political fallout from a loose zipper.

Jason's rage and frustration found a use when he was contacted by

Momma. He had been her chief terrorist hunter ever since. The money was more than good and the job satisfaction better.

He would get them all if it took a lifetime. It was his purpose in life *per aevum.*

Now he was looking at one of the men who was as directly responsible for Laurin's death as the pilots of the aircraft who had crashed into the building; he literally had Moustaph in his sights, a dream come true. It had been Moustaph who had recruited the hijackers and who had seen that their expenses were paid while some learned to fly.

Only the thoughts of the interrogation techniques awaiting the terrorist made Jason shift the scope to Bugunda.

Wearing a lime-green suit and bright-red tie against an electric-blue shirt, he was as obvious a target as if he had painted a bull's-eye on his chest. And what looked like white patent-leather shoes, too.

If Jason didn't kill him, the fashion police might.

Jason indulged himself by taking a single sip from his canteen.

He shifted his posture, spreading his legs and wiggling his elbows into firm position to support the rifle.

Bugunda, waving more to the TV cameras than to the small gathering of villagers, was approaching a microphone. Over his left shoulder, Moustaph was applauding, as were the two men next to him. Jason studied the latter two carefully. Africans in suits with telltale bulges under the left arms. Their upper faces were shielded by the reflective sunglasses so popular among dictators and tyrants of the Third World. Even so, Jason could see they were more interested in their proximity to the Arab than scanning the audience for any potential threat.

In the country's wretched economy, small bribes accomplished a lot.

Bugunda began to speak, his voice tinny as it rattled through speakers placed around the square. Jason had no idea what he was saying but he noted periodic pauses when men in uniform, outside the view of the cameras, encouraged applause. Other men, not in uniform, circulated through the audience, brandishing sticks in case the more slow-witted spectators failed to get the message.

Jason checked his watch. The minute hand still had a little space between it and the top of the hour. Time for a final check. As slowly as possible, he turned to make sure he was once again alone. He pushed the palm of his hand against the rifle's bolt, making certain it was as far forward as it would go, closed and locked.

He had killed men before in Delta Force operations, anonymous beings he had taken with a gun, a knife, or his bare hands. He had done so as commanded without remorse or qualms. He had only killed enemies of his country who, had the opportunity presented itself, would have returned the favor. A soldier's duty. Today he was going to snuff out the life of a single unarmed individual who had done him, personally, no harm. The fact that the man was responsible for the deaths of thousands, perhaps tens of thousands, was of no particular interest. But anyone who gave succor to al-Qaida was a candidate for execution. Killing them involved no more moral issues than squashing a cockroach. All concept of kindness to one's enemies, of fair play, had been burned out of Jason along with the ruins of the Pentagon that September morning.

Admittedly, there was thrill in danger: insertion into the country, the skill of getting into position without detection. It was a rush that he now realized he'd missed more than he had thought. The actual killing would be anticlimactic. Death from a distance was never as exciting as face-to-face. Still, for the pure pucker factor, it beat painting seascapes.

He returned to his former position: legs flat and wide apart, elbows resting comfortably to support his weapon. He inhaled deeply—once, twice—and centered the scope between Bugunda's eyes before lowering it perhaps a millimeter. A shot in the middle of the forehead was desirable but it was unlikely the man would survive any head shot.

With the eye that wasn't glued to the scope he watched the minute hand of his watch go straight up before he slipped off the safety and took two more deep breaths, and then a third, which he held as he gently increased pressure on the trigger.

So intent was he on holding his aim steady he either didn't notice or didn't hear the gunfire or the crack of a projectile splitting the air at ten times the speed of sound. His first real awareness came with the impact of the Heckler & Koch's recoil and the scope's circle of blood and brains splattering onto those standing next to his target.

He waited an extra second, watching the two men beside Moustaph drag him off the platform as though to protect him from another assassin's bullet. As Jason dropped the rifle, his last glance toward the village took in mass confusion. Its inhabitants had either dropped to the ground or were staring stupidly at the corpse on the platform or generally getting in the way of those trying to flee. Men in uniforms were firing their weapons in every direction, including the sky. Those Jason assumed to be in command shouted orders at deaf ears as Moustaph was literally thrown into one of the jeeps, which disappeared in a cloud of red dust.

Leaving the rifle where it was, he slipped out from under his blanket and crawled as quickly as he could to the base of a flowering magic guarri tree—a bush, actually. Its fruit was often fermented into a potent liquor and its wood was said to have magic properties, two reasons it was never used to make charcoal. At the moment it would conceal Jason's line of retreat. A rattle of automatic-rifle and machine-gun fire ripped through the grass like wind-driven rain, snipping leaves from the maize and flattening some of the millet as though by an invisible hand. He could only hope the ill-disciplined troops were firing in every direction. Still, a random bullet could kill just as easily as one carefully aimed. Ducking his head as though to present a smaller target, he stood. Keeping the guarri in line between him and the village as best he could, he moved swiftly away on a track he had predetermined with the GPS. Even as the random gunfire began to subside, it took willpower not to break into a run. The waving of the tall grass as he crashed through would not escape the notice of even the greenest troops.

The sound of gunfire had acted as a signal. Somewhere in front of him, Jason could hear rotor blades thumping the thick, humid air. From behind him there was the sound of engines.

Now Jason was in a field covered with only waist-high grass and about fifty yards across. Some sort of horned animal raised its head, spotted Jason, and fled, followed by two more of its kind.

Floating in the middle of the lake of dry grass was an old Boeing-Vertol CH-47A Chinook helicopter, the one seen on every evening's newscast during the Vietnam War as it ferried men in and out of combat. The only difference was this one was painted black and without insignia. The payload of the Chinook had made it popular the world over for both civilian and military use. It would be as impossible to trace as the sniper's rifle.

Jason waded through the swaying grass, the chopper's twin rotors, one at each end, reminding him of a pair of dragonflies mating in flight. From his right, one of the jeeps he had seen in the village emerged from the tall grass, its fifty-caliber chattering at something behind it. A lump in the backseat was wrapped in flowing white robes.

They had Moustaph!

Someone in the Chinook saw it too, for a metal ramp appeared at the lip of the large cargo door halfway down the fuselage. The jeep bounced inside.

Jason was running now. With Moustaph on board, he had become dispensable. There was no need for anyone to take further risks to make the mission a success. The helicopter levitated a few inches. Once free of the earth, it began a slow counterclockwise rotation from the torque of its twin engines.

Jason was galloping at full speed, intent on reaching the chopper. Only a blur to his right caused him to turn his head in mid-stride to see the other jeep approaching. They had seen him and were turning at an angle that would put them between him and the departing Chinook.

His straining heart seemed to skip a beat as the chopper rose a little higher. He could see one of the crew members, indifferent to the approaching jeep's machine-gun fire, standing in the doorway. Was he waving? The bastards! They were going to leave him!

No, wait. The man was signaling. He wanted Jason to stop? Jason suddenly understood. Not stop, but . . .

He threw himself forward onto the ground just as a finger of white smoke streaked to connect the Chinook's doorway with the second jeep. There was a ball of fire as the vehicle disintegrated among flying parts both body and chassis and a thunder that rolled across the field like a storm.

Smoking debris was still falling like a gentle rain as Jason stood and brushed himself off before reaching out for the hand extended from the cargo door.

"Thanks!" he yelled, trying to be heard above the racket of the engines. "That was a little close!"

The crew member, his face half hidden by the visor to the helmet he wore, pointed to the still-smoking tube of the rocket launcher, smiled, pointed to his ears to indicate he couldn't hear, and jerked a thumb at the rear of the aircraft.

There Moustaph was being helped none too gently out of the jeep, his hands cuffed behind him and his feet shackled. The crewman nodded and grinned, a smile that invited Jason's. Stepping into the rear of the cavernous Chinook, he made sure that Moustaph was alive and in no immediate danger of anything more than the discomfort of being bound and a large, grape-colored bruise that was growing under one eye.

He stared at the terrorist whose return gaze was full of fury.

Jason smiled, remembering the old Arab proverb about revenge being a dish best served cold. Jason's had been given over a decade to cool.

4

National Security Agency
Fort Meade, Maryland
11:02 a.m. Local Time the Same Day

John Odet was certain that either his eyes were playing tricks or fate was. He shuffled the stack of photographs, wiped the magnifying glass off with a handkerchief, and started over again.

Same result.

John glanced around his diminutive office. Room enough for a nice, if small, faux wood desk, two modern club chairs, and a credenza with pictures of his family. At least his mother, father, and a couple of nieces and nephews. The director was big believer in family. Probably wouldn't be a great idea to include pictures of John and Benny, though. Although the federal government prohibited discrimination on grounds of sexual orientation, it wasn't smart to flaunt such things.

Pictures notwithstanding, John liked his office, a real step up from the cubicles he had occupied as he worked his way up the GS ladder. One of the nicest things was the new furniture he got every two years whether he needed it or not. Just before October first when the new fiscal year began for the federal government, there was a rush among all bureaus, agencies, and departments to make sure every last penny in the old year's budget was spent. Otherwise, there was the risk of some hawkeyed congressperson cutting the budget of the offending bureaucracy by the amount of unspent funds. New furniture, new computers, new everything that would ensure the budget was completely gone.

New furniture, though, wasn't what had John's attention this morning. It was those mystifying pictures.

John picked up the phone and punched in a four-digit number.

"Director's office," a female voice announced.

"Is he in, Penny?" John asked.

"Who may I say is calling?"

John suppressed a sigh. Penny had been hearing his voice daily for two years now. He wondered if the director's straight callers got the same treatment.

"It's me, John."

"Oh!" A pretense of surprise. "Let me see if he's available."

If not, he had jumped out of a window. John had greeted the director this morning in the hall, and the only way to the elevators was past John's office.

"Mr. Odet!" The director's voice boomed with the false bonhomie he used with all subordinates. "What might I do for you?"

The question, John thought, was largely rhetorical. "I'd like a few minutes of your time, sir."

"Now?"

John's could imagine the man, checking his gold Rolex as he calculated whether or not the lunch plans John was sure he had might be jeopardized, plans with someone from one of the larger and better-known intelligence organizations. The director never missed a chance at upward mobility. "If possible, yes sir."

"OK, but come on right now."

The director's office might have been mistaken for the bar of an exclusive men's country club. But then, that was where the director had spent most of his time before an enormous campaign contribution had purchased his appointment. Dark paneling with trophy cases of loving cups, bowls, plates indirectly lit. John occasionally wondered if Penny's duties included keeping them polished.

In his silk shirtsleeves, the director came around an aircraft carrier–sized desk to take John's hand in both of his own. It was though the man were running for office.

He dropped John's hand and pointed to a conference table that formed the base of a *T* with the desk. "Have a seat."

When the men were seated across from each other, the director clasped his hands and, elbows on the table, leaned forward. "So, John, what do you have that is so urgent?"

John produced a manila folder and a magnifying glass. "Pictures. Take a look."

The director gave John a questioning glance before he pulled the photographs to his side of the table.

His face wrinkled in what John would have described as disgust. "Are those *bodies* wrapped in sheets in the background?"

"Yes, sir. September 15, 2011, Gleison Colliery Mine, Wales. The mine flooded. British Coal Authority never found the true cause because the source of the leak was underwater, but they speculated simultaneous failure of the pumping system and backup. The odds of that happening were estimated at over a thousand to one."

The director lifted his head from the pictures. "And just what does that have to do with us?"

John indicated the remaining stack of photos. "If you will indulge me, sir . . ."

With a frown, the director held up another photo. "And this is . . . ?"

"The *Alaska Navigator* in dry dock. January 2012. Note the crack in the tanker's side? Far too even to be accidental, according to the Coast Guard. Lucky it was discovered before the ship took on several hundred thousand gallons of crude. Would have made the *Exxon Valdez* look like puppy poop on a rug in comparison to the damage done to the Alaskan environment."

"Good for the Coast Guard. I'm sure. But I don't see—"

John got up and walked around the table. Reaching an arm over the director's shoulder, he pointed. "See that man there, just in front of the bodies recovered from the mine disaster? Looks like one of the rescue people. Kind of blurred, but you can see his face."

John moved the photo aside, pointing to another. "Now look at this man in what looks like a Coast Guard uniform standing with the group looking up at the tanker. Same guy, right?"

The director squinted, "Maybe. But I still don't see—"

John hurriedly pulled another black-and-white out of the folder and poised the magnifying glass above the lower-left corner. "Anglo-American Platinum mine, South Africa, one of the deepest mines in the world. A collapse. The Mining Qualification Authority's findings were that somebody accidentally rammed a piece of motorized equipment against not one, not two, but three major support columns. Three columns? An accident? C'mon! And look here, right under the magnifying glass. Looks like our boy, right?"

Before the director could answer, John had whipped out a final picture. "US Gulf Coast. April 11, 2010, the day after the BP *Deepwater Horizon* blew up. This is a shot of some of the civilian craft assisting the Coast Guard in searching for survivors. Recognize the guy in the poncho?"

The director pursed his lips, momentarily swayed by his subordinate's enthusiasm. Then, "Too blurred to be sure."

John shook his head. "Take a closer look. Same broad forehead, same smashed nose."

"A lot of people have noses that look like that. Particularly ex-fighters." The director pushed his chair back from the table, fingers interlocked across his belly. "Exactly what are you saying here, that this guy is some sort of disaster tourist?"

Again, the head shake. "Not possible. Every one of those photographs was taken within hours of the accident except the one from the Gulf, and that was less than twenty-four hours later. No, our friend in the pictures had to *know*."

The director was looking at John as though he had begun speaking in tongues. "Know? But how could he . . . ?"

"The only person or persons with that knowledge would be those who caused the disasters."

The director consulted his watch, a viable alternative to talking with a madman. "Ah, yes." He stood, apparently no longer willing to have his back to someone who, quite possibly, might become violent any moment. "By the way, how did you come by those photographs? Industrial accidents aren't exactly in the scope of our mission statement."

John returned to his side of the table. "Purely by accident. One of the news services complained that they thought someone, possibly outside the United States, had hacked their network. That is within our mission, is it not, protecting the communication system?"

"Yes, yes. Of course."

"Well, turns out they have had the problem before. Like when they were covering industrial disasters."

"Who would hack a news service? Be easier to buy a paper or turn on the TV."

"Unless you wanted the physical photos."

The director's answer to that was "Look, John, you do good work. Don't make me include in your next evaluation that you went off the reservation, wasting Agency time on matters that don't concern us. Oil spills, mine collapses aren't in our brief. Now, why don't you go back to your office and continue the good work?"

The tone was that of a parent convincing a small child that there really wasn't a monster under the bed.

John knew the director would rather color within the lines than paint a *Mona Lisa*. He thought inside the box because God only knew what might be lurking outside. As long as set procedures were scrupulously followed, failure would bring no censure. Besides, no bureaucrat ever won praise for solving another bureaucrat's problem. Originality of thought was a troublesome trait in government.

John and his photographs had been dismissed.

Oh well, John thought. He had tried. The folder with the photographs went into the first trash receptacle he passed.

5

Iceland
Langjökull Glacier
Three Weeks Later

The little man parked his rented Land Rover and stared at the mass of ice in front of him. Not far north of the edge, the ice cap towered 1,200 to 1,300 meters. The woman at the car rental place had told him the scenery at the top was spectacular, but he was not visiting one of Iceland's largest glaciers as a tourist, not in the normal sense.

He looked back up the gravel road he had just traveled and saw nothing but the rocky volcanic hills that had been sculpted by millennia of ice. Nothing moved. He turned his attention to the black boulders, some bigger than houses, dotting the landscape and shook his head. Too many places from which he could be observed by unseen eyes. He sighed. Too late to worry about that now. The people he worked for wanted answers and they wanted them in a hurry.

Still, caution was called for. Taking a pair of binoculars from the seat beside him, he swept a wide arc.

Nothing.

Replacing the glasses with a cell phone, one with photographic capabilities, he stepped out onto the near-frozen ground. Even though it was summer, he was glad of the heavy sweater he had brought. These days, he was subject to chills.

No wonder. He was too old for this sort of work. But he knew no other.

He took a final look around and started walking toward a series of metal stakes near the first patch of ice. If what he had read was correct, they were markers placed by one of Iceland's glacier societies to indicate the annual summer shrinkage of the ice cap, a foot or so of tundra that had been under tons of ice since last fall.

He stopped as he spied something protruding from the white in front of him. A stick? Some sort of growth. Could that be . . . ? He snapped two pictures, checked the phone to make sure he had photographed exactly what he was looking at, and stepped closer.

He squatted and reached for what was sticking out of the ice. He gave it a tug. Frozen fast. Shoving the phone into a pocket, he reached into another and produced the bone-handled jackknife he had purchased just yesterday. In less than a minute he had an inch-or-so section of a woody, sticklike object in his hand.

This was the sort of thing his employers wanted. They should be pleased. He stuffed it and the knife into a pants pocket.

He began a slow walk along the edge of the glacier, his boots squishing in the sodden moss that, along with shards of stone, were the only ground cover. He had taken just a few steps when he stopped to examine the rocks at his feet. Something had caught a ray of the sun, drawing his attention. Natural gneiss or . . . ?

He squatted again, using his hands to brush aside pebbles polished smooth as marbles. There it was. Bronze? Copper? Maybe simply iron burnished by ice scraping across rocks. No larger than a quarter, it had been sheared from something larger but the curved, sharpened edge was quite visible. He took another couple of pictures before picking it up and putting that in his pocket too.

He was searching the surrounding area when he heard the sound of stones being displaced as if . . . as if someone were walking none too carefully on them. He fought the impulse to flee, instead pretending he had not heard. He was trying to determine the direction from which the sound had come, how far away it might be.

Not that either bit of information would be of any great help, not without a weapon.

Slowly, he stood with as much nonchalance as he could muster. He took one step and then a second before he bolted.

He was not surprised at the shot that sent something buzzing past him, but his short legs churned faster. If he could reach that clump of boulders, the one resembling a church complete with square tower, he might somehow escape. He ducked as though he might somehow dodge the second bullet that sang its evil song overhead.

The rocks ahead seemed impossibly distant; they seemed to recede with every step he took.

He pivoted on one foot, swinging to his left, then back to his right. There in the open, a zigzag was his only defense.

There was no third shot.

Not yet.

The thought was more frightening than the gunfire. The shooter must be confident he was going to get close enough to make the next try successful. The theory was accurate: he could hear the footsteps behind him getting closer. There was no need to look over his shoulder. He knew who his pursuer was. Or who had sent him.

He felt the knife in his pocket. A jackknife against a gun? Absurd. But the only thing he had. If he could just reach that pile of stones, he might find a place to hide, perhaps even ambush . . .

The ragged sound of his own breath and the ache in his lungs required him to devote full attention to simply inhaling and exhaling. A stitch slashed at his side as painfully as any blade.

He was surprised when his hand touched rock. He climbed onto the massive formation.

He slipped behind the first boulder and squeezed through a crevice he hoped was only wide enough to accommodate his small body. Looking around for a possible hiding place, he spied a crack in the rock level with his chin. About a foot long, but deep. He couldn't secret himself there, but the fissure would hold his discoveries. In an instant he had slid the cell phone, the stick, and the piece of metal into the crack.

Then he had an idea.

If he could scramble down the other side of the formation, maybe, just maybe, he could creep away while the other man searched for him here. No chance. Other than a scattering of boulders, the landscape was as naked as a newborn baby.

"Boris, why do you flee an old friend?" The words were in Russian.

The little man spun about to see a man holding a GSh-18 9 mm automatic pistol. The distinctly mid-Asian flat face with the flat nose, broken multiple times, was all too familiar. "Old friends do not shoot at each other, Patrivitch."

Patrivitch glanced at the weapon in his hand. "It is my job just as it is yours to be here. Sad but true. You have been hired to find certain information; I have been paid to make sure you do not." He extended the hand that did not hold the gun. "The cell phone. Place it at your feet."

The man had been watching him take pictures.

Boris shrugged. "I dropped it during the chase."

"Empty your pockets."

Boris did so, the jackknife clattering to the stone along with a wad of Icelandic króna and the keys to the Land Rover.

Patrivitch tsk-tsked. "I would have seen the phone had you dropped it."

"If you were looking for me to drop something, no wonder your first two shots missed."

"I can search for it after I kill you."

Boris shrugged. "What happens after that is of no concern to me."

There was no warmth in Patrivitch's smile. "You always had a smart mouth."

He pulled the trigger.

Boris spun from the impact, a kick as though a horse's hoof had struck his chest. His face hit the solid rock upon which they were standing, sending a jolt of pain through his entire body. Broken nose, he thought sleepily. Odd, no pain in my chest, just my nose.

Though Boris's vision was quickly becoming dark, he recognized his assailant's shoes level with his eyes. He sensed the man leaning over him.

The coup de grâce.

He was too drowsy to care.

Patrivitch straightened up, turning his head as though scenting the air. He had heard something. . . .

There it was, the bleating of a sheep.

Cautiously, he peered around the edge of a boulder facing Boris's car. A shepherd with a dozen or so sheep. Too close not to hear the shot that would finish his victim. He mentally wavered. He could fire the fatal shot and then flee. Or he could take out the shepherd, too.

No, too risky. There might be others around. Better to report back that Boris was no longer a threat. Besides, if anyone found the phone, small chance they would look for any photographs or, if they did, have any idea as to the significance of the images they might find.

Shoving the gun into his belt, he left by the opposite side of the rock formation, keeping it between him and the shepherd. When he reached the base, he broke into a jog.

6

Isola d'Ischia
Italy
Later the Same Day

Jason didn't hear Maria step onto the loggia, the adoring Pangloss padding at her heels. She watched Jason concentrating on the canvas on the easel before turning down the sound system, reducing the joyous can-can of Offenbach's *Orpheus in Hades* to little more than a tinkle.

He turned, his puzzlement turning into pleasure. "Well, hello there! I thought you were still sleeping, fighting jet lag."

"Sleep? With the whole chorus line of *Moulin Rouge* prancing through the house?"

He gave her an admiring look. Maria Bergenghetti. Dark skin, sun-streaked hair so black it had blue highlights like a crow's wing. When she smiled, as she was doing now, she displayed a Chaucerian Wife of Bath gap between her front teeth that, if not saying she'd had it in her time, said she could have the world if she so desired. The shift she wore almost concealed a figure that women half her age would envy.

"Perhaps you'd rather hear Tchaikovsky."

She put her hands to her ears. "Those damn cannons are worse than the dancers, and the church bells give me a headache."

Maria preferred Kenny Rogers to Rachmaninoff, Hank Williams to Wagner. Although born Italian, she had gone to college and grad school in the United States, absorbing odd pieces of American pop culture as well as Americanized English with a Western twang. Her interest and passion, though, were volcanoes. She had returned to work for the government of her native land. After all, few volcanoes were privately owned.

Truthfully, Jason enjoyed American country music too; he simply couldn't paint and listen at the same time. The tragedies of deserted lovers, broken trucks, runaway trains, and the other subjects the singers lamented were distracting.

And Pangloss insisted on accompanying each with the most doleful of howls.

Jason changed the subject. "So, what time is your body on now? What time is it in Hawaii?"

She shook her head. "Two days ago, a week from now. Who knows? I'm tired of being tired. Think I'll go into town, see what's new."

"Nothing since the Normans left about four hundred years ago."

"OK, so I'll see the same old stuff. But I haven't seen it in a month. Want to come along?"

He gave the invitation some thought. "Why not? Maybe I can find a *Herald Tribune*, see how Washington's doing."

"First in war, first in peace, and last in the National League East."

He smiled at the hoary joke. The Washington baseball team had arrived from Montreal long after Jason had left the town house in Georgetown that he had shared with Laurin; but, like so many expats, following a sports team was a trace of a homeland he both missed and to which he had no intent of returning. The English-language paper also featured *Calvin and Hobbes*, a favorite comic strip long since absent from American papers.

"Suzuki or Suzuki?"

Motorcycle or car.

Upon arrival on the island, Jason had purchased a well-worn Suzuki Samurai, a small jeeplike vehicle with an underpowered engine but a clutch and four-wheel drive that were equal to the surrounding hills. Its two rear seats were almost large enough for two adults and served as carrying space for his canvasses, groceries and, when Maria was with him, Pangloss. The quality of the car had induced him to buy a used 250 cc motorcycle by the same manufacturer, a machine for which Maria did not share his enthusiasm.

"Does it matter?"

"Try wearing a skirt on the back of a bike and ask that question."

"A zillion Italian women don't ask it; they just do it."

"The cause of large families."

Robespierre appeared from nowhere and began to rub against Maria's leg. Pangloss eyed the cat with canine caution.

"If we take the car, we can include Pangloss," Maria said helpfully.

Jason was already wiping his brushes clean. "The car it is, then."

The road to the causeway consisted of more potholes than pavement, each of which produced a grunt of discomfort from Pangloss in the rear. Before Maria could begin her normal complaints about the speed at which Jason insisted on driving, he initiated a conversation.

"You were so tired when you got in last night, I didn't have a chance to ask: How was the trip?"

She related the airlines' latest atrocities, now routine in the course of air travel. "Other than that, nothing you'd find interesting. And you?"

He gave her a nervous glance before returning to concentrate on what passed for the road. "Me?"

"I'm not talking to the dog. Gianna told me you were gone a couple of days."

Jason cursed himself for not swearing the housekeeper to silence. "Oh, I got tired of just hanging out, decided to go over to the mainland."

He knew there was no chance this was going to satisfy her but it did give him a second or two to think.

He could feel the heat of her blue eyes burning into him. "Jason, you remember Casanova."

The name by which she referred to her ex-husband, a man who seemed to be as capable a liar as he claimed to be a lover. The name came up on those rare occasions Jason had reason not to tell the whole truth.

"Never met the man."

"Jason . . ."

He sighed heavily. "OK, so I had a friend in Africa who needed some help . . ."

"This wouldn't be same friend who nearly got us killed in the Hades thing, would it?"

Jason sighed again, the sound of a man who had just realized his alibi was sinking faster than the *Titanic*. "OK, so, yeah, it was." He saw the storm clouds gathering. "Why not? I mean, you were gone, off watching some volcano on the other side of the world. . . ."

"You promised."

Where was his logical mind now?

"I promised I'd have nothing to do with those people as long as we were together. I don't call your being gone a month or more at a time 'together.' What if I asked you to stop climbing around erupting volcanoes? That's dangerous, too, y'know."

She let go of the hand grip she had been holding on to as the car jolted down the road and entwined her fingers in her lap, something she did when she was giving something deep thought. "Then, I suppose, I would have a choice: quit or stay with you. I would not agree to do one thing and sneak around doing the other."

She noted the set of his jaw. "Jason, I love you. Is it too much to ask that I don't have to worry about you getting killed? Or, for that matter, my getting shot at? I never want to be forced to actually kill someone to save your life again. I mean, you yourself say you have more money than you'll ever spend. Can't you live long enough to try?"

"Not if it means letting those animals who are responsible for Laurin go free," Jason said through clinched teeth, not taking his eyes off the road. "Not if it takes the rest of my life. Can't you understand that?"

Maria turned in her seat to face him, putting a hand over his on the steering wheel. "I understand you loved her very much, still do, and I accept that. But when you're full of hatred, how much can you love me?"

Neither metaphysics nor rhetoric was a subject in which Delta Force trained its members. Neither had he taken either course in college. Jason regretted the omission.

He placed a hand on her leg well above the knee as he turned onto the narrow causeway that led to the main part of the island. "I tried to show you how much I love you last night. . . ."

She removed his hand impatiently. "I was just too tired. Besides, sex and love aren't the same. My ex demonstrated that enough. I—"

She followed his eyes. A large cement truck had turned onto the far end of the causeway. A construction company had brought several over on a special ferry from the mainland to do some work in the town. But there were no roads on this side of the causeway that would accommodate a vehicle of that size.

And there was no building going on.

"What . . . ?" Maria began.

Instantly alert, Jason shushed her with a hand gesture, looking over his shoulder. He stopped and quickly shifted into reverse and began speedily backing up, to the consternation of two motor scooters, a cyclist, and a pocket-sized Fiat 500. Two pedestrians, older women, crossed themselves as they scurried to the other side of the road.

Maria turned from staring out of the open rear flap of the Samurai's canvas top and looked at the truck approaching with increasing speed. "Is he drunk, crazy, or both?"

Jason glanced to the front too, and then backward. The end of the causeway he had just left seemed impossibly far away. "I don't intend to stick around to find out."

The truck, smoke snorting from its vertical exhaust like the breath of a dragon, was rapidly filling the Samurai's windshield. The road was barely wide enough for two small cars to pass. There was no room around the oncoming behemoth. The causeway here had been originally built centuries ago across a narrow stretch of swampland that connected the two islands. Although eventually paved, there had been no reason to widen it or to add shoulders. Leaving the road meant running into a tidal bog of unknown depth, one that, under weight, could easily crumble into the sea that had been nibbling at the edges of the road since rock, pebbles, and sand had been used to steel it from the tides.

"Jason, that truck is going to hit us," Maria said in a surprisingly calm tone.

She was right. Unless Jason could win the race to the end of the causeway behind him, there was no place to go. And it didn't look like the contest was going in his favor.

7

It was becoming obvious that Jason was losing the race. He wasn't going to get to the end of the causeway in time.

The causeway.

Shoving the lever that activated the Suzuki's four-wheel drive, Jason drove over the lip of the pavement. Tires spun, hissing a rooster tail of mud, sand, and seawater into the air.

Then the tires caught, the sudden traction sending the diminutive car jolting forward.

"Jason," Maria gasped, "you can't . . ."

He ignored her as he began a sweeping crescent with the cement mixer at its center. The problem, he thought, was that there was no way to tell where the foundations of the causeway abruptly dropped off into the sea. At any second, the Suzuki could run off the shelf, overturn, and sink with all aboard.

The truck's driver suddenly became aware his prey was about to escape and abruptly turned off the pavement also. Just as Jason had anticipated, the much heavier truck did not fare as well as the much lighter Suzuki. The second its double rear wheels left the road, a geyser of muddy mix shot into the air, and it came to an abrupt stop and listed to the right like a sinking ship.

Jason made another abrupt turn, heading straight for the larger vehicle. When he was within a few yards, he brought the car to a stop, hopping out.

"Jason! What—?"

Without pausing in the knee-deep water, he shouted over his shoulder. "Drive back onto the pavement!"

As he reached the side of the cement mixer, the driver was halfway out of the window. By now the door was partially submerged and Jason guessed it had either jammed or was being held shut by water pressure. Jason made a grab for the driver's shirt but was met with a swish of a knife's blade splitting the air.

Jason sloshed his way a few steps toward the back of the big rig, where the driver couldn't quite reach him and had to strain to see to the rear. With a leap, Jason had an arm around the one that held the knife. He took a step forward, slamming the arm down onto the windowsill. The sound of the cracking ulna and a scream of pain seemed simultaneous.

The knife splashed harmlessly into the murky water.

With both hands grabbing the man's shirt, Jason wrestled him through the open window. Jason wrenched the injured arm behind the driver's back, forcing him to kneel in the water. If the man was not an Arab, he certainly could have passed muster for one. Dark-skinned and bearded.

Jason placed a knee between the man's shoulders, forcing him forward so that his face was only inches from seawater. "Who sent you?"

Turning his head, he spat in Jason's general direction.

Leaning forward, Jason forced the struggling man's head underwater. He watched until the frenzy of bubbles calmed before he used his free hand to grab a handful of hair. Gasping, spluttering, the truck driver gulped air as though the supply might run out.

"Now, we'll try one more time: Who sent you?"

Although Jason spoke no Arabic, he was fairly certain he was hearing curses, not names.

The man's head went back underwater. This time Jason waited

until the bubbles ceased before pulling him up. At first, Jason thought he might have waited too long, but the man coughed into life like a balky car motor on a cold morning.

"Glad you're back with us. Now, absolute last chance: Who sent you?" Silence.

This time Jason had every intention of drowning his former assailant, but there was a tug on his arm.

"Jason, no!"

Maria had come up behind him. "Jason, you're killing him!"

"Maria, the man tried to run us over, squash us like bugs. What do you suggest, that I sue him?"

"You can't just drown him in cold blood!"

"There's nothing cold about my blood. I'm mad as hell."

Maria was pleading but those blue eyes were angry. "Jason, let him go."

"Why? So he or one of his buddies can try again and maybe succeed?"

"You can't just kill him."

"Watch me."

"Jason," she pled. "Violence begets violence. You kill him, then they come for revenge. It has to stop somewhere."

Maria covered her mouth with her hand. "My God!" She was pointing. "You already killed him!"

Jason looked down. There were no more bubbles. He let go and the man pitched forward, facedown. "Problem solved."

Maria's face went white. She stooped to kneel in the water and pull the man's head above water, glaring at Jason "You, you . . . you murderer!"

"Maria, be rational: He goes free, you think he's going to thank us? Maybe with a long-range rifle shot or a bomb. The only way you deal with those people, the only thing they respect, is force. They want paradise; I intend to help them get there."

The dead man began to cough. His eyes opened. Then he vomited seawater.

"Looks like this conversation is moot," Jason observed, nodding toward the spectators who had gathered on the causeway, including police.

Someone had used their cell phone to summon the authorities. Another reason to hate the things. Now there was no way Jason could finish.

8

One Hour Later

Corporal Guideo Finallia, the ranking member of the main island's three-man force, accompanied Jason and Maria to the door of the small police station. He had been assigned to this island to finish his time until retirement and was unhappy to be confronted with something more complex than a tourist whose pocket had been picked.

He ran a handkerchief across his sweaty face as he saw Jason and Maria into the street. He was clearly glad to say good-bye to Pangloss. The dog had behaved well but his sheer size could be intimidating to a stranger.

In the piazza across the street, the local open-air market was in full swing. Under canvas flaps, fish and other seafood were displayed on melting ice, to the delight of flies. Next to the fishmongers, butchers readily cut chunks from whole sides of beef, lamb, or pig or sold skinned rabbits hanging from horizontal bars, their long ears assuring the customer he was not buying a rat. Still-feathered ducks and chickens hung alongside. Farther along, fruit-and-vegetable sellers haggled with scarf-clad grandmothers and summer residents' wives in designer pantsuits.

"The mens from Naples come," the policeman said in broken English, "take this man away. He no have . . . er, proofs."

"Identification?" Maria prodded.

"*Sì,* no ident-ti-fi-cation," he confirmed gratefully. "Peoples on the road see what he do." He looked at Jason. "He take truck, steal. You no know why he try to run you over?"

It was the fourth time the officer had asked the question.

Jason shook his head. "Maybe he has something against Jap cars."

The officer put a chubby arm on Jason's shoulder. "We find out."

"I hope so. I can think of a lot better ways to spend my time than dodging cement trucks."

Finallia looked puzzled, his thick eyebrows arching into a *V* over his nose. "Dodging?"

"Er, looking out for, getting out of the way of."

The policeman smiled. "Ah, you make the joke! Americans always make the joke!" Then he became serious. "No worry. Company lock up rest of cement trucks."

"That's comforting to know."

Finallia gave Jason's hand a perfunctory pump, started to pat Pangloss on the head, and then thought better of it. "Go, have a little pasta, maybe pizza. No worry."

They had taken no more than a dozen steps when Jason stopped.

"What?" Maria wanted to know.

It was the first word she had spoken to him since they had left the causeway.

Jason nodded. "That man in front of the pottery stall. He's watching us. No, don't look up. . . ."

Too late. The man Jason had spotted turned, shoving his way through a crowd whose white sneakers, souvenir T-shirts, and sunburned faces and arms marked them as cruise-boat passengers on a day trip as surely as any brand signified ownership of a cow. Jason took two steps in pursuit before realizing the futility of giving chase.

Maria maintained the same frigid silence she had begun before they left the causeway as she walked beside him up to the top of the hill toward Angelina, the Little Fisher-Girl, a trattoria specializing in local seafood. Its limited outdoor tables were already full of diners and a line had formed beside the entrance to the outdoor dining area, a small square delineated by potted bay trees.

Aside from decent fish and crustaceans, Angelina had made a concession to the largely American clientele it enjoyed in the summer: two large-screen TVs, tuned to CNN Europe. By September, Formula One races, soccer matches, and other events appealing to locals would draw customers to sip beer, wine, coffee, and grappa. The idea might make commercial sense, but Jason hated dining to the background of the talking heads, even if their voices were inaudible above the murmur of diners' conversations.

The owner and maître d', Giuseppe, met them at the entrance, his perpetual smile firmly in place. "*Signore* Peters, *Signorina*." He bowed his head in that form of unctuousness particular to restaurant personnel greeting a big tipper. "Your table is ready."

Their table was always ready even though Angelina took no reservations. The GTAEPS principle was as effective here as it was in New York, Los Angeles or, for that matter, Singapore: "Generous Tips Always Ensure Prompt Seating"—particularly in many European establishments where the gratuity is included in the bill. It also ensured Pangloss was as welcome as any other customer.

An English couple at the head of the line muttered angrily as Giuseppe whisked Jason and Maria to a table just now being cleared by one of the waiters Jason recognized as the proprietor's youngest son. Pangloss settled by Maria's chair expectantly. A few scraps always found their way to his place at Angelina.

Seated, Jason pretended to be enjoying the view. Over a sea of red-tile roofs, the harbor was visible and, beyond, the blue of the Bay of Naples faded into a gray haze. Fishing boats, no more than open rowboats at anchor in neat rows, bobbed gently in the swell. Their nets were spread to dry on the khaki-colored rocks of the breakwater like bright orange moss.

By the time he looked back at the table, a glass of white wine was frosting its glass in front of him. Another perk of tipping. Most Italians claimed that cold killed the taste, preferring their *vino blanco* only slightly chilled below room temperature, if at all. Jason was more than willing to concede the point: dulling the acidic bite of most Italian whites was to be desired. For the euros Jason left on the table after eating here, Giuseppe would have cheerfully served the wine as ice cubes.

Maria was studying her menu, although she had been here enough to have it memorized. They always ordered one of the catches of the day, anyway. "You nearly killed that man, you know," she finally said reproachfully.

Jason felt eyes on him from neighboring tables. He leaned forward, speaking softly so he could be heard only by Maria. "You may wish I had. He has some pals already on the island and I doubt they're here to buy my paintings."

Her blue eyes peered over the top of the menu. "The man in the market? He could have been anyone."

"Possible," Jason conceded. "But he sure took off when he realized I'd spotted him. I'd bet he was surprised we weren't so much shark chum out on the causeway."

"You mean he was with the guy who tried to run us over? Why would they want to kill you?"

Jason shrugged. "I guess my popularity rating has slipped."

Maria put her menu flat on the table and leaned forward on arms crossed. The pose pushed up her breasts, giving a tempting view of cleavage. "Let me see, now: for three years we live on this island where the greatest threat is boredom. I leave for a few weeks and you do a 'friend'"—she made quotation marks in the air with her fingers—"a favor. A few days later, some unknown person appears on the island, steals a cement truck, and tries to run us down. You don't suppose there's a connection?"

"Sarcasm doesn't become you."

"Killing people doesn't exactly enhance your appeal either."

Jason was acutely aware of the silence at neighboring tables. "Any chance we can continue this discussion in private?"

She flushed as she noticed the curious faces around them. The menu went up again. "Sorry, I should have . . ."

But Jason wasn't paying attention. He was riveted to one of the television screens.

It was filled with a photograph of Al Mohammed Moustaph.

9

Getting up from the table, Jason moved to the big-screen TV, where he could just hear the news announcer's voice. The man spoke with that certain authority Americans always attribute to a British accent.

". . . Moustaph, reputed to be in the command structure of al-Qaida, was kidnapped while visiting Africa."

The screen shifted to a strangely familiar scene. It took Jason a second to recognize the black helicopter in a storm of African dust.

The film crew! The fucking TV equipment he had seen before he shot Bugunda! They must have had a cameraman in the pursuing jeep!

"Although no one has claimed credit for the abduction, an anonymous al-Qaida spokesperson, speaking on Al Jazeera, the Qatar television network, has blamed 'the criminal element posing as governments of Western countries.'"

The camera panned the open area and Jason felt a wave of nausea sweep over him. There he was, running for the chopper for all he was worth. The camera zoomed in just he threw himself to the ground.

It was less than a second but his face was clearly recognizable before he disappeared into the tall grass. The scene went suddenly blank, no doubt as the rocket demolished the jeep and its occupants.

The announcer's voice continued unruffled, as though giving the match results at Wimbledon. Moustaph's picture replaced the helicopter. "The Muslim extremists threaten unprecedented attacks on Western countries if Mr. Moustaph is not released from wherever he is being held."

"Now we know why someone wanted to kill us."

Jason had not noticed Maria come up beside him.

"Huh?"

"The little 'favor' you did in Africa for your friend," she said in the even voice she used when most angry. "Looks like it might not just get us killed, but innocent people all over the world, too. You must be very proud of yourself."

"How was I to know . . . ?"

"Jason," she said as though addressing a dim-witted child, "how many times have I told you? Violence begets violence. It is an unending cycle that must be broken to end."

Tell that to the people in the World Trade Center, he thought. Or, for that matter, at Pearl Harbor. But he said, "The man was responsible for Laurin's death. I was hardly prepared to kiss and make up."

She arched one unplucked eyebrow, an expression he somehow always found sexy. "And I am not prepared to live with a man who continues the killing."

Spinning on her heel, no easy task since she was wearing flip-flops, she whistled to Pangloss and marched out of the trattoria, followed by every eye in the place.

Giuseppe could not have hired better entertainment.

Jason caught up with both Maria and Pangloss halfway down the hill.

"Maria, you won't be safe if you leave."

She stopped and faced him, hands on hips. "And I will be safe *with* you? They will make sure I am out of the house before someone tosses a bomb into it?"

Pangloss was following the exchange as though they were passing a meaty bone back and forth.

"We'll leave. We have to leave. We'll go someplace they can't find us."

"Really? And where would that be, the South Pole? No, Jason, they saw your face, know who you are. They followed you to this little speck in the Bay of Naples, they would follow you to Timbuktu."

"I hear Northwest Africa can be quite charming."

She stamped her foot, barely missing Pangloss's tail. "Make a joke if you like, I am not putting my life at risk so you may enjoy the luxury of revenge."

With that, she turned and marched toward the car, rigid as any soldier on parade.

Minutes later, the Suzuki was straining up the hill toward the villa. From the bottom, a car had been visible, parked in front of the gate.

Maria spoke for the first time since leaving town. "Aren't you curious who that is? It might be . . ."

"I doubt al-Qaida would announce its arrival by leaving a car in plain view."

Maria wasn't so sure. She was looking around at the surrounding landscape. "Well, I guess it doesn't matter, does it? I am leaving as soon as I can get packed."

"Leaving? For where, your friend Eno in Turin?"

Eno Calligini was Maria's uncle by marriage. Given his rugged good looks, flowing silver hair, and commonality of interests with his niece, Jason had suspected the relationship might have been, at one time, more than avuncular.

Her expression obviated an answer. "I'll go where I please."

"You already do. You were off in Hawaii when I went to Africa, remember?"

She turned around to sit straight in her seat, arms folded, the cold stature of a maiden frozen in rigid marble.

Jason knew better than to even try to appease her in this mood. He drove up to the gate and, using the electronic device, opened it. The Suzuki squeezed by the other vehicle, a dusty Volkswagen Passat. On Ischia, anything that had a backseat that really could hold two adults was considered a luxury car.

10

Maria was out of the Suzuki before Jason could kill the engine. Even her well-shaped rear end seemed to have an angry swing to it as she strode across the piazza. Pangloss whined and jumped out of the car to follow.

"Ingrate!" Jason muttered, preparing to follow as well.

She was standing at the outside entrance to the upstairs loggia as he hastily climbed the stairs. "Maria . . ."

He stopped dead behind her. Over her shoulder he could see an immense black woman filling most of a sofa. She was dressed in a garishly colored loose-fitting caftan. Pangloss had his head in her lap as she scratched his ears, murmuring softly.

Momma.

Gianna hovered nearby, ready to fill Momma's glass from a black-and-white-labeled bottle of Gaja chilling in a nearby bucket.

"Please, make yourself at home," Jason said, stepping around the still-awestruck Maria.

Momma looked up from the dog as though suddenly aware of Jason and Maria. "Jason! Come give Momma a hug!"

Jason stood his ground. "At the risk of sounding inhospitable, might I ask what you're doing here?"

She shook her head, setting multiple chins in motion like Jell-O. "Doing? Well, I'm enjoying the company of your dog—Pangloss is his name? And I'm also enjoying a delightful and refreshing Piemonte this wonderful woman offered me."

Gianna shrugged. "*Signore,* I no offer ennythin'. She ast an' I . . ."

Jason nodded to his housekeeper. "I understand, Gianna. Not your fault."

With a last resentful scowl at Momma, Gianna departed toward the back of the house.

"Really, Jason, I wouldn't think you'd begrudge . . ."

He noted the customary dialect had dropped from her speech. Her English could be as precise as his when she chose. And he could guess whom she was trying to impress.

"Think again. My privacy is my own."

Maria finally spoke up. "Jason, who is this woman?"

Jason didn't take his eyes from his visitor. "We used to do business together."

Momma rose with a grace one would not expect of a woman of her bulk, crossed the room, and smothered Maria's hand in hers. "And you must be Dr. Bergenghetti. May I call you Maria?" She reached out to touch the scarf around Maria's neck. "Hermès, right? Hard to miss those beautiful colors. And all this time I thought Jason was exaggerating how pretty you are! You're so lucky! He simply adores you!"

Jason was quite sure he had never mentioned Maria to Momma. For that matter, he realized with a jolt, he'd never said anything about having a dog, either.

Jason sensed that Maria's hostility, if not melting, was at least showing signs of a thaw.

Momma led Maria back to the couch, still holding her hand. "And I understand you're a scientist, too! You certainly don't look like one."

Maria smiled weakly. "I will take that as a compliment."

Momma's effervescence was as uncharacteristic as speaking in exclamation points.

"As delighted as we are to have you here, I'm guessing this isn't a social visit," Jason said.

If she noted the sarcasm, Momma ignored it. "Actually, you're right. I do have a bit of business to discuss."

She looked pointedly at Maria.

Jason shook his head. "This is *our* home. There's nothing you can say to me you cannot say in front of Maria."

"Of course, darling," Momma oozed. "It's just that . . . well, I have no idea how secure this house is."

"Secure?" Maria asked, as though Momma might think the structure was about to slide down the hill into the sea.

"She means she doesn't know if anyone else might be listening," Jason explained. "You know, bugs."

Maria was less than happy about the implications of that. "Why would anyone want to listen to us?"

Jason was about to explain how in Momma's business paranoia was like an inoculation against a potentially deadly disease when Momma went over to a pair of French doors. "It's a beautiful day. Why don't we all sit outside?"

Maria remained seated. "No! I want to know why someone would, what is it? Bug, yes, bug the house."

Momma was already opening the doors that led out to a small balcony and a table with four chairs. "I couldn't guess, dearest. All I know is that when I arrived here an hour or so ago, all everyone was talking about was the American who nearly got run over by a cement truck. How many Americans on this island, Jason?"

"OK," Jason conceded gruffly, "but I still want to know—"

He stopped in mid-sentence. There was a man sitting at the table, a man whose skin was the color of midnight. Even seated, Jason could see he was tall, perhaps seven feet. His hands rested in front of him on the table, hands far too big for a normal person. But his most remarkable feature was his eyes. They reminded Jason of pebbles polished by a stream: smooth, shiny, and lifeless. The man slowly got to his feet, confirming Jason's original estimate as to height. Despite the heat, he wore a suit of some rough black material. There was no sign he was uncomfortable in the temperature, no sweat on his black face, no dampness under the arms of his suit. Jason recalled the stories of Haiti's zombies—men and women not quite dead but not alive, either.

"Oh, how careless of me," Momma chortled. "This is Semedi, my friend and driver." She turned to Maria. "You won't believe this, but I never learned to drive."

More likely, she had never submitted to the scrutiny of identification that went with a driver's-license application.

Driver and bodyguard, Jason guessed. But he said, "Semedi? That's patois for Saturday, right?"

"Also the name of one of our *loa*, or voodoo spirits," Momma added.

"The *loa* of death, as I recall," Jason added.

If Semedi understood any of the conversation, he gave no sign.

Momma sat on—or, rather, filled—one of the chairs, fanning herself with her hand.

Jason sat across the table from her as Maria slid into the remaining seat.

"OK," Jason began, "to what do I owe the honor of the first visit you've ever made to my home—any home?"

Although speaking to him, Momma's eyes were searching the landscape, perhaps looking for long-range spyware. "Yesterday morning I received a call from a policeman in Iceland."

Jason knew she wanted him to ask a question, but he remained silent.

"You remember Boris Karloff?" Momma asked, relevant to nothing Jason could think of.

What was this, some trivia contest? "Sure. Stage actor turned to movies in the late thirties, did a number of Frankenstein films. Even had a TV show in the fifties."

Jason swallowed his curiosity. Damned if he'd play one of Momma's games.

She shook her head, tinkling long, drooping beaded earrings. "Not the same. He was one of our—ah—contractors. Little guy, always wore a hat of some sort. I think he was Russian, Eastern European, something like that. You were"—she shot a glance at Maria—"You were investigating a fraudulent scheme by a consortium of Russians. Boris was the one who fingered, pointed out, the head guy."

Jason recalled now. An in-and-out hit job. Boris had been a minor but important player, a gnomelike little man who had put a face with a name that, left alone, would have made Bernie Madoff's escapades seem penny-ante, bankrupting several European financial institutions and, quite likely, precipitating a panic not seen since the Wall Street crash of 1929. The little guy always wore some type of head covering—to cover pointed, elflike ears? At the time, he had seemed remarkable only because few who worked for Narcom ever met others who did.

"He was so thrilled to have worked with one of our major contractors," Momma added.

Jason put out a hand: stop. "*Was* a major contractor. I said the job in Africa was my last, and I meant it." He shot a quick look at Maria and was rewarded by the faint hint of a smile.

Momma drained the last of the wine and looked around hopefully. Gianna knew when not to be available. She set the glass down on the table. "That was truly some of the best I've ever had, particularly an Italian white."

"Boris," Jason said, "you came here about Boris."

Momma shrugged, a small matter. "It seems he got himself hurt in Iceland, shot, actually, doing a bit of investigative work. He won't tell the local police anything but keeps asking for you. Narcom's number was the only one he had."

"Me?" Jason was truly surprised. "Why me?"

"As I said, he was thrilled to work with you. I suspect yours was the only name he had of anyone connected with the company."

Jason asked, "So, what does all this have to do with me? I'm retired, remember?"

It was his turn to view a huge smile as Momma reached across the table to pat his arm. "Of course you are, dear! Having met Maria now, I can see why you wouldn't want to leave her or this marvelous villa, even if it meant a nonhazardous trip to Iceland to simply see what is going on."

"Wasn't nonhazardous for Boris," Jason observed dryly.

Momma leaned over to pat his leg. "I can see your point of view. Boris was . . . was investigating something someone saw as none of his business. As the closest contractor—"

"Closest *former* contractor."

"Yes. Well . . ."

Jason suppressed a sigh. This side of Momma, charm and acquiescence, was new to him, even if her manipulative nature still showed.

He should have recognized the slow curveball.

The fast break over the plate came soon enough. "Of course, I suppose you will have to be leaving here shortly. A pity."

Maria was immediately concerned. "Leave? That is what Jason said. Do you really think we have to?"

Momma clucked sympathetically. "Sweetie, unless you believe the driver of that cement truck was vacationing here and just happened across Jason, you can bet his head-chopping friends will follow. I would be surprised if one of their filthy, hateful mullahs hadn't declared a fatwa, or death writ, against Jason. You can also make a safe wager those people don't care whom they might injure or kill—you, your housekeeper . . . anybody who gets in the way of their trying to get to Jason."

Maria looked over her shoulder, an involuntary response that said she was already alert for lurking assassins. "But where can we go? I mean, if they found us here . . ."

"I've given that some thought," Momma said, a concerned parent helping solve a child's problems. "If Jason would sign on to just investigate this matter . . . Well, there's no reason for him to get involved in the actual operation but he—and you if you wish—would be working from a safe and secure base."

"Like I said, I'm retired. Besides, there are a lot of places on the face of the earth I haven't seen yet."

Momma switched directions as quickly as an unsuccessful base-stealer caught in a rundown. She stood. "Well, don't say I didn't try, Jason. After our long relationship, it seemed fitting to offer you safe haven when you needed it, but you have always been an independent soul."

"Wait," Maria had a hand on Momma's massive arm. "Exactly where did you have in mind?"

"For the moment, Iceland, of course."

11

Ischia Ponte

"Iceland?" Maria asked, her excitement obvious.

"What's with Iceland?" Jason asked.

Momma looked at him. "I thought I said that: It's where Boris is now. In a hospital, not talking to police."

"Perfect!"

They both tuned to Maria.

"It's perfect," she said again. "About one hundred and thirty volcanoes, including Eyjafjallajökull, its monster eruptions shut down European air travel for nearly two months in 2010."

She made it sound like an accomplishment.

"Thermal volcanoes, too, like Yellowstone in the United States. I haven't been there in years." Her enthusiasm ebbed as she turned to face Jason. Why can't we go?"

Both Jason and Momma were staring at her.

Jason noted Momma's eyes narrow slightly, a sure sign something devious was going on behind them. "Excellent! If you and I can persuade Jason to manage to find out what happened to Boris, your expertise will be very helpful. Maybe my company might sponsor a trip down inside this, er, big volcano. How many people would that involve?"

Jason was instantly suspicious. "How?"

"Well," Momma said sweetly, "you know I can't divulge a confidence, but I can say Boris was in Iceland on a matter related to the geology of the place."

Jason was having a hard time seeing anyone getting shot over the study of rocks, plus Momma's penchant for scheme and intrigue was as indigenous to her nature as heat and rain to her native Haiti.

"Exactly what would you expect Jason to do?" Maria wanted to know, obviously enticed by the prospect of a funded expedition.

Momma studied thin air for a theatrical moment. "Well, honey, he's already indicated he doesn't want to be directly involved in anything risky. All I'm asking him to do is find out what happened to an old friend, come back, and tell me."

"You wouldn't expect him to participate in anything if there's trouble, anything violent?"

Momma gave her head a slight shake. "He's far too valuable to risk."

Liar, liar, pants on fire.

Jason felt like a goat being haggled over in some Middle Eastern bazaar.

"You're sure?"

"Of course, sweetie." Momma had on her most innocent face, a sure sign of deception.

"No violence, no killing?"

Momma shrugged, a human earthquake. "Just information gathering."

Momma's voice had taken on that musical lilt of Haiti's patois again, an indication she was pleased with the way things were going.

"But you don't intend to initiate violent action, and if it does happen, Jason won't be involved." A statement, not a question.

"Of course not."

Was Maria's objection to violence personal rather than generic, practical rather than altruistic? Or was the possibility of being able to fully explore a recent volcanic eruption too inviting to pass up?

Maria was silent, thinking.

Momma rose again, this time motioning to Semedi. "It's been wonderful to meet you, Maria. I hope you can find a safe place. I know you and Jason will be happy together there. But I've got a crisis to handle."

The ploy worked.

Maria also stood. "No, wait! If you can fund an exploration of the volcanic activity and you are sure Jason will only be involved in gathering facts . . ."

A fish that had swallowed the bait whole could be less securely hooked.

Narcom's operations had as much chance of being nonviolent as an NHL hockey game did.

Jason started to remind both women that it was, after all, his decision, then stopped. He could protest, decline to participate. And then? He was still going to have to move, disrupt his life again to escape his enemies, having to look over his shoulder again here in the Bay of Naples or somewhere else. Going to Iceland wasn't going to put an end to that, but it would be better than the running and hiding. Besides, his whole life had been a series of actions until three years ago. The brief encounter in Africa had reminded him how much he missed the excitement, the rush of life-and-death decisions.

In any event, he and Maria could not stay here, not with today's attack. It would be followed by others.

He kept his mouth shut and listened before asking questions.

12

From the outside door of the upstairs loggia, Jason and Maria watched Momma's departure until Jason checked his watch.

"We're gonna have to move if we're gonna make the hydrofoil. Momma might change her mind about letting us use the Gulfstream out of Naples."

Maria took a long look around. "You plan on leaving today?"

"You heard what the lady said: whoever made the try this afternoon isn't going to quit, and I'd just as soon not be home when they try again. Gianna can take care of the house as well as Pangloss and Robespierre. I'd suggest you start packing."

"I've hardly unpacked."

"So much the better, but you'd better add some warm clothes. Now, if you'll excuse me, I need to throw a few things into a suitcase."

Once alone in the bedroom, Jason locked the door. If Maria tried to get in, he would have to think of an excuse. Kneeling before an eighteenth-century chest on a stand, he felt along the bottom until his fingers found what he was probing for. There was the sound of tearing tape and he sat back on his heels, unwrapping an oilskin package. The rich smell of Hoppe's Elite Gun Oil filled his nostrils as he unwrapped his special double-edged knife in its special sheath with two straps, which he bound to his right leg just below the knee. Next, he gently unfolded the cloth from around a Glock 18 9 mm pistol and two extra clips, fully loaded. The gun was a version of the Glock 17 but with an automatic-fire option. With a thirty-three-shot double-stack clip, its firepower made up for the lack of accuracy of a barrel just short of four and a half inches. You could fill the air with a lot of lead very quickly.

Sliding back the action, he verified that the automatic already had a magazine in it. The gun went into a holster he clipped to his belt at the small of his back.

Momma was not all generosity. She knew better than to mention in front of Maria that use of her private aircraft meant not only convenience, but also an opportunity to carry weapons, a subtle way of telling him he might well need them. Hardly the peaceful intelligence gathering she had promised Maria.

Finally, Jason selected several CDs from a stack in a bedside table and placed them in a special container. He toyed with the idea of taking a few brushes and tubes of pigment before discarding the thought. No matter how alluring the possible subjects, he wouldn't have the time to paint.

He stood, looking around the room. Three of his paintings hung on the walls, depicting various scenes of Isola d'Ischia. Over the bed hung a pair of capriccios he had picked up in Rome. Imaginary scenes of architectural landscapes, they had been popular decoration in eighteenth-century Italy. In unusually shaped frames, one depicted a view of what might have been the ruins of Venice had the city fallen into decay. The other was a fanciful view of ancient Rome, also in ruins as suggested by cattle grazing before the three remaining columns of the temple of Saturn, arbitrarily juxtaposed next to what might have been the Arch of Titus, which, in reality, was at the other end of the Forum. Both paintings were topped by a sky of the rose-tinted clouds that always adorned the genre.

He would miss this place, the slow pace of life and the vistas that seemed to leap onto his canvases. But he had known somewhere deep in his mind this day would come. It was the price demanded by his other life, the one that would not stay in the past. Now that his presence had been discovered by his enemies, there was no chance he could live there. Even if the terrorist group were destroyed, there were always others. Like the Hydra, as soon as one head was removed, two more appeared. Intolerance and hatred needed little nourishment to flourish.

He grinned grimly. He was one person who could do without the job security.

Stuffing only clothes that could be washed into a small handbag along with toiletries and an iPad, he took a final survey of the room, unlocked the door, and went out.

He was relieved Pangloss was not there as he and Maria drove through the gates for what he suspected would be the last time. He didn't need the dog's howling at being left behind no matter how earnestly Jason assured him of reunion.

He stood beside Maria at the stern of the hydrofoil as it rose out of the water and turned toward Naples. Wordlessly, he watched the craggy peaks of the island sink below the horizon just as so many places he had come to love had faded out of his life.

13

Keflavík International Airport
Near Reykjavík, Iceland
The Next Evening

The tires of the Gulfstream gave the single runway a smoky kiss before twin jet engines howled in reverse thrust. A few seconds later, the aircraft sedately turned onto a taxiway and rolled past the ultra-modern terminal building to the tarmac of the general aviation area.

It was followed by a Toyota Land Cruiser. Had its white paint job with blue lettering and blue-and-yellow trim not been sufficient, the flashing blue lights announced Lögreglan, Icelandic Police. As the Gulfstream maneuvered into a spot among the few transient aircraft, its engines spooled down with a final whine and the police car drew abreast of the single door.

Jason and Maria stood in the opening as the hiss of hydraulics lowered the stairs. He fumbled in a jacket pocket for a pair of sunglasses, feeling both foolish and disoriented. Disoriented because he was looking into the glare of sunlight at twenty-two hundred hours, ten o'clock at night, local time, foolish because he should have anticipated the twenty-plus hours of daylight summer brought to sixty-five-degree-north latitudes. He was thankful he had remembered to bring both light jackets and sweaters, items used only on the rare cold winter day on the Bay of Naples. June or not, the temperatures would be bouncing between fifty-five and forty-five here, chilly for someone used to a Mediterranean climate.

A woman was getting out of the police car, hair the color of straw falling almost to the shoulders of the black uniform trimmed in white. Behind her was a man wearing the armband of Iceland's Customs Service. Iceland had no military; instead, the national police was divided between the normal police functions, a naval police similar to a coast guard, and customs. From his reading on the flight, Jason knew the entire force numbered in the neighborhood of 750.

The woman reached the top of the stairs. "Mr. Peters, Dr. Bergenghetti?"

Both extended hands and received a firm, very unfeminine grip in return.

She grasped first Maria's hand then Jason's, and moved aside so the customs man behind her could pass. He stood for a moment, admiring the interior of the aircraft.

"I'm Bretta, Lieutenant Bretta," she announced.

"Sounds more like a first than a surname," Maria observed.

She treated Maria and Jason to a brilliant smile. "It is. There are few of what you call last names in Iceland."

Jason searched deep blue eyes, suspecting he was being had. "That must make the phone books interesting."

"We have what you call 'patronymic' names. Hroarsson would be son of Hroar."

The customs man interrupted. "Anything to declare?"

Both Jason and Maria handed him their passports.

"No, nothing," Jason said. "I left in something of a hurry when I heard about the call from your police commissioner."

The man was examining the passports. "Your stay will not exceed three months?"

"Speaking for myself, I'm hoping it won't be three days. Dr. Bergenghetti here is a volcanologist. I believe she may tarry longer; she has an appointment with—"

"Dr. Pier Sevensen," Maria piped up. He's driving down from Askja, where the university's Nordic Volcanological Center is located. I hope to plan an expedition to explore the caldera of Eyjafjallajökull as soon as it finishes cooling off, maybe a month or so from now."

The customs man's eyes widened. "Explore? I would think it is too dangerous for that." He handed them back their passports. "In any event, welcome to Iceland."

"Iceland is lovely in summer," Bretta volunteered.

That remains to be seen.

By this time the Gulfstream's crew, pilot, first officer, and flight attendant were fidgeting in the aisle, eager to disembark. The customs man reached for the General Declarations held by the pilot, those papers required of all international flights listing passengers, their nationality, origin of flight, and other information whose purpose was obscure if not nonexistent. Jason suspected the true function of these documents was to give jobs to the bureaucrats of all nations who filed, stored, and created space for them. Never once had he seen anyone ever actually read a General Dec.

"The commissioner is waiting," Bretta said pointedly.

Scooping up a small overnight bag, Jason followed her to the aircraft's door before speaking to the crew. "I hope to finish my business here quickly. I'll call the pilot on his cell when I'm ready to go. In the meantime, take in the sights." To Maria, he said, "Have any idea when you and your professor might finish up?"

"We're going up to Askja tonight. He has to be back at the university's main campus here in Reykjavík tomorrow. I'll call you."

Easier said than done, thought Jason, noting his BlackBerry showed "No contacts" within minutes of leaving the airport.

May as well enjoy the local sights. The sole "sights" within the vicinity of Keflavík consisted of sheep and occasional reindeer grazing on the green moss that covered black volcanic rock with craggy, glacier-carved hills towering above. The few houses—farm dwellings, he supposed—were modest wood structures, many with sod roofs. The road itself, Highway 1, was a four lane, but every few minutes the Toyota had to slow down for humps that reminded Jason of speed breaks.

"There are no trees," he marveled.

"The early settlers cut most of them for fuel and building. Since it takes nearly fifty years for a tree to mature in these latitudes, reforestation efforts move slowly."

Bretta's explanation was punctuated with a bounce of the Toyota that sent Jason's head dangerously near the roof despite his seat belt.

"What's with the bumps?" he asked.

Bretta didn't take her eyes from the road. "The winter causes what you would call 'potholes.' The locals patch them by filling them with gravel and paving over them."

"But doesn't that slow . . . ?"

She spared a glance for him. "In Iceland, few people are in a hurry. You will note that, unlike most European countries, we have a posted speed limit: ninety kilometers an hour in the country on paved roads, fifty in town or on gravel roads."

Jason had noted the frequent speed-limit signs. He changed the subject. "You speak excellent English."

She did not seem to be complimented. "All schoolchildren are taught English and Danish from the first day."

He changed the subject again. "Your police commissioner . . ."

"Harvor, Commissioner Harvor."

"Yeah, Harvor. All he said on the phone was that Boris Karloff had been shot and wouldn't talk to anyone but me. What happened?"

Was that a tightening of the mouth, a slight squint of the eyes?

"You know this man, Boris Karloff?"

Why else would he ask for me?

"Yeah, although I haven't seen him in a long time. Any idea why he would be asking for me?"

She brought the car to a stop while a flock of sheep ambled across the road. "No, you will have to ask the commissioner."

"Do livestock always use the highway?"

She exchanged a wave with the shepherd. "They not only use it, they have the right of way."

They sat in silence for most of the rest of the fifty-kilometer drive.

Reykjavík had no suburbs. One moment they were in open country, then they passed one of the ubiquitous speed-limit signs and buildings sprung up like wildflowers after a summer rain. One or two stories, they all had steeply sloped roofs and small, narrow windows. Some were wood, others stone. Many were painted in bright colors.

"What's that?"Jason was pointing to a large dome structure sitting in an open space of about a block.

"Geodesic dome. Our power company builds them over the geothermal wells that supply the country's power. We use no coal, no gas. Iceland has the cleanest power in the world."

The last was said with a degree of smugness.

A turn brought the Toyota to a street that ran along a bay. The water was an icy blue. Mountains crouched in the mist along the far coast.

"'Reykjavík' means 'smoky bay' in Viking," Bretta said matter-of-factly. "When they first came here, the steam from the geothermals looked like smoke."

"You ever considered a job as a tour guide?"

She glanced at him quizzically. "Why would I want to be a guide? I am already a police person."

Iceland might have the world's cleanest power, the most confusing phone books, and livestock-friendliest roads; but, if Bretta was an example, it had no sense of humor. But then, there was nothing amusing about living in the dark six months out of the year.

14

734 Búastaðavegur
Reykjavík
Five Minutes Later

Landspítali Fossvogi was one of the few contemporary buildings Jason had seen in the city. Six or seven stories high, two wings were divided by a tower of an additional two levels. The car park was half full.

Bretta pulled up to what Jason guessed was the front entrance and leaned across him to open the car's door. "I will call the commissioner to tell him you are here. Room 430."

Jason barely had time to grab his overnight case, much less thank her for the ride, before she was driving off. He watched her pull into light traffic and disappear in the direction from which they had come.

Inside, he could have been in any hospital in the world. The smell of disinfectant was edged by the sickly sweet floral odor common to such institutions.

Flowers?

In Iceland?

A highly polished corridor led past a reception desk to a bank of elevators. Ignoring the woman behind the desk who could have been

71

Bretta's sister, Jason stepped inside the elevator, punched in the button for the fourth floor, and waited until the doors silently slid shut.

He had no problem finding Room 430. A policeman sat outside the door.

He stood as Jason approached, barring entry.

"I'm here to see Boris Karloff. I'm Jason Peters."

The officer was not impressed. "My orders are no one sees the man in that room without orders from Commissioner Harvor."

Swell. Fly to Iceland to speak to a mystery man I haven't seen in years about something too secret to discuss over the telephone and some flatfoot blows me off.

"Just where might I reach the commissioner?"

"You already have."

Jason turned to see a short, chubby man in police uniform extending a hand.

"Harvor."

No other name. Of course.

"Jason Peters. What's this all about?"

The commissioner was standing with his hands clasped behind his back, a pose Jason recognized from pictures of dozens of military men from Grant to Patton to McChrystal. Jason had a mental picture of him practicing the stance in front of a mirror.

"Wish I could tell you, but the man simply won't speak to anyone but you. A couple of sheepherders found him at the Langjökull Glacier. Looked like he'd been robbed and shot. His wallet was missing and there was no identification. The only thing we have is the name he gave us and how to contact you through some American company."

A mugging at a glacier? Well, this was Iceland, not New York.

The commissioner read his mind. "I know to an American a single shooting may not seem like much, but here in Iceland, we average less than a murder a year. You'll notice none of our officers is armed."

"Any idea what he was doing at the Lang, er Lang . . ."

"Langjökull Glacier. No, as I said, he won't speak to anyone but you." Harvor reached past Jason to open the door. "I suggest you ask him."

It took a moment for Jason's eyes to adjust to the dim light inside the room. The blur of a heart monitor danced across a screen, casting flickering shadows across a small white mound under the linen of the only bed. Tubes hung from racks or ran from under the sheets into bottles. Jason drew closer, making out a small head just above the covers.

No Spock ears.

The face was older than Jason remembered, eyelids the color of bruises against skin as white as the starched sheets surrounding it.

"Is he awake?" Harvor asked.

Eyelids fluttered open and bluish lips parted in a death's head grimace. It took Jason a second to realize the man was speaking, whispering. He put his head next to the mouth.

"Peters? Good of you to come."

"I wouldn't have missed it for the world."

The lips twitched into what might have been a smile. "Still the comedian, I see."

It was as if the words had tired him. Karloff's eyes shut and Jason feared he had drifted off to sleep. He stared at the pale face, unsure what to do next. The eyes flickered open and lips quivered. Jason leaned even closer.

"The glacier . . ."

Boris was struggling with each word. "The glacier . . . the southwestern . . ." His next words were unintelligible. Then: "a church . . ."

At least, that was what it sounded like he said. A church? Was the man simply mumbling or hallucinating?

Or Jason had not heard correctly. "Say again?"

"You will have to leave."

A woman's voice. A very annoyed woman's voice.

Both Jason and Harvor turned to see a figure in white fill the doorway: white hair, white uniform, white shoes.

"I am Elga, the floor nurse and the doctor has not permitted visitors. The patient has been given a sedative and you are interfering with its effect."

Harvor said something in a language Jason did not understand though there was no mistaking the tone. "I told her we are on police business," he explained.

"I do not care if you are on a mission from heaven. The patient is very weak. The doctor has not permitted visitors."

Jason sized up Nurse Elga. The woman was immense. If it came to physically ejecting the tubby police commissioner, Harvor was an odds-on second best.

Harvor pulled a cell phone from somewhere in his uniform. "How may I contact this doctor?"

"You may contact him from the hall."

The policeman outside stuck his head around the doorjamb, assessed the situation, and disappeared.

Elga put hands the size of a catcher's mitt on thighs that would have credited an NFL running back. "Do you require assistance in leaving?"

Threat, not a question.

Harvor glanced at the form under the sheets and then at Jason. "I think we better take this up with the doctor."

No shit.

As Jason turned to go, he thought he had somehow snagged his pants on part of the hospital bed. Instead, Boris's hand was holding on to his sweater's sleeve as the face on the pillow looked up at him. He was whispering something.

"You are leaving." A statement, not a question, from Elga.

Jason held up a hand: wait. He leaned over, putting his ear next to the moving lips.

"What?"

"Cravas, Nigel Cravas." There was a pause as though Boris was summoning the strength to finish. "British Institute . . . Tell him, tell him . . ." A pause. "The . . . eanies . . ."

Jason was not sure what he was hearing. "'Cravat'? 'Meanie'? 'Beanie'?" he asked.

No good. Elga pulled his shoulders up, inserting herself between Jason and the bed. "You are leaving *now.*"

15

Five Minutes Later

In the hall, Harvor tried the number the nurse had given him, fuming when he reached the doctor's voice mail. "These doctors! They think they may come and go as they please! Ever since Iceland's financial crisis a few years ago when the number of free hospitals was reduced, the doctors have forgotten they work for the state, that they are required to be on call twenty-four hours a day. Shameful!"

If you think Iceland's MDs are hard to get in touch with, Jason thought, try an American doc on a weekend.

"Exactly where is this place where the man in there was found?" he asked the commissioner.

Harvor was still distracted by the independence of his country's medical profession. "In an area of the glacier called Geitlandsjökull, the southern part of the glacier. But why? . . . Surely you are not planning on going there?"

"Why not? We can't get any information from the man in there." Jason gestured toward the hospital room.

"But as soon as I can reach the doctor—"

"Which may be after dark." Jason glanced out of a window at the end of the hall. "If it gets dark."

Apparently despairing of reaching the doctor, the commissioner returned his cell phone to wherever it had come from. "What do you expect to find there?" he asked suspiciously.

"I don't know," Jason replied, "but we sure aren't finding out by standing around here."

"How do you plan to get there? It is a two-hour drive and the rental-car agencies are closed. It is almost midnight."

Jason grinned. "I thought you might want to take a look yourself, possibly before the shooter returns."

Harvor looked at Jason levelly. "What makes you think he will return?"

"The man in there, Karloff, whatever his real name is, was trying to tell me something."

"Who shot him, no doubt."

"Maybe, but I think he was giving me directions."

"To what?"

"We won't know if we don't go there. Besides, who knows how long it will be before you have a chance to investigate another shooting in Iceland?"

Jason's stomach growled, reminding him that he'd had nothing to eat on the plane. "Is there a place I can get a quick bite around here?"

"Bite?"

"Something to eat."

"There is a very fine restaurant down the street, serves Icelandic specialties." Harvor looked at his watch. "May be closed by now."

It was.

Jason tried to ignore his complaining stomach. Reading the menu posted in the window in English and a number of other languages helped assuage his hunger: fresh herring, salt herring, broiled herring, baked herring, fried herring. And, of course, herring croquettes.

He returned to the hospital, convinced that, in this case, hunger was the better alternative.

The ride in the Range Rover took closer to three hours actually. They were no more than a few kilometers out of Reykjavík when the road went from four lanes to two to gravel. It was getting dark now, a dusk-like light that would be as close to night as the summer months permitted. Other than an occasional truck headed into the city, there was no other traffic.

Since Jason found it impossible to sleep on airplanes, even in the Gulfstream's small but comfortable bedroom, he had been awake for more than twenty-four hours. But cars were not aircraft. There was no irrational fear that something might go wrong at thirty thousand feet. The steady sound of the engine, the monotonous hum of the tires on the road were a lullaby. He dozed off, coming awake with a jolt when the car stopped. At first, he was unaware of what he was seeing. The huge white mass shimmering in the twilight seemed luminescent, almost magical, as though an iceberg had floated out of the North Sea and onto land.

"This is it," Harvor said, getting out of the car, a flashlight in his hand. "Come, I will show you where the shepherd found him."

Jason was thankful for the heavy sweater as he pulled it tighter around him. "You know the location?"

The policeman stopped, turning. "We may not be as sophisticated as your American police but we do investigate thoroughly, Mr. Peters. The officer who first responded made a map of the location as well as photographs of the scene. Can you see your way without a light?"

"Not well, but I'd prefer not to turn on the light just yet."

"Oh?"

"In case someone else is in the neighborhood, I'd just as soon not pinpoint our position."

Jason could see the gray blur of Harvor's face as the commissioner stared at him a moment. "As you wish. Mind your step."

Jason was doing just that: watching where he placed his feet. The scree left by the retreating glacier made the path treacherous, all the more so because it was difficult to see in the half-light. He was so intent on trying to avoid tripping over the rubble that he was almost upon it before he saw it.

Something made him look up. Twilight was beginning to fade into the twenty-hour day. Limned against the dove-gray sky of early dawn towered a form vaguely familiar but just out of the reach of Jason's memory.

He stopped and the commissioner, hearing no steps behind him, turned around. "What is it?"

"That rock formation." Jason pointed.

Harvor's voice bore a tinge of annoyance. "There are many rock formations here. The ice cap carves . . ."

Jason tuned him out. In daylight, he would have missed it, but in the half dark where sight was not three-dimensional, the silhouette had a square, Romanesque tower above . . . above . . . a church!

He had heard Boris correctly.

But what had he meant?

Jason was pointing. "We need to take a look at those rocks."

Harvor reached into a pocket and produced a sheet of paper. "I can't be sure in this light, but it looks like from the map the investigating officer found your friend there."

Both men were silent as they climbed the steep slope. Once at the top, they were surrounded by the formation itself.

"We cannot see without the light," Harvor observed, stating the obvious. "The rocks will block the natural light until the sun is higher in the sky."

An event Jason was unsure took place in these latitudes.

"OK, let's take a look."

The policeman played the flashlight's beam across rocks so black Jason guessed the blood from Boris's wound would be invisible.

"Can you tell from the diagram exactly where in this stone jumble he was found?"

Before Harvor could answer, something twinkled in the light to Jason's left. "Play the light over there."

The flashlight's beam revealed a space between two of the huge rocks, a narrow passage. Just beyond, something sparkled. Jason sucked in his stomach and squeezed through.

From behind him, Harvor protested, "I don't think I can get through there."

The portly policeman was right. "Go around that pillar to your right."

As Harvor came puffing up, his light picked up something shiny.

Jason squatted but did not pick it up. "Looks like a bullet casing. I'd guess nine millimeter."

Harvor leaned over. "You have experience in such things?"

Jason was turning it over with a ballpoint pen, careful not to touch it. Inside what amounted to a roofless room of stone, the ejected shell could not have gone far. The shot must have been fired within a few feet of here.

He stood, extending he brass shell on the tip of the pen for the policeman's inspection. "Your investigating officer must have missed it."

"Or it wasn't here when he was," the cop offered defensively.

How many Icelanders own handguns, Jason thought, let alone went about firing them indiscriminately?

But he said, "You might want to keep that in case there are partial prints on it."

Harvor looked at him suspiciously, his expression now visible in the increasing light. "You did not answer my question, Mr. Peters: You have experience in such things?"

"I watch *Law & Order*."

Harvor was clearly making a decision as to whether to let the matter rest as Jason slowly turned around, his eyes searching the stone chamber. Wordlessly, he took the flashlight from the policeman's hand, shining it across the face of the rock that surrounded them.

There was a noise Jason could not believe he was hearing. It sounded like, but could not be . . . a cell phone's beep. Following the persistent chirps, Jason came to a crevice that gave back the light from his flash. In one step, Jason was reaching into it. His groping fingers touched something cold, metal that had absorbed the ambient temperature of the brief night.

His hand closed around it and he drew it out. A cell phone.

He flipped it open. "Yes?"

The reply was both distinctly British and, equally certain, irritated. "See here, Karloff! We are not paying you to ignore our calls. I've been trying to reach you for hours!"

"I'm sorry," Jason mumbled, trying to imitate Boris's voice. "I've been busy. I—"

The tone went from annoyed to wary. "You're not Karloff. Where is he?"

"Er, indisposed at the moment. With whom am I speaking?"

There was a moment of silence before the phone went dead. The tiny screen displayed a number Jason recognized as being somewhere in the British Isles. He committed it to a memory long ago trained to recall names, words, and numbers.

"Who was that?" Harvor demanded.

"Someone who clearly didn't want to speak with me."

"He gave no name?"

"That is correct."

Harvor reached for the phone. "We can determine the source of the call."

Reluctantly, Jason handed it over as he stuck his other hand back into the fissure. This time he touched another, much smaller, piece of metal and what his fingers told him was a piece of string. No, a twig.

Harvor extended the hand not holding the phone. "Those, too, Mr. Peters."

"And I will take both those and the cell phone," said a voice.

Harvor and Jason turned to see a man holding a gun. His face could have been the surface of the moon it was so pocked with scars. Acne? Jason thought he recognized the black matte polymer of a Russian made GSh-18, the original, if brief, replacement for the Makarov as the standard Soviet military sidearm. The fact the man had his finger curled around the square trigger guard instead of the trigger itself reminded him the weapon had a Glock-like safety that was automatically released when the trigger was squeezed.

The stranger was no amateur.

"Unless you are a police officer, you have no permit for that weapon," Harvor said with a huff. "You can be sent to prison for even possessing such a thing."

Jason didn't take his eyes from the stranger. "I don't think he's overly worried about the possibility. I'd suggest you do as he asks."

The man gave a sharklike smile exposing teeth the color of old ivory. "And I suggest, Commissioner, that you do as Mr. Peters says."

The English was near perfect, yet there was an accent. Russian? Eastern European?

Jason kept his face frozen, unwilling to register surprise the man with the gun knew his name.

Harvor did not. "How did you . . . ?" He faced Jason indignantly. "Did you know this man was here?"

Jason shook his head. "No, but it was a good guess."

The intruder extended the hand not holding the gun, motioning for the demanded items. "The phone and whatever else you found. Questions later."

There might not be a "later." Jason had no doubt this man had intended to kill Boris, most likely to protect whatever secrets the camera-enabled phone, the twig, and the scrap of metal might reveal. Why would he spare two strangers who discovered what Boris had hidden? As soon as he had what he wanted, it was probable Jason and Harvor would suffer the same fate.

Jason swore at himself silently. The Glock was still in his bag in the car. He had hesitated to strap on the holster in front of Maria, listen to her reproachful reminder that this was a mission to get information, nonviolent.

Harvor was extending the phone. If Jason was going to act, now was the time, gun or not.

16

Jason stood by as the police commissioner extended the phone and the two other items. He watched the man with the gun stuff the cell phone, the twig, and the piece of metal into the pocket of his jacket.

"Who hired you?" Jason asked.

He didn't expect an answer. The question was simply a play for time, something he had absorbed long ago from the psychological training to which every Delta Force member was subjected. The more desperate the situation, the greater the need to start a conversation or do anything that served the purpose of delay. The longer disaster could be postponed, the more likely it could be averted.

The man looked at Jason, surprised. Men like this one rarely revealed their employers if, in fact, they even knew who was really paying them. "You don't need to know."

Jason's back was against one of the stone walls. He was moving his shoulder back and forth as though scratching an itch he couldn't quite reach. "Oh, but I do! You know who I am, you know I'm not without means. I'm sure whatever your employers want, I can provide in a much more, er, civil, manner."

The man grinned. He had heard pleas like this before and obviously enjoyed them. "They are not interested in your money, Mr. Peters. Or should I say, the money of the company for which you work."

Jason was reaching a hand behind his back, trying to scratch a really pesky itch, when Harvor broke in. "Surely you do not mean to kill us? You will certainly be caught and imprisoned."

Again, the shark's smile. "I will take that chance. Now, if . . ."

He never finished. Harvor began to tremble, tears in his eyes. "I have done you no harm. I have a wife, a family who will suffer if anything happens to me. . . ."

The pudgy policeman was either terrified or an extraordinary actor. Jason really did not care which. What mattered was the gunman's attention was riveted on the weeping, pleading Harvor, allowing Jason to use his shoulder more freely to work the stone he had felt at his back, a loose bit of rock he hoped to wiggle free.

Harvor was making what Jason guessed was a final plea for his life and it was clear the man with gun was enjoying it. Some men he had known received an almost sexual pleasure from wielding extreme power over others. The power to take a life was the ultimate form.

Jason felt the piece of rock come free. He grasped it with his right hand as he fixed his gaze on a point behind the man with the gun as if seeing something of interest there. Far too much the professional to be taken in by such a basic trick, the lunar-faced man ignored the ploy, listening to Harvor's seemingly terrified babble. Jason guessed he had only seconds before the commissioner was a dead man.

He worked a smaller piece of stone free with his left hand.

He was going to get a single chance.

Better than none at all.

Moving his left arm slowly from behind him, Jason tossed the smaller rock, a pebble really, onto the stone on which the men stood. It make a plink, hardly audible but enough to make the gunman move. Or more accurately, merely flinch, his gun swinging away from Harvor.

Better yet, he took his eyes from his prisoners for an instant.

Jason came over the man's shoulder with the larger rock, his version of a Major League fastball. But he had no intention of it catching the plate.

The man with the gun caught the movement with the corner of his eye.

The gun swiveled toward Jason and went off an instant before the rock knocked it from his hand.

Jason felt as though he had been bludgeoned in the left shoulder with a club. His back struck the rock hard enough to knock the breath from his lungs. He fought knees no longer willing to bear his weight.

Through vision blurred by shock or tears or both, he saw the weapon spin across the rocky floor. By reflex, he made a dive for it just as his antagonist did the same.

The other man had the shorter route. He had his fingers closing around the grip of the automatic when Jason, prostrate on the stone, saw a booted foot come out of nowhere and stamp the other man's hand. In spite of the howl of pain, he could hear the bones snap, shattered between the boot and the unforgiving rock.

Jason had the gun in his hand now, rolling quickly onto his back to grasp the weapon in both hands. "Hold it right there!"

The other man either didn't hear or didn't care. He was half standing when he sprang, arms outreached.

Jason could hardly miss. Still, he made himself center the white forward sight before he squeezed the trigger. The sound of the GSh-18 bounced off the rock walls and the weapon jumped in Jason's hand. He brought it to bear for a second shot.

He never got it off.

The man's leap carried him onto Jason with a force that sent a shockwave of pain radiating from his wounded shoulder through his entire upper body. Gritting his teeth, Jason tried to wrench the gun free before he realized there was no resistance.

The weight lifted as Harvor tugged the inert form away.

"Are you all right, Mr. Peters?"

The gun still in his hand, Jason struggled to his feet, leaning against a rock wall for support. "I'm alive, thanks to your stomping the bastard's hand at just the right moment."

Harvor was staring. "You've been hit!"

No shit!

Jason stuffed the automatic into a trouser pocket, using the other hand to grip his wounded shoulder. "I'll be OK if you can get help here soon."

Harvor took one last look at Jason, then at the body of their former assailant. There was a bloody foam on his lips and each shallow breath seemed an effort.

"Our friend there isn't going to make it without medical attention pretty quick. Looks like a lung shot. He'll either suffocate or bleed out."

Harvor still wasn't moving. "You hit his gun hand with that rock."

"I sure as hell wasn't aiming for the strike zone."

"The what?"

"Never mind. How quick can you get help?"

"The radio in the car. I'll call for a helicopter."

"You don't have a cell phone?"

Harvor shook his head. "At these latitudes, anything that operates from a satellite is, how do you say it? Unreliable. Besides, it would be very expensive to equip every police officer."

From what Jason had seen of this thrifty country, the second explanation outweighed the first, as evidenced by the anonymous call he had received on Boris's hidden phone. "Whatever. You really need to get help here."

He watched the rotund policeman head off in the direction of the Range Rover before making a closer examination of his damaged left shoulder. Hurt like hell and was bleeding like a fountain but didn't look like anything vital had been damaged. Now, if he could find something to slow the loss of blood before he became dizzy. . . .

The man was sprawled across the rocky floor of the open chamber. The flannel of the shirt under his jacket would be perfect: soft and absorbent. And its present owner wasn't going to have much use for it, not with the front soaked in blood.

Only when Jason reached the shallowly breathing body did he remember. A quick search of the pockets retrieved phone, twig, and scrap of metal.

"Peters . . ."

A whisper.

Jason looked down at the man he had shot. Pale, eyes sunken back into his head. One hand feebly motioned Jason closer. He put his ear next to the mouth, still bubbling blood.

"If you're smart . . ." There was a spasm of coughing and a spray of blood. "You'll leave here and forget . . ."

Jason was tearing a strip from the shirt. "You'd better worry about yourself. We need . . ."

There was a grunt that Jason guessed was meant to be a laugh. "Me? I failed. I'm good as dead. You still . . . you still have a chance."

Jason was holding the man's head in his hands, trying to make him comfortable. "Who sent you?"

Blood-smeared teeth showed in the rictus of a smile. "For me to know, you to find out" was only partially audible.

Jason shook him. "Who?"

There was no reply.

Jason looked down into eyes staring into eternity.

17

Landspítali Fossvogi Hospital
One Hour Later

Jason lay on his back, imprisoned by the rails of the bed. He had only a faint, dreamlike memory of being placed on a stretcher and loaded into a helicopter. Arriving was a total blank. But the bed, the room, the smells, and the IV drip in his arm left no doubt he was, in fact, in a hospital.

Woozy from the loss of blood, he thought he might even be hallucinating. The sounds of disembodied voices over the speaker system, the smells of disinfectant, the white-clad figures returned him to Walter Reed Hospital on that otherwise flawless late-summer day in 2001. For six frantic hours he had haunted the hallways, praying Laurin would be in the continuous stream of ambulances ferrying the injured from the smoking hole in the side of the Pentagon. In the next several days, a week, he was never quite certain, he had abandoned the normal functions of sleeping and eating, spending every hour at the entrance to the emergency room. The acceptance of reality came painfully, leaving him only the hope for recovery of the body, a chance to see Laurin one final time. Even that dire possibility faded. He was denied the grim satisfaction of a flower-covered casket, the commitment to the earth. His only solace had been the ring he wore on the gold chain around his neck. Memorial-service preparations and enduring the sympathy of friends failed to cure a void that, he was certain, would last forever no matter how hard he tried to fill it with alcohol and self-pity.

All of that came back to him in the semi-dream of delirium induced by loss of blood and analgesics. His mouth felt like it had been stuffed with cotton.

There was a face swimming above him, one vaguely familiar. The kindly and understanding hospital chaplain who had tried in vain to comfort him as the trickle of those who were injured but survived the blast dried up without Laurin? No it was . . . He struggled to put a name with the face.

"Can you hear me, Mr. Peters?"

The revelation came as though from on high: Harvor. Harvor the Commissioner of Police. "Loud and clear. Can you get me some water?"

"The doctors have removed the bullet from your shoulder. You are quite fortunate: a few millimeters over and you could be dead."

Jason had never considered being shot particularly fortuitous. "Lucky me."

"We have searched for the cell phone and the other items but they were not on the dead man's body."

Jason suddenly became aware that, other than the standard open-backed hospital shift, he was wearing nothing. If Harvor or his minions searched his clothes . . .

"I'd really appreciate some water."

Harvor reached for a table beside the bed and poured water from a carafe into a paper cup. The sound made Jason run his tongue across dry, cracked lips.

Harvor held the cup in his hand. "Perhaps you have some idea where these things might be?"

Jason's eyes were fixed on the cup. "Have you searched that rock formation?"

"Thoroughly."

Jason struggled against the drugs to prop himself up on his

elbows. The effort made his head spin and he feared he would black out. "The water . . ."

"Oh, yes, the water."

The police commissioner proffered the paper cup. Jason emptied it in two swallows. He had never enjoyed anything more, even the single-malt scotch he favored, but it was like pouring water on desert sand: it seemed to evaporate in his throat.

He handed the cup back. "Another, please."

Harvor set it down on the bedside table. "I'm not sure how much liquid the doctors want you to have, Mr. Peters. I'll have to check. But first, we need to talk about the missing phone, that piece of string or whatever it might be, and the scrap of metal. Then there is also the matter of the pistol you were carrying in your bag when you arrived here in Iceland in addition to the one you took from the man who died. Normally, the penalties for possession of such a weapon are quite severe, but in view of the fact you saved my life, I have simply confiscated yours to be returned when you depart Iceland."

Jason tried not to look at his clothes hanging in an open closet by the door. Why the police had not searched the pockets was a mystery, as was the reason he desperately wanted to keep the missing objects himself, to make them give up whatever answers they might hold, rather than turn them over to the police.

He could also see the small overnight bag he had brought on the plane to Iceland. With any luck at all, once they had found the Glock, they hadn't rummaged through the bag's contents. The knife, his specially designed blade, should still be in there. He might be without the Glock, but he was not weaponless.

Harvor was about to say something when a uniformed officer, face flushed with excitement, burst into the room. "Commissioner?"

Harvor replied in a language Jason did not understand, the tone implying annoyance at being interrupted. Jason did catch the name Karloff.

Ignoring the wave of vertigo, Jason sat up. "Something has happened to Karloff?"

Harvor gave him a curt glare. "Something indeed, Mr. Peters. Something that is police business."

The commissioner followed the uniformed officer out of the room.

In seconds, Jason had the IV out of his arm and was trying, despite a wave of dizziness, to step into his pants. In less than a minute, he was fully dressed. He was gratified to find his pockets still contained the objects Harvor wanted. He bent over to tie his shoes and nearly passed out. The laces would have to remain loose for the moment.

Using the corridor wall for support, he stumbled his way toward the elevator. From the room numbers on the doors, he knew Room 430 would be one floor up. After what seemed eons, the elevator doors hissed open and Jason lurched inside and pushed "4."

The doors parted, revealing a scene that could have come from an old Keystone Kops silent film: Police uniforms dashed about without apparent purpose. People in white lab coats shouted orders no one seemed to obey. The impression was of a fire drill where no one knew the location of the exits.

Jason grabbed the lapel of one of the white coats. "What happened?"

The woman looked at him as though he might have been the only person in Reykjavík who did not know. "Happened? Happened? The patient in 430 . . ."

Jason didn't wait for a full explanation. Filled with dread, he shoved his way toward the room, ignoring a swimming head and legs that felt more like spaghetti than bones. At the door of the room, he slid past a protesting uniform and stopped.

What he saw brought burning bile to his throat. For an instant, he thought whatever he had eaten in the last twelve hours would find its way to the floor. Then he remembered he hadn't eaten at all. Three of the room's walls were decorated with an abstract pattern of red splatter now turning a rusty brown. Even the ceiling had spots of blood. Boris was face-up, his upper torso dangling from the bed's blood-soaked sheets toward the floor like some malignant growth. Beneath his chin, a red-encrusted slash grinned obscenely, its crimson lips still dripping blood.

Judging from the mess, he had continued to struggle even after his throat had been cut.

"Mr. Peters!" Harvor was at Jason's side. "You should be in bed, under observation, where you can be cared for."

"Like Boris there?"

"Boris?"

"The man with the slit throat. Last I saw of him, he had a police officer outside his door."

"The officer assigned seems to be missing," Harvor replied stiffly.

I'm sure he is.

"You must return to your room!"

And wind up sliced and diced?

Obediently, Jason turned and left. He took the elevator down to his assigned room, where he made sure his shoes were tied, took the sweater from its hanger, and walked out of the hospital without notice. A cab took him to the airport, where the Gulfstream and crew waited.

He entered the small general-aviation passenger area and took out his BlackBerry to call Maria. At first he feared a possible lack of network coverage as Harvor had mentioned, but she answered on the second ring.

"I'm at the airport," Jason informed her. "I think I got all the information about Boris I'm going to."

There was a pause. Then, "Can you stay over another couple of days? Pier and I are just getting started on planning the expedition."

From "Dr. Sevensen" to "Pier" in less than twenty-four hours? Not a good sign.

"Something's come up. I need to leave."

"You need to go somewhere else or you need to get out of Iceland?"

Damn, but she knew him too well.

"I promised you to avoid any violence . . ."

Explaining a bullet wound wasn't going to be easy.

Her tone was wary. "Well, if you're keeping your promise . . . Where is it you are going?"

Jason was caught flatfooted. He literally had no place to go. The villa at Ischia Ponte was definitely out. He was effectively homeless.

"Washington, briefly, and I'm not sure after that."

"OK. I'll call or text you in a day or so when I know for sure how much longer I'll be here."

How long did it take to plan a trip into a volcano's crater? he wondered. The thing was probably no more than a single square mile.

He concluded the conversation just as the Gulfstream's captain approached.

"All fueled up, Mr. Peters, ready to go. But I need a destination to complete the flight plan."

Washington it was.

It took only a few minutes to complete the aircraft's flight plan. As the Gulfstream screamed off the runway and turned southwest, Jason comforted himself that Harvor did not yet know he was gone.

He stuck a hand in a pocket, touching the phone. What made it and the accompanying twig and metal shard worth killing for? And by whom?

And what, if anything, had any of it to do with him?

Nothing.

He hoped.

He would have the twig analyzed along with the metal, take a look at what numbers or pictures were on the phone. . . . He reached for it and withdrew his hand. First he would shut his eyes for a few minutes.

The lack of sleep, the anesthesia and painkillers from the hospital, the loss of blood, all were making him drowsy.

He got up and made his way to the plane's small but comfortable stateroom. Removing his shoes and gingerly struggling out of his jacket and the sling cradling the arm of his wounded shoulder, he sat on the side of the bed while he pulled down the collar of his shirt. The bandage on his shoulder was as pristine white as it had been in the hospital. No more bleeding. He stretched out, staring at the ceiling only a few feet from his head.

For the first time he could remember, Jason drifted off to sleep aboard an aircraft in flight, dreaming of figures in white carrying knives far larger than surgical scalpels and Laurin speaking with Boris.

18

Calle Luna 23
San Juan, Puerto Rico
The Same Time

The man who called himself Pedro spoke with a Slavic accent. His high cheekbones and blue eyes were not like any Latino whom Francisco had ever seen either. And his nose looked as though the man might have been a professional fighter: Flattened so that it covered a good part of his face. But jobs in Puerto Rico were hard to come by, and asking questions was discouraged, particularly inquiries as to exactly what Pedro and his ever-changing coworkers actually did.

The town house itself was also like none other Francisco had seen in the city. The exterior was normal enough, except for the fact its stucco was a pale blue rather than the muted reds, greens, and yellows favored by the other buildings, only one or two rooms wide, that sat along the curbs of the narrow blue cobblestone streets of Old San Juan sharing common walls.

That was not the only difference. The place had been modified far beyond what Francisco guessed was allowed by the strict rules of the city's preservation council, a body dedicated to keeping as much of the sixteenth century intact as possible.

During Spain's construction of the fortifications of San Juan beginning in 1539 and extending over the next two and a half centuries, the eighteen-foot-thick walls of the fortress guarding the harbor—San Felipe del Morro—and a number of storerooms and magazines had been built to facilitate the speedy delivery of provisions, powder, and shot to the fort's garrison.

The English and Dutch had been a constant threat, mounting campaigns from their Caribbean colonies. Sir Francis Drake attacked in 1595, barely escaping when a cannonball pierced the cabin of his ship. Four years later, the duke of Cumberland succeeded in a land assault and siege against the city, only to retreat six months later when dysentery decimated his forces. In 1625, the Dutch sacked the city but were unable to breach del Morro's walls.

After the fort fell into disuse at the conclusion of the Spanish-American War, the storage spaces honeycombing the city's walls were deserted, available to squatters, beggars, or whoever chose to take them over. Soon, respectable facades were added, along with upper stories, and the former usages were forgotten.

Calle Luna 23 was such a house, with some notable additions. Instead of the blank wall at the rear that had been the inner part of the fortifications, a banquet-sized room had been carved out to accommodate a battery of computers and other communication equipment that Francisco did not recognize. He only knew they were connected to the third floor, an area forever locked off from the rest of the house. The shutters of the floor-to-ceiling windows facing the street were steel rather than wood and were never opened, not even in the evening when every house in the old town was wide open in hopes of catching the breeze that would dissipate the damp mustiness of the air-conditioning that made Old San Juan habitable this time of year.

At the moment, Francisco was finishing sweeping the stone floor. His cleaning job was as mysterious as everything else here. First, the floor was littered with cigarette butts. Not the usual filtered Marlboros or Winstons sold at the bodega across the street, but cardboard-tipped, foul-smelling things with black tobacco. Francisco had never seen such a brand elsewhere in Puerto Rico. Where had they come from? Then, his first task each of the three days a week he came to clean was to empty a large wicker basket of shredded paper into the municipal garbage bin down the street. What was so important, so secret, that it needed to be shredded? Finally, there was the third floor. The door from the stairs was always locked and secured by a chain. Apparently no cleaning was required there. What was so valuable that it had to be locked away? And who were the men who came to and went from Number 23? None of them appeared to be Latino; almost all looked Slavic like Pedro. They spoke a rough language Francisco could not understand, even though he had taken several language courses before a slumping economy had forced him to drop out of the university at Ponce on the southern side of the island. They did occasionally speak English, particularly over the cell phones they all carried. But the speech was always oblique, never referring to anything Francisco was aware of. He surmised that the words they said stood for something else, a code.

Sometimes, though, they spoke clearly. That was even more confusing. Things about attacks on Japanese whaling fleets, cutting long lines in the Bering Sea, or sabotaging lumbering equipment in Brazil. Who cared about things so far away?

GrünWelt, GreenWorld, the international society publicly and politically dedicated to stopping the supposed rape of Planet Earth. That's who, although the name meant nothing to Francisco.

Its world headquarters were ostensibly located just down the street from the US embassy to Switzerland and Liechtenstein at 19 Sulgeneckstrasse, Bern. An impressive building had been purchased and renovated with sums donated by concerned conservationists from around the world. The society's announced policy was to fight whatever it saw as destruction of the environment with whatever peaceful means might be at hand.

That was the public persona.

Activities that might not stand the scrutiny of the authorities, or that skirted local or international law, were planned and put into practice here in San Juan, away from the hordes of well-meaning, if ill-informed, members whose dues and contributions provided the only source of income. At least, as far as the public knew.

Like many parts of the world lying between the tropics, Puerto Rico's police had the laissez-faire attitude common to those latitudes plus the unique Anglo concept that, no matter how suspicious, premises could not be entered by authorities without some form of probable cause. In short, as long as the inhabitants of Number 23 caused no problems in San Juan, they were left alone.

Francisco was aware of little, if any, of this. He did know Pedro was talking to someone in the States, because he had been behind him and seen the 202 area code on the screen of the cell phone.

"I am relieved to hear if our problem has not been solved, it has been located there. Are you sure you can handle it?"

His silence while the question was answered implied satisfaction. "It is imperative you recover the objects. Yes, I understand it may not be easy. Dispose of the carrier. If you need assistance, call."

Francisco thought that odd too. For an organization concerned about faraway whales and Brazilian rain forests, recycling would seem to make more sense.

19

Dulles International Airport
Chantilly, Virginia
7:01 the Next Morning

The Gulfstream's tires kissed the runway an instant before Jason was shoved against his seat belt by howling twin Rolls-Royce BR 725 engines in reverse thrust. Had Momma not permanently sealed the windows, he would be getting his first view of his native land in . . . what, three years?

He thanked the flight crew and accepted a ride to customs and immigration in the main terminal, general aviation's version not opening for an hour yet. As the shuttle rumbled across taxi and runways, Jason looked beyond the perimeter fences at what he could see of the western Virginia landscape. It could be anywhere: Europe, Asia, the Middle East, venues where he had arrived and departed so frequently that such facilities and their surroundings took on a certain anonymous sameness. That was both curse and blessing. Blessing because it lessened the acute awareness of how many times he had landed here and over at Reagan National when he had a wife and home to go to. Curse because landing at either reminded him Laurin would not be waiting with cold drinks and the latest neighborhood or office gossip. Now being in the land of his birth had no significance other than the fact he had to leave Iceland and had nowhere else to go. He was as effectively homeless as those mendicants one sees on the streets of major cities. The only difference was that, for some of those, choices made in their lives rendered them financially and emotionally unable to sustain permanence. The choices made in Jason's had made a permanent residence a liability.

"Where to?" the cabdriver wanted to know as Jason tossed his single bag into the backseat and climbed in.

"The Pentagon," Jason replied automatically. "With one stop in between."

The Dulles Corridor Metrorail Project had not visibly progressed since Jason's last trip in from the airport. A section of Highway 123 between Scotts Crossing Road and the I-495 Beltway was still closed, forcing more traffic onto highways designed to carry far less. Like most residents of DC and northern Virginia, Jason had long ago despaired of the project's completion within his lifetime—or, for that matter, his grandchildren's lifetime had he any grandchildren. Between cabdrivers' vociferous objections to loss of fares inflated beyond reason, local residents' fears that rail service would spread Washington's crime into their suburban communities like some deadly virus, and labor unions' constant push to sup at this trough, the rail line had become a political football in which the spectators, not the players, were the losers.

Nearly an hour later, the cab pulled up to the Pentagon's south parking lot. Jason, two dozen white roses in the arm not in a sling, climbed out.

"Sir? Sir?" The cabbie asked nervously. "I can't park here, not without a permit. There is no public parking."

Jason didn't even turn around. "So, circle the building a couple of times. I'll meet you right here."

"Er, sir, I can't do that. Company regulations require I collect the fare when you exit the cab."

Jason stopped, turned, and walked back to the waiting taxi.

He lowered his face until it was even with the driver's. "I know you don't make company policy. I also know it's not your fault that the idiots who designed the memorial I'm about to visit didn't provide parking. If you do not allow me to deliver these flowers to the site dedicated to my wife, that *will* be your fault. Do we understand each other?"

The cabbie took one look at Jason's scowl, weighed the possibility of the mayhem implicit therein against an enhanced tip, and said, "Yessir, yessir. Perfectly. I don't know how long I can stay here before they make me move but—"

Jason was already striding away.

At the southwest corner of the Pentagon, slightly fewer than two acres were dedicated to those who perished there on 9/11. Crape myrtles in their summer splendor were scattered about the gravel lot as were 184 terrazzo-finished sculptures that resemble diving boards over small lighted pools. Each sculpture bears a name and is arranged in a timeline from the youngest victim of a few months to the eldest in his seventies. If the person was one of the eighty-eight who were aboard the ill-fated aircraft that crashed into the building, the viewer looks skyward to read the name. If inside the Pentagon, one faces the building.

It took Jason only a few steps to stand beside Laurin's memorial. He had first seen it on that mournful afternoon in September 2008, when the little park was dedicated in front of family and friends of the victims.

Kneeling, he placed the roses beside the small pool. He was fully aware that the park's keepers would remove all flowers when they shut down for the evening, but he didn't care. For a few hours, visitors would know someone had cared for Laurin Peters very much. She had no other site to deck with flowers on her birthday or special occasions, no gravestone memorializing the dates of her life. Only this, an abstract sculpture among many abstract sculptures, a pool among many pools.

He stood, his vision blurred. He made no effort to wipe away the hot tears coursing down his cheeks as he turned and walked to the waiting cab without a look back.

"Now where?"

Jason had to think a moment. He needed someone to look at the stick, the piece of metal, and the pictures from the phone's camera, someone who might have an idea of their significance, of why they were worth killing for. What better place than DC with its universities, government-funded research centers, and laboratories both civilian and military?

"Thirteenth Street, Bolling Air Force Base."

Between the Potomac and I-295, Joint Base Anacostia-Bolling was the base for the Air Force's honor guard and band. There were no flight operations there. In fact, its tree-lined streets housed far more dependents than service personnel. The BOQ (bachelor officer quarters) just off Luke Street were spacious, anonymous, and usually with vacancies the command support staff would be delighted to have filled by transient service veterans.

An hour later, Jason had checked into a small suite, showered, changed clothes, and made an appointment with the base clinic to have his bandage changed the next day. He was ready for something to eat. The clerk in the lobby directed him to the officers' club, barely two blocks away. Twice, women pushing baby carriages passed him on the sidewalk, each wishing him a cheery good morning. The tidy individual base housing units with their neat lawns, many displaying Big Wheels, tricycles, and swing sets, gave the impression more of a small town rather than a military base.

Jason would be comfortable there. Better yet, he wouldn't be there long enough to get bored.

20

The man called Pedro scowled as he looked at the message on the computer screen dated the previous day: "Package arrived per flight plan. Temporary help in place. Smith."

The obtuse language was a precaution against possible interception by ECHELON, even though the practice was under attack by the European Parliament as an instrument of industrial espionage. Whether the outrage was warranted or the result of the system's exposure of six billion dollars in graft paid by an aircraft manufacturer to French officials, Pedro neither knew nor cared.

Behind him a younger man also watched the screen. "Package?" he asked in Russian. "I do not understand, Colonel."

Pedro whirled around, snarling. "Better you should stumble than misspeak! Do not ever refer to me so! My name is Pedro!"

Realizing the greater part of his anger was the result of several shots of vodka, not the other man's indiscretion, he relented slightly. He produced a pack of Russian cigarettes, black tobacco with cardboard filters, and offered one to the other man. "Is better we speak Spanish. Or better yet, English."

The other man shook his head in a polite "no thanks" to the tender of the cigarettes. "I still do not understand. I was sent out here by my commander. . . ."

Pedro struck a match and inhaled hungrily. The odor reminded the younger man of the smell of silage on his family's farm near Kiev.

"You *volunteered* to serve the cause of saving the planet." Pedro corrected. "And I am glad to see you, Sergi, er, Carlos. We worked well together in the past."

Carlos smiled. "I am flattered you remember. You were *polkovnik*, a colonel. I was a mere *mladshiy leytenant*, a junior lieutenant. But our mission here is not clear to me. I do not understand Russia's interest in such matters as saving species such as the little fish, the snail darter, in the United States, or preserving the range of the Arctic polar bear."

Holding the cigarette between his lips, Pedro turned off the computer, thankful for an excuse not to have to deal with others for the moment. He put an avuncular arm around Carlos's shoulder, leading him into what served as the house's living room: cheap chairs made of canvas slung over metal frames. "Come, share a vodka, and I will explain what our superiors in Moscow did not."

Moments later each man stood, glass in hand. "*Tva-jó zda-ró-vye!*" they said in unison, tossing down the liquor in a single gulp.

The older, Pedro, refilled the glasses while the foul-smelling tobacco smoldered in an ashtray. "Most of the world believes Marxism is dead," he began. "At least in the West. But it is not. It has simply changed names and methods."

Carlos said nothing, a questioning look on his face.

"That is why GrünWelt and related entities exist, my young friend, to continue the struggle against the capitalist oppression of the working classes."

The younger man ignored his refilled glass. "I do not see what attacking Japanese whaling vessels has to do with Marxism."

Pedro had tossed back his drink and was refilling. "It may or may not. That is not the point. The point is that by embracing and furthering the cause of saving the planet, we weaken the industrialized Western imperialists."

Carlos started to ask a question, but Pedro held up a restraining hand. "For instance, just here in Puerto Rico we and our allies forced the closing of a US naval gunnery range on the island of Vieques, insisting it was creating an environmental disaster even though only a small part of the island was involved. A few years ago, our protests forced the US Navy to quit testing antisubmarine sonar off the coast of California because we claimed the sound disturbed whales. One does not pull a fish out of the pond without effort, eh?"

Carlos was impressed. "Surely no sane nation would compromise its defenses for the sake of a few whales?"

Pedro started to pour him another vodka, stopping when he saw the previous glass was untouched. "It gets better yet. Our friends in America have so far prevented or severely limited new offshore drilling, increasing America's dependence on foreign oil, a source we hope to cut off with the help of our Arab friends."

"Arab friends?"

"The Arab nations."

"Nations? More like tribes with flags!" Carlos snorted derisively. "We have allies in America?"

Pedro shrugged. "They are unwitting allies, people devoted to green causes even at the expense of their own country. Each year they protest the building of nuclear power plants. Or any power plants, insisting electricity can be generated by windmills and solar power panels sufficient to run the industry of the land. They scream that dams that generate hydroelectricity prevent the spawning of salmon. Or will cause the demise of the small fish you mention."

"The snail darter."

"Yes, that is it." Pedro, his face becoming flushed, laughed loudly. "When American industry shuts down for lack of fuel, perhaps the people can eat snail darters, eh?"

"Global warming has become an issue," Carlos observed. "I suppose we oppose carbon emissions."

His hand wavering, Pedro filled his own glass again. "Absolutely. But we have to do little. The American people fear world industrialization has caused the problem. In fact, one of their former vice presidents flies about the world in a private jet preaching just that. He also heats and cools several homes."

"The people do not realize how much carbon that jet puts into the atmosphere? I would think it would be hundreds of times more per-passenger seat mile than a commercial aircraft."

"And for this he won a Nobel Prize! The American people love causes and man-made global warming is the current cause."

Carlos only sipped at his glass rather than downing it all at once. "And is the planet warming? And is it man's doing?"

"Who knows? Who cares? When one burns wood in the fireplace, one does not ask who felled the tree, eh? The final result is centuries in the future, long after our bones have become dust. What is important is that we must not let this opportunity to finally topple the capitalist system slip our grasp."

Carlos shook his head at the proffering of the bottle. The young Russians were not as inclined to binge drink as their elders. Or to spout old aphorisms. "And how does that relate to the operation that has just begun in America?"

Pedro wagged an unsteady finger at him. "This man Peters has possession of certain . . . certain things that could be damaging to our cause, the cause of preserving Earth." He snickered, holding up his glass in yet another toast. "The cause of GrünWelt!"

"You will try to gain possession of these, er, objects?"

"Of course. We will use professionals, some of our former military friends who have no connection to GrünWelt. Should they be apprehended, they cannot be traced to us."

He extended an arm as though in another toast, staggered forward, and would have fallen had not Carlos stood just in time to catch him under the arms. "Come, comrade. It is afternoon, time for the siesta the people here love so much."

Pedro was already snoring by the time Carlos laid him out on a couch.

21

267 Beisihuanzhonglu
Most Serene Development Company
Haidian, Beijing
The Day Before

Wan Chu stared out of the windows of his tenth-story office, where the outline of the 2008 Olympic Stadium could be seen. Although less than a quarter of a mile away, the massive structure appeared ghostlike in the brown haze that most residents of China's capital city had come to accept as normal. The facts that most local factories were fueled by high-sulfur-content coal and that the city's natural air circulation was limited by its location in a shallow valley combined to produce some of the foulest air on Earth. Rationing permits for operating private vehicles inside Beijing's Inner Ring Road and mandating alternate days when each car, motorcycle, or truck could operate had not helped.

The Most Serene Development Company, being entirely owned by the government like most Chinese companies, was not subject to such bothersome regulations.

A knock at Wan Chu's office door announced the entry of Chunhua, his secretary. In the three years Chunhua had been employed, Wan had never seen her when her face was not partially covered by the surgical mask so many Chinese wore in the forlorn hope it would screen out some of the air's pollutants. Such was the price to be paid for the world's fastest-growing economy, one that would soon be greater than that of the United States. Not only was China a major creditor of the Western democracy, it was more productive.

Wan Chu, like most Chinese, was puzzled by a country that would intentionally cripple its own industry with a plethora of laws and regulations that were making the stamp "Made in the USA" obsolete while sending manufacturing jobs out of the country at a rate rivaling the migration of lemmings, those rodentlike animals that supposedly drowned themselves by the thousands.

Now that the Soviet Empire had self-destructed, the United States was the sole remaining enemy of the People's Republic of China, the one obstacle to Asian, if not world, domination. If it also chose to self-destruct, so much the better. Soon, the Chinese Navy would be strong enough to simply take back Taiwan while the United States did little more than whine to the United Nations. They certainly would not have the stomach for armed conflict over the island, no matter what their guarantees of Taiwan's independence said. After that, US interest in the East could easily be terminated, either peacefully or by threat of a force the Americans would have neither the material or will to oppose.

But that was the future.

Chunhua placed a printout of an e-mail on the otherwise empty desktop and turned to leave.

"Comrade Secretary," Wan stopped her, using the largely outdated form of address, "we have discussed this before: It is unfitting for one of the People's employees to display that mask. It implies the People are unable to produce air fit to breathe."

It was an old and likely dead issue, but Wan felt it his duty to bring it up anyway.

"Comrade," Chunhua replied, "it is not the air I fear. It is the many diseases spread in the People's air by evil spirits."

Wan had made as little headway in dispensing with the woman's peasant superstitions as he had with the removal of the mask.

He sighed, conceding both matters for the moment. "You have read the e-mail?"

She bobbed her head. "Of course, Comrade Employer. GrünWelt is having a problem."

When wasn't GrünWelt having problems? Letting an operation be run by Russian thugs had been a mistake from the beginning. Of course the company's European operation was having a problem. GrünWelt was ostensibly a Swiss eleemosynary institution dedicated to saving the world from being ravaged by a greedy mankind. As did most organizations controlled by the People's Republic, it had three layers.

First were the members, those well-meaning if ill-informed people who, for whatever reason, believed, or professed to believe, the earth was in imminent peril from man-made global warming. They ranged from Birkenstock-shod vegans to businesses that capitalized on "going green" by manufacturing everything from self-decomposing plastic bottles to environmentally friendly laundry detergent.

Next came the Russian ideologues, those former Communist Party members whose equally firmly held beliefs told them that capitalism could be destroyed by use of the green/global-warming movement. Their methods could be and frequently were illegal and violent, carried out with the fervor of zealots, including sabotage of enterprises deemed Earth-unfriendly, such as mining and petroleum operations, nuclear plants, and an endless list of industries. As long as they remained untraceable to GrünWelt, Wan Chu cared only that they achieved the goals set in Beijing, through Switzerland. As far as these men knew, the fifty- or hundred-dollar donations of its members actually supported GrünWelt and its global operations.

Nothing could be further from the truth. Those pitifully small gifts were not enough to pay for a single attack on a Japanese whaler or sabotaging a single pipeline or oil well. GrünWelt was actually funded by the profits from trading fraudulent carbon credits. At first Wan Chu and his Most Sublime Development Company had been skeptical as to the gullibility of the West. Put a value on each metric ton of carbon dioxide released into the air and then trade credits for each ton below that assigned by the European Carbon Exchange or the Chicago Environmental Credit Exchange? Who would be so stupid as to admit they had exceeded the quota assigned by some government?

Western corporations, that's who. Europe, where such foolishness was regulated or the United Sates, where big companies feared public opinion. If power company A exceeded its carbon limit, it could find manufacturer B who had not reached its limit and buy "credits." The same amount of carbon dioxide was released into the atmosphere, of course, but those who bought credits either stayed within the law in Europe or got good press in the States.

Wan Chu had come up with the idea of purchasing a number of small plants in France, Holland, and Belgium, along with their assigned carbon limits. The factories, marginally profitable anyway, were shut down, thereby producing nothing but credits, which were sold. The idea became so profitable, the People's Republic repeated the process in every country in the European Union except Greece, which manufactured nothing that Wan Chu could ascertain rated emissions restrictions. That done, phony manufacturers were incorporated and did nothing more than hiring phantom workforces to pretend to produce items actually made in China and collecting more salable carbon credits. It had been a jewel in Wan's crown when one of these bogus companies had actually been cited for its carbon efficiency by the American most prominent in the war against global warming, the same American who heated and cooled half a dozen vacation homes and flew about in a private jet.

Wan returned his thoughts to the woman standing in front of his desk. "What sort of a problem this time?"

"The American, Peters."

"And?"

"Intelligence has located him in Washington by scanning airline passenger manifests. Surveillance from our embassy has tracked Peters to an Air Force base in the city. Perhaps the San Juan, er, office, might like to know."

The Russians in San Juan. They would not even have to cross a border. They were crude but deadly when efficient. He would not have to worry about Peters much longer. Chunhua might be an ignorant, superstitious peasant, but she was quite capable.

He dismissed her with a "Thank you, comrade. You have been most helpful."

He watched her departure. Now the Most Serene Development

Company and all it had achieved was threatened because of a lucky find in a glacier and this American called Peters. Peters was the last-known person possessing what was found in the glacier, and the Russians had let Peters escape in Iceland even though they had taken care of the little man who used the name of a long-dead movie star. You could hardly trust people who daily drank a liquor that tasted like gasoline and who used violence rather than subtlety or patience to achieve their ends. But that decision had been made higher up the food chain than Wan. Much higher.

Turning to the computer keyboard, he typed an encrypted message, which, even if decoded, would only have read "The package you seek is in Washington. Location upon your arrival."

For some reason, he had a bad feeling about this. Joss, experience, whatever. Peters was trouble.

22

Jason was speaking into his BlackBerry. "There are a couple of things I need. First, I had to leave the Glock in Iceland."

Momma's voice came across the vapor as mellifluous as if she were standing there. "Easy enough. I can have another over to you in an hour, hour and a half, with a coupla extra clips and National Security permit. Anything else?"

Jason didn't want to ask how she could arrange for a concealed-carry permit when it took weeks of investigation, mounds of forms, vetting, and a biography almost pre-dating birth. City of Washington permits simply didn't exist, no matter what the Supreme Court said.

"Yeah. I need a name of someone at the laboratory at the Department of Agriculture, as well as someone who can do a metallurgical analysis."

There was the sound of a pen scratching on paper. Momma was a believer in making old-fashioned lists rather than relying on cyber entries that could disappear on a whim.

"Anything else? I mean, the PX got your brand of scotch? Your love life OK?"

"What love life? After you cooked up that expedition to get Maria out of the way, I'll be lucky to see her in six months."

A deep chuckle, the sound of logs crackling in a fireplace. "By that time, this problem be solved. She'll never know what you did."

Manipulative old woman!

But he said, "I hope not."

The phone went dead.

Forty-five minutes later a package arrived by private courier. It included a business card of a Seymore Watt, PhD, Department of Agriculture. Jason had no idea how a firearm and ammunition got past the guard shack at the base's entrance. He had just finished making sure the Glock was in good functioning order when his BlackBerry pealed off the ominous opening bars of Beethoven's Fifth Symphony, his personalized ring tone.

Momma was as good as her word.

"Jason?" Maria's voice was excited. "Where have you been? I've been trying to reach you for hours!"

"Er, been in DC. No reason there'd be a reception problem. Things going well with you and . . . ?"

"Pier Sevensen. They're going great! Did you get the pictures I sent?"

"Haven't checked for messages lately."

"Well, you'll see. This afternoon, we went out to a volcanic field, geysers all over the place, like your Yellowstone Park."

A whole field of geysers? She sounded as excited as a child on Christmas morning.

"Jason, you have no idea! Iceland is a volcanologist's dream, every kind of volcanic activity you can imagine!"

Not exactly a recommendation Condé Nast's glossy travel magazines would give, Jason thought.

But he said, "And the expedition, how's it coming along?"

"We should have it fully equipped in a week. Your friend Momma has been a perfect angel. Everything we need arrives almost as soon as we ask for it."

I'll bet.

"After it's all set I'll come home until Eyjafjallajökull has sufficiently . . . Speaking of home, where are we going to go if we can't go back to Isola d'Ischia?"

A decidedly reproachful tone.

"I'm working on that."

"In other words, you don't know. Jason, I hope you've learned your lesson. Doing violent things only brings more violence. If you hadn't gotten involved in that shooting in Africa, we would still be at our villa . . ."

And you wouldn't be among all those geysers and volcanoes.

Gently, Jason put the BlackBerry down, reached across a small table, and unscrewed the top of a bottle of Balvenie single-malt scotch. A bargain at the PX at only seventy-five bucks a fifth. He could still hear her voice if not the words as he crossed over to the kitchenette, filled a glass with ice, and returned. Picking up the BlackBerry, he murmured assent, put it down, and filled his glass.

". . . I don't want to have to move for fear of our lives again. I just hope you'll listen to me this time . . ."

"I always listen to you, Maria."

She *hmph*ed her indignation before changing the subject. "I hope so, Jason, I really do. Don't forget to look at the pictures I sent you. Well, have to go. I'm having dinner with Pier."

Herring, no doubt.

"Don't forget: No more violence."

"Don't worry. I'm only gathering information."

"Love you."

"Me too."

The BlackBerry went silent.

Taking the iPad from his overnight bag, Jason put his buds into his ears. He leaned back in the room's most comfortable chair, sipped from his glass, and let the swift violin strokes of the opening concerto of Vivaldi's *Four Seasons* take over. Priest, composer, violin virtuoso, the man left his native Venice for Vienna seeking the patronage of the emperor Charles VI only to die a pauper in a foreign city.

Jason supposed there was a cautionary tale there somewhere, something about leaving the safety of one's native land for adventure abroad. If so, it thankfully eluded him.

23

The US Department of Agriculture is housed in two buildings connected by an enclosed bridge. Both are of an architecture a purist would describe as classicism. Jason thought of it as Government Gothic, the continually replicated, unimaginative cubes that house the bureaucracy along the National Mall. The sameness of the stone and minimum adornments were less than pleasant to his artist's eye. That, he surmised, is what you get with the lowest bidder.

The uniformed security guard informed him Dr. Watt's office was in the second building. Even if Jason had not known it was the south building that housed the laboratory, his nose would have tipped him off. The faint smell of chemicals permeated the air, the walls, and even the elevator he took to the second floor.

Chemistry had not been the highlight of his academic career. The second time he had been unable to recall whether water must be added to acid or vice versa had resulted in his banishment from a damaged college chem lab. Geology had proved a safer and less volatile fulfillment of his science requirements.

113

He hoped the next Jason Peters was not in the lab, at least not until the present one cleared the building.

Just as he stepped out of the elevator into a hallway, he was greeted with "Ah, Mr. Peters! I've been expecting you."

A smiling, round-faced Asian woman with jet-black hair tied in a knot on top of her head was wearing an ankle-length lab coat. As she approached, she extended her right hand. "I'm Miriam Wu. Good to meet you."

Jason looked up and down the hall. "I was meeting a Dr. Watt. . . ."

Her smiled widened. "I know. He had an emergency of some sort. A corn fungus in Kansas, I think." She frowned. "Or was it the return of the potato beetle in Idaho? No matter. He asked me to meet with you since I'm the one who did the research your foundation requested. Hope you don't mind."

"'Foundation'?"

She looked at him, puzzled. "Yes. I believe it was the Food for the World Foundation or something like that, someone Dr. Watt knew."

Rather than put his foot in his mouth, Jason said nothing.

He felt a firm grip as they shook. "I appreciate your seeing me, Dr. Wu."

She did not let go of his hand but led him into a large room where beakers, vials, and other chemical paraphernalia were lined up on tables. Against one wall, bottles held liquids of all colors. At the front of the room were two smaller tables with microscopes.

"Our lab," she said needlessly. "Not the sort of thing you'd see over at the FDA, but good enough. Sometimes we get ignored, you know." She snorted. "Just because botanists aren't searching for a cure for cancer, we get only the scraps from the budget."

"But so many medicines have come from plants," Jason said tactfully. He tried desperately to think of one. "Like penicillin from mold. Mold *is* a plant, is it not?"

She gave him a dazzling smile. "Yes, a fungus, actually. Like mushrooms. But the government's bean counters don't get the bang for the buck with herbal medicines that they do with chemical drugs." She giggled. "Oh, my, I'm running on! You're not here for departmental squabbles. Please, have a seat."

She indicated one of two stools at one of the smaller tables.

"So," Jason said, assuming the pleasantries were at an end and it was time to get down to business, "what did you find about our mysterious twig?"

Her mouth twisted into an expression of puzzlement. "What I think I found doesn't jibe with anything I've seen before. Where did you obtain the specimen?"

"Iceland."

"No, really? You couldn't have."

It required no sensitivity training to perceive Dr. Wu's skepticism. Reaching into his jacket pocket, Jason produced three photographs he had printed from the digital images on Boris's cell phone. "The person who found the, er, specimen took these pictures." He handed them to her. "I think they show the thing growing out of a glacier."

She sat down hard on one of the stools, her eyes focused on the pictures. "Unbelievable!"

Jason sat beside her. "Want to share with me exactly what is so hard to believe?"

She put down the prints and stared into space a moment, composing her thoughts. "What we have here, what you gave me isn't a twig; it's a vine of the species *Vitis vinifera*."

"Forgive me, Doctor, but Latin was never my language."

"A grapevine. But in Iceland? Talk about hard to believe! I mean . . ." She swallowed audibly and continued. "That isn't the half of it. A little botanical history, if you will indulge me. The first grapes were what we call dioecious, that is, they had either male or female flowers, depending on pollination from bees, wasps, bats, whatever, just as do any number of vegetables and fruits today. Obviously, the process was haphazard. A bee isn't interested in pollination, just pollen. He might well pollinate our early grapes with pollen from, say, non-fruit-bearing flowers, resulting in very small grapes, inedible fruit, or no grapes at all.

"Then, somewhere along the line, evolution stepped in: The species mutated, producing what we call a perfect flower, one with both male and female parts. The grapevine became hermaphroditic. We're unsure of when this happened exactly. The first mention of wine-quality grapes we know of is Sumerian from the third millennium B.C., but we have no way of knowing if this was before or after the mutation. We do know that one of the Spanish explorers of North America mentioned a large, white grape growing along Cape Fear, North Carolina, in 1504, most likely a scuppernong. No doubt these grapes had mutated.

"Samples tested for DNA tells us your grapevine is not hermaphroditic."

"Meaning?"

"Meaning it isn't of recent origin."

Jason asked, "Define 'recent.'"

"That's what I don't know. What I can tell you is that in the early 1800s the roots of most European vines were infected with a species of fungus known as phylloxera. Wiped out most vineyards. North American vines were resistant, so European vines were grafted onto American roots. DNA also tells us your specimen pre-dated that graft."

"So, the vine from the glacier pre-dates the early nineteenth century."

Dr. Wu picked up the woody piece of vine, using it as a pointer. "I can't prove it to a scientific certainty, but the fact that this vine pre-dated the mutation I mentioned would make me think it is far older than that. One more thing."

Jason was having a hard time digesting what he had already heard. "And that is?"

"This vine is of the genus *Assyritko*. Not exactly, but a close relative."

"Isn't that a Greek wine?"

"Not just Greek. It is a white grape originating on the island of Santorini, which, as you may know, is of volcanic origin."

"Possibly the greatest volcanic eruption in history, if I recall. When? Sometime in the first millennium B.C.?"

"You'd have to ask the Department of Natural History. But what is significant, now that you told me where the specimen came from, is that I understand there is a great deal of volcanic activity in Iceland. The same sort of soil found on Santorini would be there as well."

Jason took the twig, turning it over in his hand. "It couldn't be all that old, could it? I mean, wood rots."

"Not if encased in ice where oxygen can't get to it. I . . ." Dr. Wu paused, looking toward the back of the room, where a young woman stood. "Excuse me a moment. One of my assistants."

As the two women conferred in the back of the cavernous room, Jason turned the piece of vine over in his hand, trying to both digest what he had just heard and fit that information into what he knew. Grapes in Iceland? What about that fact was worth killing for? And what was the possibility the scrap he held had been accidentally, or intentionally, dropped into the glacier? And what part, if any, did the little piece of metal play?

He hoped he would have the answer to the last question shortly after leaving Dr. Wu.

The botanist finished her conversation and returned. "Wanted some help on an experiment. Where was I?"

"Grapevine in a glacier in Iceland."

"Oh, yes. Glaciers aren't my specialty, but I do know some of our more remarkable discoveries have come from bits of vegetation found in them, plants long extinct, evidencing climatic conditions we never knew existed."

"Like a climate warm enough to grow grapes."

"Like, for instance, we know from the rings of frozen trees carried along by ice caps, glaciers, that there was what is known as the Medieval Warm Period, a time when the earth was unusually warm, between roughly 800 and 1300."

Jason thought about this. "So, you think this grapevine might have come from that time period."

She nodded. "That's the only logical explanation I have."

"Is it possible someone planted that bit of vine there?"

She shook her head. "Possible, I suppose; but from the photo it would have to have been there a long time to be that deep in the ice."

"How long?"

Again, the head shake. "As I said, glaciers aren't my specialty, but from what little I do know, it would have taken centuries for that bit of vine to be that deep in the ice."

Science wasn't as precise as Jason had hoped. "And how did a Greek variety wind up in Iceland?"

"Again, just a guess, but the Greeks were great traders. That particular genus could have found its way north from the Mediterranean, maybe carried by Viking raiders who plundered from there to the North Sea. No way to be sure."

"I still can't get my mind around grapes in Iceland."

"Stranger things have happened." She shot the cuff of her lab coat, glancing at her watch. "Now, if you will excuse me, Mr. Peters, I have the taxpayers' work to do."

24

Another ugly building on the National Mall. At least this one housed not an anthill of bureaucrats but a division of a private foundation, the Smithsonian Institution.

Jason entered under the suspended re-creation of a mammoth blue whale, the world's largest animal, and went to the information desk. Following directions, he took another elevator. The corridor was lined with offices. Judging by the space between doors, closets had been subdivided. He stopped in front of the one that bore the name-plate that matched the name on the piece of paper he held, Dr. Sewell Sutter, professor of anthropology, University of Maryland.

The good professor also worked at the Smithsonian part-time.

"Come in!" Sewell responded to Jason's knock.

A smallish man sat behind a desk that must have seen generations of government employees come and go. Surprising for an academic's office, its top was cleared, other than the stack of papers the man behind it had been reading.

119

"Dr. Sutter?"

The man stood, revealing rumpled seersucker pants matching the jacket hanging on the nearby coatrack. He had a short beard, more gray than dark, and peered at Jason through owlish glasses with eyes that twinkled as though with a joke he was about to share. "Mr. Peters?"

The hand that gripped Jason's across the desk was calloused. Dr. Sutter engaged in some form of manual labor, something more strenuous than peering at artifacts.

He came around the desk and moved a stack of papers from the room's only guest chair to the floor. "Last term's exams," he explained. "My grad student has graded them but I still look them over."

Jason took the vacated seat. "I'm sure your students appreciate that."

Sutter retreated back behind his desk, smiling. "I doubt it. You know how it is with students: It's 'I *made* an A' but 'Professor Sutter *gave* me a C.' But you're not here to hear of the hardships of academia." He reached into a desk drawer, produced an envelope, and shook out the sliver of metal. "You want to know about this."

Jason said nothing.

The professor picked it up, holding it between thumb and forefinger as if exhibiting it to one of his classes. "We don't have much metallurgical equipment here, but a few simple tests told me this is iron alloyed with a touch of tin. It has traces of carbon less than a tenth of a percent."

Jason raised his eyebrows, a question.

"That small a percentage of carbon tells me the iron was not tempered, fired over charcoal. Doing so realigns the iron molecules, forming steel. But you can look at the thing and see it was forged, beaten out. In fact, a microscopic investigation revealed traces of the hammer. That is about all I can tell you for certain."

"That's it?"

The professor put the bit of metal back in the envelope and carefully placed it in the center of the desktop. "I can give you some well-reasoned speculation, if you like."

Jason leaned forward in the chair. "Please."

Sutter ran a hand across his chin, his beard making a scraping sound. "First, this is part of something old. Some of the marks would suggest it was whetted with stone, plus the fact that iron tools, as opposed to steel, haven't been made in centuries. The concept of age is reinforced by the fact it was formed by an early process, water-powered bellows and blast furnace. That procedure came into use shortly before the 1300s."

He paused and Jason asked, "Any idea what it was?"

"Based on the fact that it at one time had a cutting edge, I'd say it was some sort of tool, an agricultural implement. Again guessing, I'd say a late Middle Age billhook."

"A what?"

"Billhook. A knifelike tool shaped somewhat like the letter *J* lying on its side. That also is speculation, based on the fact that the iron is, as I said, not tempered and therefore not weapon-grade like, say, a sword or even a hunting knife. That leaves tools, and the suggestion of curvature suggests a billhook, a common agricultural tool used for cutting, pruning, et cetera."

"As in pruning grapevines, perhaps?"

Sutter looked surprised. "Why, yes, I'd think it could be used for that purpose. Why?"

"Just curious. Can you date it with any sort of precision?"

The professor picked up the envelope, holding it up to the light as if studying the outline of its contents. "I can't get any closer than what I've already said: late thirteenth century at the earliest. When was the hand-forging of iron replaced by machines? I have no idea. Sorry I couldn't be more helpful."

Standing, Jason took the envelope and slipped it into a jacket pocket. "But you have been, Professor."

They shook hands again and Jason was on his way, this time taking the stairs, his mind groping for answers: grapevines in Iceland centuries ago? A pruning tool that could well be seven, eight hundred years old? Interesting, perhaps, but . . . There must be something else. A key to some secret yet to be known. Whatever that secret might be, it had already caused the death of Boris.

He stopped halfway down the stairs.

Boris.

What was it he had tried to say just before Jason and the police commissioner had traveled out to the glacier? What were, in effect, his last words?

Something about meanies or beanies? A British institute and someone named . . . named? Cravat, that was it. Like the precursor of the necktie. No, Cravas.

The meanies or weenies or whoever made no sense at all but were the only clue Jason had at the moment. That and whoever Nigel Cravas might be—clues that might save his life if he could interpret them.

He had seen a small, windowless room with a number of computers on his way in. At that moment, no one was there. Taking a seat in front of the one most distant from the door, it took only seconds to get onto the Internet and Google.

Nigel Cravas, British Institute at Collingwood College, Durham University. He paused. Durham. . . . Cathedral town in . . . northern England.

As Jason read on, he knew he would soon be taking a trip.

25

267 Beisihuanzhonglu
Most Serene Development Company
Haidian, Beijing
08:40 Local Time
The Next Day

Tan Ching made Wan Chu nervous. It wasn't just that the older man was with the Ministry of State Security, China's intelligence service, or even his chain-smoking American Marlboro cigarettes that made Wan's office smell as bad as the industrially polluted air that filled the city's skies. It was the man himself, his half-lidded lizard eyes that missed nothing, his habit of nodding from time to time as though Wan had revealed some significant secret. The fact he had sent people who displeased him to Qincheng, China's political prison, gave no reassurance either.

Wan was unsure of the exact meaning of the man coming here rather than summoning Wan to his office as would ordinarily be the case. And uncertainty did nothing to control the nerves that made it difficult for Wan to sit still.

Ching exhaled a gust of smoke, a fire-breathing dragon. "Your people have secured the problem with the American?"

Wan glanced around for something to use as an ashtray. His only choice was the cup from which he'd just finished his morning jasmine tea. He slid it across the desk.

"Not yet. But they will get him. That's what they do."

Ching turned eyes cold as stone toward Wan. "And if he discovers the significance of whatever he took from the glacier first?"

Wan shrugged. "Their significance is subject to debate, comrade."

Ching's fist came down on the desk so unexpectedly, Wan flinched. "We do not need 'debate,' comrade! We need results!"

"Perhaps you have a suggestion?" Wan asked meekly.

The man across the desk lit a fresh cigarette from the butt of the previous one before dropping it into the teacup, where it hissed and went silent. "What motivates these men, these Russians?"

It took a second for Wan to understand the question. "They believe weakening capitalist nations to the point of collapse is a prerequisite for the return and ultimate triumph of Marxism. They see the global-warming cause as one that will move their agenda forward."

Ching snorted, sending smoke gushing from his nose. "Fools like that are useful. But what really motivates the men who do the work, the ones who you say will ultimately kill this man Peters?"

Wan looked at him blankly.

"Money!" Ching bellowed. "Political idealist or not, cash gets faster results than slogans or agendas." He stood. "Tend to it."

"Of course, comrade," Wan said, thanking whatever gods existed that the meeting was at an end.

26

Calle Luna 23
San Juan
At the Same Time

Although the hour was not late, especially by local standards, the number of cars with tinted windows drew attention in this otherwise quiet neighborhood. The vehicles each came to a stop in front of the house. Car doors opened and men got out of the backseats. None of these men was Latino. Instead, they looked *norteamericano* or, perhaps, European. Each carried a small bag or suitcase as though they had just arrived from the airport. As each passenger climbed out of an automobile, he hurried, head down, inside the house as though fearful of being seen.

The few locals who had not tired of speculating as to the meaning of these events had varying opinions as to their significance. Señora Valequez, age eighty-six, was certain she was witnessing one of the drug deals featured almost nightly on the TV news and wanted to call the police. Juanita, her married daughter with whom she lived, cautioned that those who interfered in such business frequently met with violent ends. Señor Hermez, from next door, noted that, from what he could see, the men were not members of any local gang he recognized. He was certain there was a plan afoot to move the Guantánamo Bay detainees to Puerto Rico. After all, didn't the Anglos send much of what they did not want to Puerto Rico since the US territory had no say in national politics?

As the last of the cars disgorged its single passenger and pulled away, equally wild guesses faded along with curiosity.

Inside Number 23, a dozen men were gathered, an assemblage somewhat larger than the downstairs room could comfortably accommodate. The men were all middle-aged and large. They looked hard. Many had scars, noses that had not been set properly after being broken, or gaps where teeth should have been. None of them had mustaches, beards, long hair, or any other tonsorial or grooming feature that might attract undue attention. A polyglot series of conversations was going on at once, the principal languages being Russian or English, although several other Slavic dialects were represented.

The man who called himself Pedro descended from the stairs and the voices died like a CD being turned off in mid-recording. He edged his way through the already tightly packed crowd, making his way to a table on which a laptop computer had been attached to a projector. Acknowledging greetings with a simple nod of the head, he went to the back wall and pulled down a screen, then turned to face the assembly.

He raised his voice and began in English, "May I have your attention!"

The request was unnecessary. The only sound was the straining of the air-conditioning unit in a losing battle with the increase of heat generated by so many bodies in such a small space.

A man's face flashed on the screen, its grainy quality suggesting the photo had been taken at a distance. It was replaced by another view of the same person.

"This is the man," Pedro said. "You will want to study his face so as to remember it."

A hand went up somewhere in the back. "What else do we know about him?"

"He has been professionally trained. He succeeded in killing the man we sent to Iceland."

A murmur of concern circled the room. "Professionally trained by who, military? Intelligence?"

Pedro held up his hands for silence. "It does not matter. What is important is that he be taken care of quickly. He poses a serious threat."

Pedro knew these men cared little for his cause. They were veteran Spetsnaz, Russia's equivalent of Navy SEALs or the Army's Delta Force. The breakup of the Soviet Union had sown chaos among the armed forces. Equipment left unrepaired, payments late or not whole, and scarcity of rations and supplies all brought disillusionment with the military. Some of the elite forces were assigned civilian duties, such as fighting an increasingly violent criminal element and protecting the country's leaders against attempts to dismantle the government by assassination. Many of the special forces quit in disgust at working under police bureaucrats. There were jobs providing private security for Russia's newest elite, the capitalist businessman. Some worked as mercenaries, finding lucrative employment training troops in African civil wars. Others simply hired out their weapons and abilities, never asking why their new masters were in need of both.

Money, not causes like GrünWelt, interested such men.

"We will pay five hundred thousand dollars to the team who rids us of this man," Pedro announced.

The offer was greeted by cheers and whistles.

"I have killed presidents of countries for less!"

"This man must be very hard to kill indeed."

"How will we claim the prize as the killer, bring you his head?"

"His balls would be easier!"

"You alone would know the difference between one man's balls and another's."

Only the last question drew a response. "Each of you will be assigned to a team, just as you were in the Army. Each team will be assigned to a specific geographic site where we know this man is likely to be. . . ."

The plan was similar to the way Spetsnaz had operated its programs of assassination of enemy political leaders in the past.

"I want to be assigned to wherever his woman is! There he surely will be, sooner or later," a man in front said.

The comment brought jeers and hoots.

"You do not even know if he has a woman," someone remarked.

"Such men always have women, frequently several."

Pedro let the increasingly ribald comments continue for a few moments before signaling for quiet again.

He held up a glass jar with a number of folded slips of paper in it. "These pieces of paper have numbers on them. Each number corresponds to a number on an envelope. Each envelope contains a location. The paper will be drawn from the jar by each team's leader as soon as I read off the names of the members of each team. You are not to discuss your location with anyone not on your team. That way, if one group should fall into the hands of local law enforcement, they will know nothing. Do you understand me?"

There was general nodding of heads and affirmative words until one man, perhaps slightly older than the others, asked, "Only one team will get the money. The multiple number of teams makes the odds against that being any one team. If I wish to gamble, I will do so in a casino."

There was grumbling agreement.

"I have thought of that. Each team will consist of four men, four teams. The leader of each team will receive one hundred thousand dollars in whatever currency he wishes when he leaves here tonight. That money may be divided however the team desires. That should at least pay your expenses."

There was a wave of indistinct voices with a tone of approval.

Pedro picked up the jar, holding it in both hands as he offered it to a man whose left eyelid drooped under a scar running from his left eyebrow to the right part of his chin. "Anatoly, you pick first."

An hour later, only the four team leaders remained in the house. The increase in the efficiency of the air-conditioning was noticeable. The four men lounged in canvas chairs, tossing back shots of vodka.

Anatoly was studying the slip of paper he had drawn. "This is strange. Why would my target be at this place?"

Pedro made an exaggerated gesture of putting a finger to his lips. "We are not to discuss the various locations."

Anatoly wouldn't quit. "I'm not discussing any specific location. I'm just saying this one is peculiar. Some of the men in my team may question if they are being given a fair chance at the bounty you have offered."

Rather than quarrel, Pedro got clumsily to his feet to peer over the other man's shoulder. "This is the location of the organization that sent the little man to Iceland in the first place. Had they not done so, the Americans would never have sent our friend Peters there. If the target knows who first was in touch with Karloff, he will go there."

Anatoly drained his glass of the clear liquid at a gulp. "*If*' is a word we do not like in our business."

Pedro collapsed into his chair. "You are not being paid to like it, but to act on it."

27

King's Cross Station
Central London
13:40 Local Time
Two Days Later

Jason was being followed.

He had confirmed the tail at the St. Pancras tube station as soon as he had stepped off the last of a series of trains he had taken from Gatwick. He had chosen a randomly circuitous route with the sole purpose of identifying anyone shadowing him. It had only been at St. Pancras he had been certain. There he had recognized a man of indeterminate age he had seen on a leg of the trip away from the station on the light-blue Victoria Line. The scar across his face was as unique as a fingerprint.

He had not seen the man on the Piccadilly Line but he had reappeared right here where the London Tube shared a station with the UK East Coast Mainline, rail service north. His absence on part of the meandering route told Jason the job was being conducted by two or more people, people experienced in observation techniques. He recalled the procedure from Delta Force's covert surveillance training: one person to keep the subject in view while using some means to communicate with one or more confederates to pick the trail when the present one dropped off. The point was to reduce the chances of the subject recognizing a single tail.

Exactly where these people had picked him up initially was uncertain. Most likely, it had been at the airport. Passenger manifests of airlines were insecure enough to almost be in the public domain and the carriers cared about as much about their passengers' privacy as they did about their comfort. If not Gatwick, keeping an eye on rental-car companies or one of several tube stations would work as well. No matter. The time of the horse's departure from the barn really didn't make much difference. The object of the exercise now was to terminate the unwanted attention.

As if to confirm what he already knew, Jason watched the man speak into a cell phone, no doubt alerting one or more that he, Jason, was headed for the GNER, the high-speed rail service.

Jason sighed heavily. So far this had been less than a pleasant trip and Scar Face and his as-yet-unseen pals weren't likely to improve things.

It had started the day before yesterday when he arrived at Dulles International. Even in first class, the days of luxurious and pleasant air travel had gone the way of age and weight restrictions on female cabin crew.

First class could not shield the passenger from the precooked cuisine microwaved out of the possibility of flavor, glop that hardly appealed to the taste. Why the airline didn't simply have McDonald's or some other fast food operator cater meals and thereby reach at least the bottom rung of mediocrity, Jason could not understand.

At least he had not had to wait to use the tiny restroom minutes before landing. A quick shave with the safety razor included in his first-class packet made him feel much better, as if it scraped away the grime of travel. A crisp white shirt replaced the rumpled knit polo. Neatly rolled khakis replaced jeans that looked as though he had slept in them, as indeed he had tried unsuccessfully to do.

Generally, he felt much better.

Until he had to contend with Scar Face & Co.

Pausing to lean on his wheeled board bag, Jason looked around the modernistic station. It was well lit by banks of lights over the track, giving the illusion of a skylight. Perhaps thirty or forty passengers milled about along the single platform before climbing aboard cars behind the slant-nosed GNER Voyager that would make the 254 miles to Durham in slightly over three hours before continuing on to Edinburgh and Glasgow. To Jason's left, a young man in jeans coaxed the haunting sounds of the *erhu*, the Chinese violin, from his odd-looking, two-stringed instrument. An occasional passerby dropped a coin into the musician's cup. To Jason's right, passengers were entering onto the platform from the stairs from above, many carrying plastic bags bearing the logo of the station's eight restaurants and food servers. Some had packages from the several shops.

Jason's attention centered on one of them, a man who could have been Scar Face's twin in size and bearing. He wore a pair of sunglasses although the light was far from harsh. The slight turns of the man's shaved head allowed Jason to size up the scene in front of him. An almost imperceptible nod directed Jason's gaze to where Scar Face himself rested a foot against a bench as he pretended to tie a shoe.

Jason was between the two men, and the new arrival was between him and the exit. He regretted he had not taken the time to use a contact in the City to acquire the weapon he could not have carried aboard the airline.

Jason's first impulse was to board the train and barricade himself into his first-class compartment. An instant's thought revealed the impracticality of the idea: in the narrow confines of a British rail car there would be little room to maneuver, particularly if he had to face two or more opponents.

Scar Face, finished with his shoe, was moving toward Jason, his gait idle as he pretended to study the adverts posted on the station's walls: shows opening off Piccadilly Circus, English taught in ten days, the newest chain of fish-and-chips shops. Without moving his head, Jason darted his eyes in the other direction. He was not surprised to see Skin Head moving in his direction too.

Both men held their right arms rigidly at their sides. Jason had little doubt each man had a knife up his long sleeve that would drop into a hand with a swing of the arm.

The move was familiar enough. Jason had seen it in a dozen training films somehow stolen from the Russian Spetsnaz Vympel, those übercommandos whose specialty was silent death behind enemy lines. Their trademark was proficiency with the combat knife, eight inches of balanced steel bearing a slight similarity to the American Bowie knife in that not only was the cutting edge razor sharp, but the first two inches behind the point were also honed to perfection, giving the weapon the ability to stab or slash in either direction. The Soviet-equipped groups also carried a clasp knife and a "fling" knife, a blade balanced for throwing.

The memory was less than comforting.

Jason searched the platform. Ah, yeah. There, in the middle, helping an elderly lady with her bags, a uniformed policeman.

The automatic weapon slung across his chest indicated he was with the Transportation Division of the Metropolitan Police, one of the few British police who routinely carried firearms, commonly seen in tube and rail stations since the bomb attacks of July 7, 2005. Now he stood, one hand behind his back, as he watched passengers move back and forth; the other held what looked like the oversized 1980s version of a cellular phone.

OK, now what?

Assuming Jason could get to the cop, what was he going to do, point out the two men as *possible* assailants?

With as much indifference as he could muster, Jason sauntered along the platform, a passenger looking for the car whose number matched that on his ticket. His bag's wheels hummed soothingly across the smooth concrete.

Unarmed, Jason stood a slim chance against one man with a blade, none against two. His daily workouts had kept him in physical shape and he remembered his military training well. But two professional assassins? It was the stuff of James Bond movies. Unless he had the advantage of surprise.

Surprise.

There was another part of his long-ago, if well-recalled, Delta Force preparation he was calling upon, those situations where trainees were placed in near impossible situations, forced to rely on their wits and whatever was at hand.

Scar Face and Skin Head were closing the gap, their eyes flicking between Jason and the cop. So far, neither man seemed particularly concerned. They came to a halt as Jason reached the officer.

Jason recalled an article he had read about the tube. Luckily for the tranquility of its passengers, cell phones rarely worked in the underground system. Since the bomb attacks, however, this seeming benefit had become a hazard: What happened if there was another emergency? The problem had been solved in January 2009, when TETRA technology had established emergency cellular phone contact between special handheld sets issued to police and others working in the network.

Jason held up a copy of the multicolored diagram of the system. "Excuse me, Officer, but could you tell me how I get to Victoria Station?"

Conditioned to questions from tourists unable to read the simplest of maps, the cop reached for the sheet of paper Jason was proffering with one hand.

Jason instantly snatched the bulky cell phone from the astonished policeman and depressed what he hoped was the Speak button. "Bomb!" he yelled. "Bomb!" He had read that the phones had locator devices but now was not the time to verify reports. "At King's Cross Station!" he added.

The cop was trying to grab back the gadget as pandemonium broke loose. One woman's corgi had slipped its leash and was tearing at ankles. Baggage was deserted where it had fallen. People were shoving one another to get to the exit, a tide that swept both Scar Face and Skin Head along with it. Jason broke free of the officer's grasp and hurled the bulky phone against the nearest wall, where it shattered. There would be no countermanding this report.

Having failed to retrieve his phone, the officer grabbed Jason by the collar. "You'll be coming with—"

With both hands, Jason swung his roll-aboard, catching the surprised policeman's knees, which buckled like a felled oak. The instant he let go of Jason to try to prevent a fall, Jason was off, running with dozens of panicked passengers.

The exit was jammed, not only by those trying to get out, but also by uniforms from the adjacent tube stations trying to get in.

Scar Face and Skin Head had disappeared.

28

Metropolitan Police (New Scotland Yard)
8–10 Broadway
Victoria, London
Two Hours Later

The morning had seemed the precursor of an enjoyable day for Inspector Dylan Fitzwilliam: Tonight, Shandon, his wife, would return from a five-day visit with the grands in Manchester. No more takeaway dinners, no more shoddy cleaning by the charwoman. A series of snatch-and-grabs in the Petticoat Lane Market that had the print media in an uproar had been solved as of yesterday, the malefactors safely in the nick, and, finally, two days of unseasonable drizzle had lifted, bathing the city in sunlight.

That was this morning.

Now there was the American.

As per the inspector's standing request, he had been notified of any "unusual" activity in the tube stations and a false bomb threat was, well, unusual. Fomenting a panic like the one that had ensued at King's Cross, it had been mere luck no one had been trampled to death if the security tapes sent over by the British Transport Police were to be believed. As it was, there were enough complaints of cuts and bruises and at least one possible broken arm.

Someone who thought a prank like this was funny was seriously sick. Next time someone might get killed. Or, worse, a real bomb threat might be viewed as crying wolf one too many times. The bloody Yank would have to be apprehended before one of his "jokes" caused serious harm. No doubt he was, in fact, an American according to the officer whose radio he had used.

Fitzwilliam felt the beginning of a headache. Scowling, he reached for his empty pipe and sucked on the stem. The damn health Nazis had forbidden a man smoking in his own office. By the time he took the creaky, 1960s vintage lift down to the Leper Colony, the name the employees had given the outdoor smoking area, and he enjoyed a half bowl of tobacco as much as standing around outside would allow, he would have wasted half an hour. Nothing to do but smoke and make idle conversation with chaps he barely knew. That and look at the building itself. From any angle, it suggested a ship's bow. Fittingly enough, since the structure had originally been intended to house part of the Admiralty. Instead, it had become home to the boffins at MI5 before being turned over as a hand-me-down to the Metropolitan Police.

The American.

Hold on a bit! The Yank had been in a rail station, right? A rail station would suggest he was on his way somewhere other than the inspector's bailiwick, spreading his brand of mayhem into someone else's jurisdiction.

Fitzwilliam put his pipe back in the perfectly clean glass ashtray he had not been able to use for six years now. He shook his head. No, he couldn't just dump his problem on some unsuspecting constable out in the shires, could he?

His ill mood deepening by the minute, he reached for the phone on his desk and punched a single key. "Patel? Could you pop by? Yes, now."

In less than two minutes there was a gentle tap on the door and a dark-faced man with a brilliant smile stepped inside, standing rigid as a ramrod. "Sah!"

Patel must have used the stairs to get here this quickly. Commendable. Still, his military-like bearing made the inspector slightly nervous. Even though his subordinate had grown up in a family who had spent generations in the colonial regiments, he did wish Patel would not act as though he were on review by the royal viceroy. Fitzwilliam supposed he should be thankful the man didn't stamp both feet when reporting. There would have been complaints from the floor below.

The only things more annoying was the smell of curry that seemed imbedded in the man's skin and the fact he was always smiling, even when being dressed down. People who smiled all the time did not understand a policeman's world. Or, for that matter, any world Fitzwilliam knew.

"You are aware of what happened this morning at the King's Cross tube station?"

Patel's eyes were centered on a spot above Fitzwilliam's head, another annoying military legacy. "Yes, sah!"

Whatever his shortcomings, they did not include a failure to keep apprised of what was going on around the cop shop.

"We can't let this man, this American, run loose around London until he causes a riot." Fitzwilliam picked up his pipe, peering into the blackened bowl. "You may need a pen and pad."

The two items appeared in Patel's hands as though by magic.

"First, I want to know if anyone spots this man. We have a number of pictures from the station's security cameras. If he shows up on a camera, I want to know about it."

The inspector referred to the number of surveillance cameras placed around London. A nervous public had reluctantly agreed to this mass intrusion on its privacy during the years of random bombings by the IRA. Like most government programs initiated for specific expediency, this one lingered long after the emergency passed, now justified as helping to reduce crime.

"If we find him," Fitzwilliam continued, "I think we have ample grounds for arrest, what with the trouble he caused at King's Cross."

Patel's eyes stared over the top of his pad. "Arrest?"

"Arrest. Charge of public disorder, inciting a riot in a tube station, whatever. We can at least detain him before someone gets killed, put him on a plane back to wherever in the States he comes from. I suggest you start by having the security people at all rail and tube stations keep an eye out for him. The pictures show him with a bag, luggage. That would suggest he's in transit. That's just a guess, of course."

"You are quite good at guessing, sah."

29

Euston Station
London Underground
A Few Minutes Later

Jason had been waiting for more than two hours for the excitement to settle down at the St. Pancras/King's Cross station just a few blocks away. From a fish-and-chip takeaway across the street, he had watched a procession of armored bomb-disposal vehicles, helmeted bomb-disposal personnel with body armor thick enough to make them resemble turtles, and sniffer dogs with no armor at all.

The British took his threat seriously, as well they should. But now there was no way to know what lines were still operating and the only train to Durham might well be delayed.

Worse, the uniformed beat cop had peered into the fish-and-chip shop with increasing frequency. Perhaps it was the bag that had aroused suspicion. Jason had wiped his face and fingers and left the tasteless and half-eaten meal still oozing grease into the newspaper on which it had been served. He ducked into the Underground, gratified to notice the police were no longer blocking the entrance. Perhaps he could get on his way after all.

It was a young woman in uniform who caught his attention just as he reached the bottom of the escalator. And not because she was young, rosy-cheeked, and rather pretty in that wholesome English way. She was studying a photograph Jason instantly recognized as himself, taken in the King's Cross station only hours before. Involuntarily, he raised his eyes to meet the glassy stare of a camera surveying the platform and those upon it.

The realization his picture might well be all over London made him think he was about to lose the fish and chips right here.

Carefully keeping his back to the young woman, he relaxed slightly as the next train whooshed into the station from his left. He stepped into the first door that wheezed open, shouldering aside a disembarking elderly gent complete with bowler on head and umbrella under one arm.

In response to the justifiable glare, Jason muttered an apology without slowing down. Instead, he reached the end of the car and stepped onto the small platform between it and the next. He continued at as a brisk pace as possible until he reached the fifth and final carriage, where the end was unlike the American subways to which he had become accustomed. The last car did not end in an opening simply barred by a spring gate. He was facing a locked steel door. Had it been that long since he had been in London?

A glance out of the window brought home another unpleasant unfamiliarity: there was no room between tracks even had he been able to leave the car. The London trains passed within inches, not feet, of each other, unlike their cousins across the pond.

A sound behind him made him turn around. A plump grandmotherly type was settling into her seat, eyeing him suspiciously over a large shopping bag that testified to a recent trip to the greengrocer's.

This was not going to work: if he were spotted on the train, police would be waiting at the next station. Bumping shoulders with several more passengers, he exited the train back onto the platform, his bag grasped tightly as the wheels bumped over uneven spots. Keeping his face to the ground, he forced himself to shuffle, not rush, to the stairs to the National Rail station above. He paused twice, both times to rub a hand along the stairs, accumulating a palmful of grime.

This time, his memory served him well. On the concourse to platforms 1–3 was the paper-doll-cutout sign for toilets. Besides the row of urinals, half a dozen stalls waited behind closed doors. The operation was not one run by the London Underground but private enterprise, as indicated by the man in the white mess jacket seated by the door who caught and misinterpreted Jason's urgency.

"That'll be fifty p, sah," he said pushing open the door to a vacant stall.

Jason handed the man a full pound, slamming the door behind him as he entered. First, he applied gritty palms to his face. Seated on the toilet, he rummaged through his bag until he found the wrinkled polo shirt and jeans. His clean shirt and khakis replaced them in the bag.

As he exited, the attendant made no effort to divert his stare or surprise. A quick glance in the mirror above the washbasins revealed the reason: Jason's face was streaked with dirt, his clothes looking very much like he had slept in them, quite likely on the street.

The attention of the people on the platform was focused on the arrival of half a dozen more uniformed officers. No one noticed the man at the end, the one who looked like he had slept in the tube as some of the city's homeless, scorning council housing, were wont to do. He was filthy: dark smears of soot across his face and hands that looked like they had handled coal dust. Bag tucked under one arm, he shuffled along with the gait of one who simply has nothing left in life to lose.

In London as in most American cities, street people are near invisible. The existence of the phenomenon has in recent memory become an embarrassment. The hobos and tramps of another era who survived on odd jobs and individual charity are today mere beggars, likely the victims of mental illness, addiction, or something else rendering them offensive if not potentially dangerous to the public. Collective charities have unwittingly soothed the common conscience by minimizing the sight of such people like the one dragging his feet along the platform now with soup kitchens, shelters, and counseling. None of those has removed the homeless from the streets but instead simply centralized them at such places as the Salvation Army's Faith House on nearby Argyle Street, no doubt this man's destination.

Consequently, no one paid the slightest attention to the rumpled, filthy wretch as he got onto the Up escalator and disappeared from sight.

Outside, Jason stepped off the curb and attempted to flag down a cab. The black Morris missed him by inches. A second effort with another taxi yielded the same result.

Of course. What hack driver was going to take a dirty—and very likely smelly—street person as a fare?

The third time, Jason moved as the taxi stopped for a light. Opening the door, he climbed into the backseat.

"Now, see here," the cabbie began angrily, turning in his seat.

Jason proffered a twenty-pound note. "Twenty-four Grosvenor Square."

London cabbies are famous for their encyclopedic knowledge of the city, so Jason should not have been surprised when the man asked. "US embassy? Are you daft, man?"

Apparently street people did not frequent embassies.

Jason sat back in the seat. "You have your fare. Drive."

Other than audible muttering, not another word was spoken during the trip.

The United Sates embassy to the Court of Saint James is in London's posh Mayfair section. Specifically, it takes up the western side of Grosvenor Square (which is actually circular), the street being closed to vehicular traffic since 2001. Statues of General Eisenhower and Franklin Roosevelt stand in the gardenlike green space at the center of the square. Nine stories (three underground) of white postmodernist architecture is capped by a huge gilt eagle. The style and statuary clash somewhat with the eighteenth-century Georgian town houses for which the square is known. One of them housed John Adams as the first American ambassador to England. It is likely the local residents will not be sad to see the embassy move to its proposed location in the Nine Elms section of Wandsworth. With one possible exception: the ground upon which the embassy presently stands is leased from the duke of Westminster because he would sell the site only upon the United States' return of Virginia—land seized from his family by the rebels during the Revolution.

Jason watched as the cab drove along Hyde Park and turned into Park Lane. Two blocks ahead was Grosvenor Square. Already Jason could see a line of people waiting for admission in hopes of obtaining visas. For some reason, the London embassy receives more than twice as many such applications than any other in Western Europe.

GREGG LOOMIS

"This will do," he said, opening the taxi's door and reaching for his roll-aboard.

The cabbie mumbled what might have been a thank-you before driving off.

Bag trailing behind, Jason walked beside the increasing line. Asians, Middle Easterners, some of undeterminable origins, but none conspicuously British. For some reason, it must be easier to enter the United States from the UK than from other countries. A few glared at him resentfully as he made his way to the guard shack at the front gate, where a US Marine sergeant in blue pants, khaki blouse, field scarf, and white cap stared straight ahead to where two corporals herded people through a metal detector before admitting them to a second, much shorter, line.

"Sir," the sergeant said, barely moving his lips and his head not at all, "you will need to go to the back of the line to fill out a visa application."

Jason wasn't aware he had been in the man's line of sight. He took out his passport and held it up. "Don't need a visa, but I do need to see someone in the trade attaché's section."

This time the Marine swiveled his head slightly, taking in Jason's disheveled and filthy appearance. "And just who in the trade section might that be?" he asked, amusement in his voice.

"Anyone above the rank of clerical help will do, for starters."

A smile broke across the man's face. "And just like that you expect me to call for some unknown person in this embassy to do exactly what?"

"Above your pay grade, Sergeant . . ." Jason made a show of reading the man's name tag pinned over the left pocket of his blouse. "Sergeant Kiwoski. You put me in touch with someone in the trade section on the double or I promise you you've seen your last days in this cushy Marine Security Guard deployment. Fuck with me, Sergeant, and you'll be on your way to the head shed at Eighth and I for reassignment to the sand-box before you have time to pack your sea bag. Understood?"

Perhaps it was Jason's familiarity with Marine jargon (Eighth and I Streets being the location of US Marine headquarters) or maybe it was his tone, which had all the softness of one or more of Kiwoski's former drill instructors. Possibly it was the man in the shabby outfit's eyes, hard and cold as glacial ice. For whatever reason, Kiwoski picked up the phone at his elbow, spoke no more than half a dozen words, and said, "Someone will be here in the next three minutes."

"Thank you, Sergeant."

Sure enough, barely ninety seconds had passed before a young man appeared. With emphasis on *young*. Despite the dark suit, club tie, and starched white shirt, the kid didn't look old enough to have graduated from high school.

He extended his right hand. "Wandsworth, George Wandsworth."

When he saw how grubby Jason's hand was he looked as though he might withdraw his own.

"Jason Peters."

"Follow me, Mr. Peters."

With brief stops at a metal detector and to examine Jason's bag, Wandsworth led Jason to a bank of elevators. As a door silently slid open, he motioned Jason in, followed him, and punched an unnumbered button. The car began a steady descent. They exited into what could have been a corridor in any office building, except there were no windows to the outside.

At the third door on the left, Wandsworth stopped, indicating Jason should enter. He did. The room was small, furnished with a government-issue metal table and four uncomfortable-looking chairs. The place reminded Jason of the interrogation rooms he had seen on TV cop shows.

Wandsworth indicated the closest chair and slid into the one across the table. "OK, Mr. Peters, what can your government do for you today?"

It had taken Jason less than fifteen seconds to spot the two cameras partially concealed in the ceiling. "That, Mr. Wandsworth, depends on your duties here."

Wandsworth put his elbows on the table, entwining his fingers. Somehow the gesture seemed feminine. "I'm not sure what you mean. As trade attaché, this office acts as a sort of chamber of commerce for the United States. If an English manufacturer, for example, is considering perhaps opening a plant in, say, Alabama, we do whatever we can to expedite the operation. That sort of thing."

Jason was shaking his head. "Then, the answer to your question as to what you can do is to let me speak to the head of section."

Wandsworth's eyes narrowed. "You're some kind of spook, aren't you?"

"Second time since I got here someone's asked me a question that's none of their business. You got a pen and paper?"

The young man patted his jacket pockets, producing a small spiral notebook and a pen.

Jason tore out a blank page, briefly wrote on it, folded the page, and handed it across the table. "I suggest you give this to your chief of station without delay."

Wandsworth was skeptical. "And then what?"

"Trust me, you'll receive appropriate instructions."

It took a full twenty minutes before the door to the little room opened. A man in his mid-forties stood with Jason's note in his hand. He was average height and weight with hair seriously thinning on top. He was, in other words, totally unremarkable.

He carefully shut the door behind him before stepping next to Jason. "Mr. Peters, I'm Howard Cassidy."

Jason rose and shook his hand. "Don't tell me, let me guess: your friends call you Hopalong."

A grin flickered and died. "Yeah, sometimes."

"And stimulating trade is not your mission here."

"Right again. Just like half the people in embassy trade attaché offices around the world. That's why I'm familiar with Narcom. And that's why it took me so long to verify your employment and check with Langley. They told me to give you whatever you wanted as long as it didn't involve killing somebody."

Jason wasn't sure the restriction was a joke. "Nothing that serious. I just need to borrow a car for a couple of days."

Hoppy was clearly relieved. "I think I can arrange that." Then he frowned. "Our bean counters are going to want to know why you can't use public transportation."

"Just tell them security requires it."

Not entirely untrue, since Jason's picture by now had probably been circulated to every cop at every rail station and airport in the United Kingdom.

"Any particular flavor?"

"Mid-range or lower. British-made, preferably."

"The ambassador's private secretary just bought a nice used Vaux-hall VX220."

The mid-engine, targa-topped two-seater was tempting but Jason said, "Something a little less eye-catching."

Besides, his experience with British sports cars—from the MG, Austin Healy, and Triumph to the last of the pre-Ford Jaguars—had been one of dependable undependability. The parts that regularly fell off of them were, at least, of the highest British quality.

"We, the embassy, own an old Morris Minor. Been around so long no one wants to part with it."

"Perfect."

30

Duke of Wellington Pub & Inn
Darlington Road
Durham, England
20:22 Local Time
The Same Day

After a refreshing shower and change back into khakis at the embassy, it had been a long drive north on the A1(M), made even longer by the Morris's lack of both interior space and speed. Jason had stopped twice, once to refill the Morris's tank and call to reset the time of his meeting, and once more to postpone the rendezvous again.

The latter call had resulted in a pause before the peevish reply. "Really, Mr. Peters, we're getting into the dining hour. Perhaps you'd like to meet me at the Duke."

"The Duke?"

"The Duke of Wellington. On Darlington Road. Anyone in town can tell you how to find it."

The professor had been right: everyone on the street could, and did, tell Jason how to find The Duke. Unfortunately, no two sets of directions were alike.

Jason decided to at least enjoy this medieval town built on the hill that was the fifty-seven-acre peninsula formed by a bend in the River Wear. The low skyline was dominated by a Norman cathedral and fortress, stones dragged from a nearby quarry shortly after 1072. The church housed the relics of the Venerable Bede, eighth- and ninth-century historian and ecclesiastic, a sure draw for the mediaeval pilgrim trade. The castle had served as the Episcopal Palace until the bishop gave it up in 1832 to found Britain's third university there at Durham.

Touring Durham was fine but not the purpose of Jason's long drive, or, for that matter, the reason for his journey to England.

Near the outskirts of town, a woman was riding a bicycle, her long shadow painted across the road by the late setting summer sun.

Jason pulled the Morris up beside her. "Ma'am? Excuse me, ma'am?"

She shot him a glance but didn't stop pedaling.

"Can you tell me how to get to the Duke of Wellington?"

Evidently his accent identified him as an American tourist, not one of England's rare but highly sensationalized serial murderers.

She stopped, putting both feet on the shoulder of the road and pointing. "D'ya see that row of buildings?"

At least, that was what Jason thought she said. The burr was almost as blurred as the Scottish dialect a few miles north. He nodded.

She was still pointing. "D'ya na see the sign, the one that says 'Duke of Wellington'?"

She rode off before Jason could thank her. If thanks were due.

He parked the Morris and took in the glass-fronted establishment.

Jason stepped inside a traditional British public house. Dark mahogany bar, dim tulip-shaped lights on chandeliers and—unusual in pubs of the past but becoming more common—a small wine selection in a glass case, but . . . Something was missing. The low murmur of conversation as the clientele leaned against the bar sipping their pints was the same as was the sporadic exclamations from the group gathered around the dartboard on the far wall. The smell was of old beer, fried food, and . . . no smoke. The clearly visible air, the stale tobacco odor, all gone the way of the red British phone booth and the personal privacy of the royal family.

The health gestapo had prevailed in Great Britain.

Jason waited until there was an opening between the bodies crowding the bar. He stood patiently until the publican spotted him and sidled up, his eyebrows raised in a question.

"Draft bitters," Jason said, not looking forward to a beer served at room temperature. But then, it seemed all beer in Great Britain was served that way. "And I'm looking for someone, a Professor Nigel Cravas."

The barkeep was using one hand to hold the pint glass and the other to pull the beer tap. He jutted a jaw to Jason's left. "That's him, the chap in the last booth. Will you be having dinner with us tonight?"

Jason put a five-pound note on the highly varnished bar top and waited for his change. "Thanks. I'll know in a few minutes."

The smell of old grease made the possibility less than mouthwatering.

Hunched over to protect his glass from patrons not always careful against whom they bumped, Jason made his way to the far booth. "Dr. Cravas?"

The man glanced up from a plate of what looked like cremated beef swimming in grease. A stained napkin hung from his open shirt collar. A glass of tea-colored liquid was at his elbow. The slice of cucumber told Jason it was a Pimm's Cup, a mixture of dry gin, aperitif, lemon soda or ginger ale, and spices. Like New Orleans's Sazerac Cocktail, the drink's origins lay somewhere in the eighteenth century and no two establishments made them exactly the same way. In typical English fashion, the Pimm's came with no ice.

Cravas's red-rimmed eyes and the slight slur of his voice told Jason this glass was not his first of the evening. He made an effort to stand and sat down hard, settling for a "Mr. Peters! Do have a seat."

Jason did that, watching Cravas finish off the meat using both knife and fork in the English and European manner. He used the napkin to wipe a dribble from his chin before draining his glass. He was a roundish man of about fifty, his face puffy, jaws beginning to sag into fleshy bags. The burst capillaries along his cheeks were the badge of the heavy drinker.

He put down knife and fork. "Forgive me for not getting up."

Jason was settling into the seat across from him. "And forgive me for my tardiness. I had a bit of a problem getting out of London."

"Hmph! And who doesn't these days? I try to avoid the place whenever possible."

Jason was unsure where to begin. "How long have you been with the British Institute of Science and Climatology?"

Cravas lifted his glass, noting with disappointment that it was empty. "Ever since I joined the faculty of the college in the eighties. School was only founded in 1972, y'know. Newest college at the newest university." He gave what could have been either a laugh or a grunt. "Newest and newest. That's interesting." He looked toward the bar. "Say, be a good chap and fetch me another libation, would you? Conversation dries my throat. Jake there at the bar knows what I want. He'll put it on my tab."

Jason struggled out from the tight confines of the booth even though he had barely taken two sips of his own beer.

He caught Jake's eye. "Another Pimm's for the professor."

Jake was concentrating on filling a pint glass, this time half Guinness, half ale—a black and tan. "And who'll be paying for the good professor's glass now?"

Jason had a feeling he knew the answer. "He said to put it on his account."

Jake handed the drink to a customer, the heavier stout clearly delineated from the lighter ale. "Did he, now? And did he say when he might be paying up? The matter's gotten more than a month behind."

Jason put another five-pound note on the bar. "Take the Pimm's out of this."

Cravas had been watching. He jerked his head toward Jake and the bar as Jason slid back into his seat. "That dobber! I've been patronizing this place for years. They know I'm not going anywhere."

Jason took a sip of his bitters, which had somehow gotten even warmer in his absence. Time to get down to business. "You, or your institute, hired Boris Karloff to go to Iceland. Why?"

If the abrupt shift in conversation surprised the professor, he didn't show it. "Karloff? Like the movie actor who played Frankenstein? Is that what he told you his name was?"

"That's what he told me, but I'm curious as to exactly what he was doing in Iceland and why someone would kill him for doing it."

"We, the Institute, had been hearing rumors about the ice floe, the glaciers, there. Word was flora, plants, kept showing up in it, plants that don't grow at that latitude. Not bloody likely the university would put money into any kind of research by someone without the proper degrees, right? It took a bit of arm-twisting, as you Yanks say. Seems the material you sent me from your Dr. Wu has confirmed the rumor is true."

"He got killed over a rumor?"

Cravas took a sip of his Pimm's. "I would think at least part of that would be obvious."

"Tell me anyway."

"He found something someone didn't want known."

Jason drank from his glass. "A piece of a grapevine on a glacier. And what was likely a tool?"

"Quite damning, don't you think?"

Jason put down his glass and placed both elbows on the table. "Why don't you explain that to me."

Cravas reached for his glass, withdrew his hand, and sat back. "As you are no doubt aware, the current scientific bugaboo is so-called global warming, possibly industrially caused by spewing carbon gases into the air. Finding a grapevine in that glacier, particularly an ancient species of grape, would indicate that the climate, at some time, was conducive to growing grapes. In other words, warm. That, in turn, would indicate that warming periods have nothing to do with human activity. There are a number of respected scientists who question the existence of global warming and certainly question any human causation."

At one time scientists thought the earth was flat, too, Jason thought. But he said, "I thought the polar ice caps are receding."

"Not quite. In 2007, Antarctica set a record for more new ice since 1979. Only along the Antarctic Peninsula is there significant melting, an area about one-fiftieth the size of East Antarctica, where ice has been growing.

"Just as glaciers in Iceland, Norway, Argentina, Chile, New Zealand, and the Himalayas are advancing. Even some in your country, like the Nisqually and Emmons glaciers on Mount Rainier are growing, as are some in Alaska. In fact, over ninety percent of the world's ice caps are growing, not shrinking. Hardly conclusive evidence of global warming."

Was this guy drunk, or was what he was saying real? "But I've seen pictures . . ."

This time Cravas did take a drink. "Dear boy, the pictures are rubbish. You take a photo in the winter when the glacier is at its greatest size, then photograph it again in the summer. The loss of ice is entirely seasonal. Have you heard of the hockey stick?"

Jason wasn't sure he had heard correctly. "Hockey stick? The thing hockey players use?"

Cravas reached under the table and retrieved a briefcase Jason had not noticed. He drew out a sheaf of papers, spreading them on the table. He pointed to a horizontal squiggly line that curved upward at one end like the blade of a hockey stick.

"This is a graph prepared from various data fed into a computer by a geoscientist from the University of Massachusetts named Michael Mann in, I believe, 2004." He pointed. "See the dates along the bottom? You will note the sudden upward swing in about 1900, just the time widespread use of coal and natural gas for heating were putting significant amounts of carbon dioxide into Earth's atmosphere. This graph gave credence to every man-caused global warming advocate on Earth.

"The problem is, Mann mishandled his data, as revealed by a couple of Canadian scientists a few years later. In fact, Mann's programs magnified data that tended to increase the hockey-stick effect while minimizing that which didn't. Mann and his theories have been pretty well debunked. Just like the Climatic Research Unit at the University of East Anglia here in Britain."

"Climatic Research Unit?"

"Back in '09, someone hacked into the center's computers, published a number of e-mails that clearly demonstrated data adverse to the theory of man-made global warming was being destroyed, particularly when Information Act requests were made. The advocates of man-made global warming have a history of, shall we say, less than academically honest research. For that matter, the disgraced CRU director, Phil Jones, admitted global temperatures have remained essentially the same for the last fifteen years."

"There are a lot of politicians that don't know that."

"Or don't want to admit they do."

"But what about the melting glaciers causing rising sea levels, inundating small Pacific islands?"

"What islands?"

"I read about—"

Cravas waved a dismissive hand. "More rubbish! Dr. Paul Kench of Auckland University measured twenty-seven small Pacific islands where historical data showed sea-level increases of two millimeters a year over the last twelve to sixty years. Only four of the twenty-seven had diminished in size. The other twenty-three had remained the same or increased. The natives of those islands know an opportunity when they see it: The industrialized world has caused something that threatens their land. They want 'compensation.' In American vernacular, 'Pay up, sucka!'"

Jason took another sip of his insipidly warm bitters, not sure what to believe. "I still don't understand why someone would kill over something that is, at best, a theory."

Cravas looked at him the same way he probably regarded one of his students who had come up with a wrong answer. "Good God, man! Do you have no idea of the billions, if not trillions, of dollars spent by private industry on the 'green' craze? Low- or no-emissions automobiles and hugely expensive modifications to power plants are just a couple of examples. Not to mention the amount of money various governments have and will continue to spend to rid the air of CO2? To suddenly announce that global warming was so much bunk or that mankind had nothing to do with it would cause entire economies to collapse. Worse, it would make politicians look foolish, not to mention a great number of scientists who have staked their reputations on the phenomenon. And think of the institutions like Greenpeace and the Greenies! Why—"

Jason's head jerked up. "Say that again."

Cravas was confused. "Say what? About the ruined reputations?"

"No, I thought I heard you say 'Greenies.'"

"Oh, that's what we call Grünwelt, one of the biggest, most aggressive, and well-funded environmental organizations in the world."

Not weenies, not meanies, but Greenies. Jason finally understood what Boris had been trying to tell him.

"What can you tell me about Grünwelt?" he asked.

Cravas went a long way toward emptying his glass. "Not much that

I haven't already. Extremely vocal about environmental causes. Some consider the blokes ecoterrorists. Hasn't been proved, of course, but there are those who connect them with 'accidents' in coal mines in Wales, sabotaging oil rigs in the Gulf of Mexico. I've had more than one threat I suspect they might be behind. Chaps aren't real good at tolerating views that don't coincide with theirs."

"Threats?"

"Nothing the police can act on. 'We will take action,' 'Your lies will not be tolerated,' that sort of rubbish. Plus, anytime anyone at the Institute of Science and Climatology speaks somewhere, they always have their yobs there to try to shout him down. There have been a couple of scuffles."

"I'll look them up on the computer."

This time Cravas drained his Pimm's. "You won't find much, other than the propaganda they put there." He regarded his glass sorrowfully. "Say, don't you want dinner? Jake will be turning the grill off soon."

Jason thought of what he had seen on the professor's plate. He started to wiggle out of the booth. "I'm staying at the Marriott. I'll get a bite there. If you find anything . . ."

"Oh, I have plenty of Grünwelt's own adverts for contributions. If you like, I'll bring them 'round in the morning. Say about oh-eight-hundred?"

"I'd appreciate it, thanks."

Jason made a hasty retreat before the professor could find an excuse for another drink.

31

Durham Marriott Hotel Royal County
Old Elvet, Durham

With that polite but distant manner peculiar to British hotels, the desk clerk had assured Jason his room not only had a view of the bend of the River Wear but of the cathedral and castle on the other side. Not that it mattered. It was dark and beginning to mist—that cold, dank blanket that Jason associated with this part of England. He could not have seen the Great Pyramid had it been just outside his window.

He declined the assistance of a bellhop with his single bag. Heels clicking on the marble between imitation Oriental rugs, Jason made his way across the faux mahogany lobby to the elevator and then the third floor. The room contained a queen-size bed, two chairs upholstered in a beige that more or less matched the walls and bedspread, and a wooden chair in front of a small desk. Botanical prints in matching frames hung above the bed and desk.

The decorating equivalent of a dial tone.

Jason checked his watch, then the menu in a folder on the desk. If he hurried, he could make the later closing of the hotel's two dining rooms for dinner. Not that he had any great expectations of culinary grandeur. This was, after all, England, where rare roast beef was only seared on the inside rather than burned and flavor had meticulously been cooked out of vegetables. On the upside, though, he had seen Scottish salmon on the list of entrees, a dish even the British seemed unable to ruin.

The room's phone rang.

"Mr. Peters? Sorry to disturb you, sir, but there's a gentleman here to see you, a Dr. Cravas from the university. Shall I send him up?"

Jason hesitated before replying. Surely the professor hadn't followed him to the Marriott to continue drinking. He had hardly had the time to fetch the Grünwelt material he was to deliver in the morning.

"No. I'm just out of the shower. Can I speak to him?"

Jason was unable to hear the conversation between the desk clerk and his visitor.

"Mr. Peters, he says he needs to speak with you face-to-face."

Warning bells began to go off.

"Tell him I'll be right down soon as I'm dressed. Under no circumstances are you to give him my room number."

The clerk sounded offended a guest would find the instruction necessary. "Of course, sir."

Jason threw on a fresh pair of pants and shirt and stepped into his shoes. He stuffed the room key in his pocket and went into the hall, pausing to moisten the knob and attach a hair, a telltale sign that would alert him on his return if anyone had entered the room. He passed the bank of elevators, going instead toward a set of doors marked as a fire exit. The doors led to a stairway. At the bottom, he could see an exit out of the hotel.

Instead, he opened the door, finding himself in a normal hotel corridor. Keeping close to the wall, Jason went down the hallway until he had a limited view of the lobby. There were only two people in it: the desk clerk and a man who sat facing the elevator.

The angle was such that Jason could not see the man's face but to the experienced eye, there was little doubt he was armed. Specifically, a shoulder holster. A man with a gun at the small of his back tends to reflexively sit stiffly so the gun butt does not jam into his back. Someone carrying a pistol in an ankle holster would never cross his legs as the man Jason was watching just had. To do so would be too likely to expose the weapon hiding just above the cuff of his trousers.

This guy, then, had no back or ankle weapon. But the way he unconsciously tugged at his jacket, keeping it zipped despite the indoor warmth, suggested he had something under it he had rather not be seen.

Jason turned and retraced his steps to the exit.

He shivered in the cold mist as he hugged the building's outside wall. He crept along it until he had a view of the small car park across the street, where the hotel parked guests' vehicles on a first-come, first-served basis. A silver Alfa Romeo 159—a small, sleek four-door sedan—blocked a lane just inside the exit. The plume of exhaust from its tailpipe disappearing into the night told Jason the engine was running. Its driver did not anticipate being there long. Or intended a speedy departure. A speck of orange glowed from the right front. The driver was smoking a cigarette as he waited.

Jason had a good idea what he was waiting for.

Bent double so as to make as little of a silhouette as possible, Jason made a dash for the parked cars. It took him less than a minute to find the Morris. Now, if only the boot was unlocked . . .

He took a relieved breath as the trunk opened easily. Jason's fingers probed the small space until they closed around the tire tool, a bar of iron about two feet long.

Still crouched, Jason approached the Alfa from behind. Creeping to the left rear, the closest thing the car had to a blind spot, he jumped onto the bumper with both feet. Before the car had fully rocked from the impact, he was on all fours, scrambling around the front bumper.

He waited at the rear right fender as the driver's door flew open. Jason could see a large man framed against the hotel lights. Though his back was to Jason, he would have bet he was looking at one of the men from the train station. And he was certain that was a gun he saw in the man's hand. The bulging sound suppressor at its muzzle suggested he intended to use it.

32

San Juan
A Few Hours Earlier

Carlos was looking over Pedro's shoulder as they both read the cryptic message on the computer screen: "Missed rail connection north. Will follow to next stop."

"How do they know where he is going?" Carlos wanted to know.

"Simple enough. Where else would he be headed? Remember, the British Institute of Science and Climatology is in Durham, several hours north of London by train. They are the ones who hired the man we took care of in Iceland. It is likely Peters is going to meet Dr. Cravas. We follow the professor and Peters will fall into our net."

Carlos cracked his knuckles as he stretched. "The Dr. Cravas. Why not eliminate him too?"

"Too risky. Something happens to one of the main cogs of the Institute, something suspicious, and we have a criminal investigation. Plus, it is far better to discredit the man than make him a martyr."

"How do we know taking care of Peters will silence everyone else who knows about the grapevine? The two people he consulted in Washington, for instance. . . ."

"Once we have Peters, he will tell us where the grapevine and the photos showing it in the glacier are. Without those, grapes in Iceland become just one more lie told by those who do not believe in human-induced global warming."

"But what makes us more believable than them?"

Pedro took a box of Russian cigarettes from his shirt pocket. With one between his lips, he rasped a wooden match across the sole of his shoe. "The essential gullibility of those who hate the American rich. Anything that harms the big corporations is desirable to them and therefore true. That is the marvelous thing about the global-warming cause: It pits the industrialized countries, particularly America, against the environment. No one wants to admit they don't care about the environment."

"But both China and India originate much more CO2 than America. Why do our members not protest?"

Pedro showed teeth the color of old piano keys in a smile as he exhaled a jet of smoke. "You have done what the Americans call 'your homework.' Both China and India are 'developing' nations. Would you deny them their chance to become fully modernized? That is hardly the social and economic justice so loved by our friends in America and Western Europe."

Carlos fanned the smoke away from his face. "But the corporations are *owned* by American capitalists. And retirement funds, pension plans . . ."

"The American politicians have done a marvelous job of making the very beneficiaries of the capitalist system forget that fact. They vilify the corporations as though the companies exist on their own instead of being comprised of millions of stockholders, many of whom are retired teachers, steelworkers, policemen. That is one more reason we shall prevail."

"And we *will* prevail?"

The question hung in the air like the cigarette's smoke before Pedro nodded. "Of course."

33

Durham

The first thing the man with the gun did was to turn toward the back of the Alfa Romeo, the source of the jolt to the car. It was a mistake Jason had counted on.

Just as the man's other foot touched the pavement of the parking lot, Jason lunged. The sound of movement made the car's driver spin, his face meeting the swinging tire tool with a crunch that crushed his right orbital bone, eye cavity, and blinded the other eye with a bloody mask.

Before his victim could even scream with pain, Jason backhanded the iron rod, bringing it up smartly against the wrist of the hand holding the weapon. The gun clattered to the pavement.

Pain, severe pain, tends to momentarily paralyze, and Jason used that instant to bring the tire tool down again, this time against the man's knee, a blow that sent him sprawling with a shriek of agony. He lay face-up on the pavement.

Snatching up the gun, Jason tucked it into his waistband and sat astride the man now moaning as he cradled his ruined face in his hands. Placing the iron tool across the man's throat, Jason leaned forward. Not enough pressure to close off all breath, but enough so the man got the idea.

"Move and your neck snaps like a matchstick," Jason growled. "Understand?"

The head nodded.

"Good. Now, I'm going to ask a few questions. For every right answer, I let up a little on the pressure. For every wrong answer, you strangle. First, who sent you?"

"Fuck you."

The words were followed by a gurgling sound as Jason leaned forward, putting more weight on the bar across the man's neck.

"Wrong answer. Let's try again. Who sent you?"

"Get fucked."

Jason sighed. His interrogation techniques simply weren't working these days. On the bright side, Maria wasn't here. He put his full weight on the tire tool. Even in the dim light from the hotel across the street, he could see the undamaged eye bulge. Killing a man like this wasn't what he had in mind, but this guy's effort to kill him in the train station this morning didn't discourage him either.

"Last chance."

The form beneath him went rigid and then limp. Playing possum, or passed out from lack of oxygen? Jason wasn't inclined to take a chance. Replacing his hands on the bar with his knees, he began to search the inert form's pockets. His first find was the long Spetsnaz knife. He tucked it into his belt next to the gun. A few pound notes in a wallet, along with a British driver's license Jason would have bet was a forgery. A jacket pocket proved more fruitful: a matchbook with printing on it, too dim in this light to read. Probably just advertising, but even the language might give more of a clue than Jason possessed at the moment. Professionals like this guy didn't normally carry around stuff that might disclose where they had been. But smokers kept matches.

A moan from the ground redirected Jason's attention to the man prone on the pavement. His pal in the hotel lobby would be returning to the car when Jason didn't come downstairs. Jason wrestled the semiconscious man out of his jacket and took the knife from his waist to slash the sleeves into strips with which he bound hands and feet.

He balled up the remaining material and used the knife's tip to pry the waking man's jaws open before stuffing his mouth with the fabric. An effective gag if reflexive retching didn't choke the man on his own vomit.

Jason had neither the time nor inclination to concern himself.

He opened the Alfa's small trunk and felt around the edge of the inside. He could discover no inside release as required by the ever-meddlesome US Department of Transportation, probably one of several reasons Alfas were not sold in the United States. That, along with lack of side airbags and the Italians' understandable disinclination to crash-test an otherwise perfectly salable car. Though largely socialist in their politics, Europeans did not favor the nanny state where their automobiles were concerned.

Jason dragged the bound man to the rear of the car. Despite desperate wriggling and muted grunts of protest, he managed to get the man draped over the edge of the trunk and then dump in the lower torso. He slammed the lid shut and climbed into the driver's seat to wait.

Pulling the pistol from his waistband, he was not surprised to recognize another GSh-18 like the one he had seen in Iceland. He pushed the catch and dropped the clip into the palm of his hand, holding it up to make sure it was fully loaded before clicking it back into place. As he eased back the slide, brass gleamed from the chamber. The weapon was loaded and cocked. He put it on the passenger seat while he reached for the box of cigarettes the man in the trunk had left on the dashboard.

Jason did not have long to wait. A form hurriedly exited the Marriott, blurred in the penumbra between the hotel's lights and the night's drizzly gloom. Turning his head away from the approaching figure, Jason lit a cigarette with a match from the book he had taken. Without thinking, he inhaled, sucking a caustic stream of smoke down his throat. He had to struggle not to give himself away by coughing.

The passenger door opened and the courtesy light confirmed that this man was one of the two he had seen at King's Cross that morning.

"Do come in and have a seat," Jason said mildly, pressing the automatic against the underside of the other man's chin as he stubbed out the cigarette. "But be sure to keep your hands right there on the dashboard."

The man silently complied. "Where's Uri?" the man asked before his lips tightened.

"Inspecting the baggage, I'd imagine. Now, keep your hands where I can see them.

"Good boy! Now, take your left hand and slowly, and I mean real slowly, reach inside your jacket, remove your pistol, holding it between your thumb and forefinger, and drop it on the floor."

Jason sensed, rather than saw, a flicker of resistance, an instant when the man was considering his options. He pressed the gun's muzzle a little harder against the bottom of the man's chin. "Don't even *think* about not doing exactly as you are told. I really would prefer not to make a bloody mess of this nice car. But then, I'm not the one who would have to explain to Mr. Hertz."

The gun came out from under the jacket, held between thumb and forefinger like the tail of a dead rat.

"You're doing swell. Now drop it."

The pistol thumped against the car's carpeted floor mat.

"Now the knife."

The man spoke for the first time, the accent light but noticeable. "What knife?"

This time Jason jammed the gun's business end into the soft flesh under the chin. "We're not playing games, Ivan. Either the knife hits the floor or your brains hit the ceiling. Your choice."

The knife followed the gun.

"Very good. Now I'm going to ask you a few questions. . . ."

"Fuck you."

Spetsnaz training must include a pretty limited English vocabulary. Jason tipped the barrel of the automatic down and squeezed the trigger. It was no contest between the shot muffled by the silencer and the terrified shriek of the man who was now looking at a hole in the slack of his trousers just between his crotch and his leg.

The sound suppressor was against the man's jaw again. "Unless you have ambitions to join a girls' choir, I'd suggest you answer the question."

Even in the dim light, Jason could see the man's eyes widen in fright.

"First and last time: Who sent you?"

Jason could almost smell the panic seething beneath the surface. "The sex-change operation will commence on three. One, two . . ."

It happened so quickly, Jason was caught off guard. With a lunge, his captive opened the car door and was rolling across the pavement. With the grace of an acrobat, he was on his feet and sprinting into the darkness. Jason blamed himself for not locking the Alfa's door or at least making sure it was fully closed. He never seriously considered shooting. The potential consequences—police, indefinite detainment, explanations—far outweighed any benefit. Besides, the man's anguished yell may well have the local constabulary on its way already as it was.

As indeed it had.

The desk clerk was either too sleepy or too polite to ask questions about a mid-evening departure when Jason signed the credit card slip for the entire night despite his brief stay. As he turned from the desk, keys to the Morris and single bag in hand, he could see forms across the street silhouetted against flashing blue lights.

He handed the clerk a twenty-pound note. "A favor: after I've been gone about twenty minutes, suggest the police check the trunk, er, boot, of the Alfa."

He was repaid by a puzzled expression and the polite disdain the British have for invasive questions.

34

Delta Flight 1204
Eight Hours Later

Jason hated transoceanic flights, even more so in economy class. Hours of being crammed into close quarters with nearly two hundred strangers, none of whom had paid the same price for their ticket. Even military transport was more generous with legroom.

Add to that the all-night drive from Durham to London that had forced him to drink what he guessed was more coffee than the little car's gas tank would have held. Certainly enough to make him promise his souring stomach that he would swear off the stuff for the next twenty years.

In the wee hours of the morning, he left the Morris beside the embassy and handed the keys to a somewhat puzzled Marine security guard at the gate. By this time, the Underground's first trains of the day were beginning to run. A quick check revealed the number of police in the tube stations from the day before had been sharply reduced: only one automatic weapon–carrying officer that Jason could see. Still, he made himself extremely camera shy, shielding his face from the overhead lenses as much as he could without being obvious.

He had dozed off during the ride to St. Pancras Station, where he purchased a Eurostar ticket for the two-hour-and-fifteen-minute Chunnel ride to Paris, falling asleep again as the train left the station. From de Gaulle he would return to Washington by a route he hoped sufficiently circuitous to have eluded anyone looking for him, whether Scotland Yard or former Spetsnaz.

The airline, of course, had nearly frustrated his plan. During multiple coffee breaks on the drive back to London, and the equally frequent stops necessitated thereby, Jason had used his BlackBerry to book a first-class ticket Paris–Washington, reservations he had electronically confirmed upon his arrival at Gare du Nord in Paris before getting on the Métro for Charles de Gaulle.

His arrival at the airport revealed a somewhat different story: Yes, of course his reservations were in the system, the pretty young Frenchwoman assured him in delightfully accented English. But what did the system know, she asked with that Gallic shrug that says there is no understanding to be had. The equipment had been changed to an aircraft with a smaller first-class section. The row including Jason's seat had been eliminated. Management had not told the reservations people, she confided, this time with a forefinger tugging at a bottom eyelid, the French gesture that says the words are not to be believed.

A seat was available in economy. She smiled with this information as though Delta was doing him a real service just to let him on the airplane. No? There would be plenty of first-class seats on the next flight.

When would that be? he wanted to know.

She checked her watch as though it displayed airline timetables rather than the hour. Its scheduled departure was only an hour or so away.

Jason wasn't going to get screwed by the airline twice in the same day. "Could you give the actual departure time?"

There was a hitch: the next flight, the one with a surplus of first-class seats, had a small problem. Something about some silly little light that would not go off no matter how many switches, buttons, and levers the pilot had used on the flight over earlier that day. It should be no problem: the necessary part was on its way, being trucked over from Orly, Paris's other international airport.

Jason had flown enough to be wary of both "minor" maintenance problems and flights with a plethora of available seats. Since admission of a *major* mechanical problem was bad PR, all glitches were classed as 'minor.' Second, a flight with a number of empty seats, particularly transoceanic, was likely to be canceled for some fabricated reason other than the real one: that the airline would lose money on it.

He took the seat in coach.

With his single bag in the overhead bin, he shoehorned himself into a middle seat that had obviously been designed by someone with minimal knowledge of human anatomy. Or a sadist. To his right, next to the window, was a gray-haired woman who began to unload a collection of travel guides to France from a voluminous purse. Why she would find the attractions of, say, the Loire, of interest when departing the country was a mystery.

Just as the cabin door was about to close, a young woman with a bad blond bleach job plopped down in the aisle seat to Jason's left. She also carried a purse that could have served as a suitcase. From it she began to unload a collection of cosmetics: face powder, mascara, eye liner, and a number of items Jason could not have identified had he tried. Once the items were arranged in her lap, she began to apply them with the aid of a small mirror. Another mystery: where was she going in the next eight or so hours where such an effort would be necessary?

At least he had nothing in common with his seat mates sufficient to provoke an effort at conversation. Enduring a recap of some stranger's recent vacation, business trip, or whatever was not what Jason had in mind. To make sure, he stood, unzipped his suitcase, and took his iPad out and put the buds in his ears. If relaxation would have been difficult with the seat back released to its customary six inches, it was impossible in the pre-takeoff upright or rigid position.

Religious music, per se, was of little interest to Jason but J. S. Bach's *Mass in B Minor* was a composition of pure beauty regardless of the subject matter. Like all of this composer's work, vocal or instrumental, this was more of a journey than an experience, returning over and over to same or similar themes and patterns. The a cappella choral prelude was blending into strings when Jason looked up to see a flight attendant who was saying something.

He removed the ear buds.

"Sir, as has already been announced, electronic devices must be shut off before takeoff. The captain will announce when it is safe to use such devices. You need to check the in-flight magazine to see which electronics may be used on board."

Both of Jason's seat mates were scowling at him, someone who was carelessly endangering their safety. Jason knew from his own flight training that iPads, cell phones, e-readers, and the like had as much influence on the aircraft's navigational systems as the wizard Merlin had had on raising up Stonehenge. Neither legend would die, however. The difference was the airlines had a motive in promoting theirs: a passenger allowed unlimited access to his own electronics was far less likely to pay for earphones to watch the in-flight entertainment.

Reluctantly, Jason made a show of turning the contraption off.

He put it in the seat pocket in front of him. His fingers went to his own pocket. The matchbook he had taken from the assassin in Durham.

He pulled it out, examining it. HOTEL EL CONVENTO, 100 CALLE CRISTO, SAN JUAN, PUERTO RICO was embossed on its cover.

What was the connection between a Spetsnaz killer and a hotel in San Juan? Not much of a clue, but the only one Jason had.

35

Joint Base Anacostia-Bolling
Officers' Club
That Evening

Jason had been disappointed to learn that Thomas, Roosevelt, Captain, United States Marine Corps (Ret.) had checked out. In fact, the bachelor officers' quarters seemed deserted. There had been nothing to do but take his single bag to his quarters and retrieve the package he had left before flying to London: the Glock, two clips, and a box of ammunition. He could have checked the gun in a bag on the plane but that would have required waiting at a baggage carousel, risking delay, and becoming a stationary target. Plus, there was also the risk the British might discover the weapon, subjecting him to criminal penalties at worst and lengthy questioning at best.

He took the opportunity to stop by the base clinic to have a doctor look at his shoulder's healing gunshot wound.

The doctor was a woman. She wore no makeup. Thick black-framed glasses, blond hair pulled back into a knot at the nape of her neck, white lab coat at least two sizes too big. Her name tag labeled her as Ferris, J. The bronze oak leaves on her collar denoted her rank as a major.

She pulled off the bandage, gently pressing around the area. "Hurt?"

"Not as much as it did last time I was here, a couple of days ago."

She cocked her head, still staring at the shoulder. "Looks like a bullet wound."

Jason said nothing as she perused his brief chart. "Says here it *is* a bullet wound, sustained outside the country."

Again, Jason said nothing.

"Also says here you're retired Army. If you're retired, how come somebody shot you?"

"Accidentally, self-inflicted."

She made no effort to conceal her incredulity as she taped a new bandage into place. "As an Army officer you should know how to handle firearms safely."

"The human mind is always capable of learning. And make that a *former* Army officer."

She snipped the last bit of tape. "Hopefully quickly. The next 'accident'"—she made quotation marks with her fingers—"might be fatal."

"I'll keep that in mind, Doc."

She stood. "For that bit of advice, Captain, I'll allow you to buy me a drink at the officers' club at, say, twenty hundred hours?"

"As long as the sun has gone down, Doc."

"Captain, somewhere on this old earth the sun has always gone down."

It was not until he was walking back to his quarters he had realized he had something very much resembling a date.

Well, why not? Maria was still in Iceland with her damned volcanoes, too busy to call or even text these last couple of days and . . .

Not her fault she's in Iceland, the small voice in his head argued. *She's there 'cause you let Momma manipulate her so you could take the assignment she had for you.*

Maybe. But I didn't stop her from even so much as an e-mail. I mean, what's she doing with this guy . . . ?

Sevensen, Pier Sevensen.

Yeah, him. What's she doing with him that's so important she can't stay in touch?

You got problems with the global chip in your own BlackBerry?

Well, it's really not a date, anyway. Just two officers having a drink.

The internal argument came to an end as Jason passed the officers' club. He went inside to the room where he had seen the computers. Calling up Google, he entered "Hotel El Convento." He was rewarded by a picture of a pale-yellow stucco Spanish colonial building. An adjacent map located it in the middle of Old San Juan. A brief read informed him the place had, as the name suggested, begun life as a convent, specifically of the Carmelite order, in 1561. Later years had been anything but benign, turning the structure into a dance hall, a casino, a flophouse and, finally, a parking area for garbage trucks. The renaissance of Puerto Rican tourism began shortly after the end of World War II and the old place had been restored as a hotel, one visited on at least one occasion by Ernest Hemingway and an impressive list of other luminaries.

Interesting, but what connection did a former nunnery have with Grünwelt? Perhaps the Greenies had an interest in Puerto Rico's rain forest. But wasn't that already a national park, protected by federal law? Another Google excursion confirmed that the El Yunque predated American possession, having been set aside as a national park by the Spanish Crown in 1876. The place had been off-limits to development for nearly a century and a half.

Swell, but what interest would a radical and potentially violent conservationist group have in an area already protected?

The only answer Jason could come up with was none. There was some reason other than global warming why the persons Jason believed had been sent to England to kill him would have been at that hotel in San Juan. The problem was finding out what that reason was.

So far, he had a strong suspicion Professor Cravas had been right to the extent that this environmental group, Grünwelt, was behind the attacks. As far as specifics, he had only two clues: the name Uri and this hotel in San Juan.

Not a whole lot.

Unaware he was tapping his lips with a ballpoint, Jason reached into a pocket for his super low-tech address book. He was unwilling to entrust years of telephone numbers to a computer system that could—and frequently did—swallow them at will. He flipped through the pages until he found what he was looking for. Then he entered a number in his BlackBerry.

"Sybil? Jason Peters here. Will you be available day after tomorrow? No, I'm not sure of the time yet, I'll have to check the airline schedule."

A few minutes before eight, he was sitting at the bar at the officers' club, toying with a short glass of single-malt scotch, regrettably not Balvenie, on the rocks. The bartender, a chief master sergeant, was polishing glasses. A comradely hum of conversation formed an audio backdrop for soft instrumentals of long-ago showtunes.

Then it all came to a stop. Except for the recorded music. The talk ceased abruptly. The barkeep put down the glass in his hand and stared at a point over Jason's shoulder.

Jason swiveled his bar stool around and had to stop himself from gawking.

Ferris, J., had undergone a metamorphosis that even Ovid could not have contemplated. The lab coat had been replaced by a red dress that did nothing to conceal a figure most eighteen-year-old girls would have killed for. The blond hair had been unleashed from its knot and hung in bountiful waves to just above her bare shoulders. The heavily rimmed glasses had disappeared in favor of artfully applied eye shadow.

She walked into the room and climbed onto the bar stool next to Jason's. He found the whisper of her stockings as she crossed her legs very, very sexy.

"Buy a girl a drink, Captain?"

A stemmed martini glass appeared on the bar as if by magic. She nodded her thanks to the sergeant as she withdrew a toothpick upon which a pair of olives were impaled. Putting it to her mouth, she used her tongue to remove the olives.

"You seem to have gone quiet, Captain."

"That trick, taking the olives off the stick with your tongue. How do you do it?"

"Only with lots of practice."

Standing where only Jason could see his face, the bartender rolled his eyes. The major was a regular here.

"Live on base, Major?" Jason asked, more to make conversation than curiosity.

She shook her head, sending blond ripples rolling. "Nope. Have a condo in Alexandria. And by the way, I'm Judith, not 'Major,' when I'm off duty."

Jason finished the dregs of his drink and motioned to the bartender. "If you'd told me, I could have met you somewhere else, saved you the drive."

She took a sip of the icy-clear liquid in her glass. "Getting you to meet me here was a slam-dunk. Getting you to venture off base might have been a bit dicey."

"I can't believe you have a hard time getting men to do anything."

She looked at him over the rim of her glass. He had not noticed earlier how green her eyes were. "Have you always flattered women?"

"Only the pretty ones."

"Touché!"

They were both silent for a moment, preparing for the next round.

"Hope you like Kinkead's," she said.

"The seafood place on Pennsylvania Avenue? Love it. Why?"

She checked her watch. "Because we have reservations there in about twenty minutes."

"Let me get a couple of things from my room."

The last time Jason had dined at Kinkead's had been with Laurin, a thought that flashed through his mind as the cab pulled up to the thirteen early nineteenth-century town houses that had been joined when the eight-story office complex, part of the tony Shops at 2000 Penn and Red Lion Row, had commenced construction in the 1980s. Now the old homes housed upscale shops, galleries, and Kinkead's. The restaurant hadn't changed: light wood, a jazz trio playing downstairs beside an open square bar that had its own menu. Upstairs was a more traditional restaurant specializing in seafood dishes.

With every step, heads turned. Watching the skirt stretch tight across Judith's derriere as she climbed the stairs interrupted more than one conversation.

And was something more than one husband would hear about later.

Noting the season, Jason ordered the clam and oyster chowder as a prelude to tempura soft shells with green papaya salad and a fruity dipping sauce. Judith opted for the crab cakes with the Eastern Shore corn flan. He was delighted to find a Gaja on the wine list.

Jason learned that Judith came from a small town in Iowa. The Air Force had put her through medical school, obligating her to five years as a military doctor. At the end of her tour, she had decided to reenlist.

"No hassles, no med mal insurance, no Medicare forms," she explained. "And even if the pay isn't all that great, the travel benefits are. But what about you?"

Jason became instantly defensive. "Ah, I served my time. Got married and was planning on moving into civilian life when 9/11 came along. Both my wife and I were in the Pentagon. I survived; she didn't."

Judith's hand went out to rest on top of his. "I'm sorry. . . ."

Jason made no effort to move his hand. "You had no way to know. Anyway, my plans changed. I went to work with a civilian contractor."

She looked at him, half smiling. "I can imagine what a former Special Operations Command guy would be doing in the private sector."

He looked at her quizzically.

"It's in your service jacket. We routinely download all patients' service records when they come in for treatment. Yours is the first I've seen that has more classified than specified. I don't know what you're doing for your civilian contractor, but I sure hope you're paid enough to make getting shot worth it."

"I got shot at for a lot less money in the service."

By the time they were at the maître d's stand awaiting the arrival of the cab they had requested, Jason had successfully deflected most questions about his personal life. Easily done when the other person is encouraged to talk about themselves.

Judith checked her watch. "Where's the cab? I've got an oh-seven-hundred staff meeting at the clinic tomorrow."

"I called the cab ten minutes ago," the maître d said defensively. "Maybe someone hijacked it en route."

As in most large cities, cabbies were not above picking up a fare on the street on their way to responding to a call. If the street fare was short enough, they could make both it and the call. The results were an additional fare and a delayed response.

Jason stepped toward the door. "I'll see if I can flag one down while we wait."

Outside, Jason stepped into a wall of heat and damp that was a Washington summer night. Built on a drained swamp just like most of New Orleans, the two cities shared a muggy humidity.

Training embedded so deeply that it had become reflex rather than thought took over as Jason scanned the empty street. At this hour, Pennsylvania Avenue was quiet. Parked cars lined the curb, their windshields giving back the pale orange of the sodium-vapor street-lights. Each had a residential parking permit sticker, a prerequisite for not getting towed in DC, where cars overwhelmingly outnumbered parking places.

There were no cruising cabs in sight.

His eyes followed a Metrobus lumbering in the direction of the George Washington University/Foggy Bottom Station. As his eyes followed the bus, he noted a Lincoln Town Car at the curb across the street. The make and model was common enough in the District, usually hired with driver to ferry the area's nobility, politicians, from place to place. But this one did not have the windshield sticker that would allow temporary parking anywhere in Washington. And it appeared empty, no dark-suited chauffeur smoking a cigarette while he waited for his patron to finish whatever had brought him into the neighborhood.

An anomaly. Like a jungle suddenly gone silent, a junk car in an upscale residential section of town, an open door late at night.

Careful to seem to be doing nothing more than looking for a cab, Jason searched the shadows, potential hiding places for whoever had arrived in the Lincoln. Of course, it was quite possible the occupants of the car had not included a hired driver but only patrons of the restaurant who would appear at any moment, loud with alcohol and cheerful after a good meal, and drive away.

But Jason wasn't prepared to bet his life on it.

There! Was that movement he had seen between two parked cars about fifty feet away? Could have been some nocturnal animal, a cat, a stray dog. Something had definitely moved.

He turned and went back inside.

Judith smiled. "No cab?"

"No cab." He took her hand, leading her away from the door. "Come on, we're leaving."

"But the door's back there," she protested.

"Not the door we're using tonight."

Years ago, he and Laurin had noticed a senator across Kinkead's dining room, one currently in the news for his purported involvement with a young intern. Jason had noted the senator's departure was in the opposite direction from the entrance, no doubt to avoid the cadre of reporters who dogged his every move. Ergo, there was an exit somewhere other than the one used by the establishment's customers.

Jason and Judith walked quickly past the open square of the bar and into the kitchen, where, in their frenzied activities, none of the white-clad staff seemed to notice. Straight back was a doorway. Beyond that, an alley.

Jason guessed the narrow space had originally been for deliveries and garbage removal from the row of town houses. Now it served the same purpose for the restaurant and adjacent establishments. The faint odor of rotting vegetables confirmed the hypothesis

Judith slipped her hand from his. "Hold on! What exactly . . . ?"

Jason could only see her outline in the dusky alley. "We can talk later. Right now I want to get out of the dark."

The alley ended at H Street. Jason took a right, finding himself on the open, well-lit, tree-studded quad of George Washington University.

Judith stopped. "OK, we're out of the dark. Now, what the hell . . . ?"

Was that movement at the base of a massive oak?

Jason put a finger to his lips. "Not out of the woods yet."

She was looking over his shoulder. "Do you know those men?"

Jason whirled around. Two figures, their faces in the shadow of baseball caps, were advancing slowly from the direction he and Judith had come. A quick look over his shoulder revealed two more coming from the opposite direction.

"Are they students, you think?" Judith asked.

Jason was cursing himself for not checking on the cab ride to Kinkead's. Not that a tail could have been spotted in city traffic. "I doubt it."

"Muggers?"

"Not likely."

"But what—"

He took her hand again, this time backing up slowly until he was in front of the door of the law school. Fortunately, Judith had spotted them before Jason had no chance of finding a position to protect his back.

He reached under the back of his jacket, producing the Glock. "You know how to use this?"

She looked as though he were handing her a serpent. "I've only fired a pistol in basic training, but I think I remember."

"Try. Don't shoot unless you have to, though."

If the approaching quartet had intended to use firearms, they would have done so before Jason has seen them, certainly before he had managed to back into a defensive position. No reason to announce what was happening to the local and campus police. They were armed, though, Jason was certain. If he showed any move toward gunplay, they would respond in kind, worrying about cops later.

Now he could see something in the hands of two of the men, something that reflected the light. Something like long-bladed Spetsnaz knives. The other two had hands inside their jackets, ready in case guns were needed.

Four against one wasn't good odds in a shoot-out. Even worse in a knife fight.

36

Calle Luna 23
San Juan
At the Same Time

The man called Pedro smiled as he looked at the screen of his cell phone. The other hand held a glass of chilled vodka. It was far from his first of the evening.

"*Prekrasniy! Chudesniy!* Peters has left the sanctuary of the military base. Anatoly's team has Peters cornered in the American capital."

His younger companion was not quite so sanguine. But then, he had consumed far less vodka. "In English, remember?"

"OK: awesome, fantastic. In any language we will soon be shed of this Peters person."

"Let us not celebrate too early. What do the Americans say, something about numbering eggs? Or is it hatching eggs? Besides, we do not know for whom Peters works. Who says they will not send another on the same mission."

"Another American saying tells us not to jump off a bridge until we reach it." A puzzled expression crossed Pedro's face. "Why would one jump from a bridge in the first place? Anyway, we know the English-man, the professor . . ."

"Cravas."

"Cravas. He contacted the man who went to Iceland . . ."

"Karloff."

"Yes, Karloff. He must have been the one who hired Peters or his employer."

"Too bad he's dead. Otherwise we might have some idea who that employer might be."

Pedro reached out and gently slapped the other man's cheek before tossing back the contents of his glass. "Do not be critical of your superiors. The decision to have Karloff die was made in Switzerland, not here. If the man had already spread the professor's poison, how could we be sure it went no further?"

He refilled his glass and continued, "An obscure professor in northern England, that is one thing. Besides, these scientists are always bickering like married people: The world is getting warmer; the world is not getting warmer. Who takes them seriously anyway? Now that Karloff is gone and Peters soon will be, who will interfere with our mission? No one, that's who! I'm ordering half of the teams to converge on the American capital immediately. Peters won't escape us now!"

Carlos wasn't quite so sure.

37

Law School Building
George Washington University
Washington, DC

Jason pushed Judith against the doors of the building. "Watch my back."

Then he stepped toward the two men with knives. He could see clearly now that his guess had been correct. A basic Spetsnaz tactic was for one or more men to try to finish the intended victim off with the silence of knives under cover of comrades with guns. Should the blade-wielding soldiers fail, the target could be handled with more effective, if less secretive, gunfire.

Bending slightly forward, arms extended from his body, Jason circled the two assailants. The quad was well lit enough for him to see the grins on their faces. Two experienced knife fighters against an unarmed man backed up by a frightened woman with a single pistol . . .

Well, they seemed to be saying, this isn't even sporting.

Jason waited patiently, knowing what to expect. The Bowie knife-like shape of the Russian blades dictated the method of attack, an attack that was not long in coming.

The man on Jason's left feigned a move to his own left, then swiped at arm's length, slashing a blur of steel from his right.

Jason thought he heard a cry from Judith as he easily danced away. The thrust had not been intended to be successful but to distract Jason from what would come next, a similar but more deadly move by his partner.

It came exactly as expected. Instead of stepping out of the arc of the slicing blade, Jason stepped into it, into it far enough that the knife was behind him. At the same instant, Jason's right arm went forward with a motion similar to a baseball pitcher releasing a fastball. The momentum flung the customized killing blade that had been strapped to his arm from its scabbard and into his hand.

Had he the time, Jason would have to thank whatever deity had reminded him to return to his room before going out and to strap the weapon on.

Before his immediate assailant could recover from his own strike, Jason was below his arm, thrusting upward. The finely honed steel entered just at the armpit, journeying upward until deflected by a shoulder bone. The man shrieked in pain as he reflexively spun away, dropping his own weapon. The move allowed Jason's narrow blade to slide free. Not a fatal wound but one that would keep the man out of any further activity tonight.

Jason's other opponent, anticipating the second or two Jason would need to work the knife free, charged. The look of surprise on his face when he realized his mistake would have been comic had its consequences not been fatal. Dropping to one knee, Jason simply held up his knife, letting his enemy's inertia impale him upon it. The blade entered under the rib cage and upward to the heart.

The man went down without a sound, dead before he hit the ground.

But Jason didn't see him fall. Instead, his attention was snatched away by the sound of a single shot.

Judith, Glock in both hands and in a shooter's stance, was watching one of the two who presumably were carrying firearms as he slowly collapsed on the steps of the law school not twenty feet from where Jason stood.

"He was going to shoot you," she said unsteadily. "Shoot you in the back."

Jason had not noticed the weapon on the ground at the man's feet.

That left one. . . . There he was, slipping silently toward Judith among the shrubbery that concealed him. Since he hadn't shot her, Jason had to guess he had it in mind to take a hostage. But he might change his mind in a hurry if Jason warned her.

Jason stooped, reaching inside the loose jacket of the dead man. His fingers closed around what he was searching for.

By the time Jason was on his feet, the man was within a few feet of Judith. Time for a single try.

Something made Judith's would-be assailant turn toward Jason at the last instant. He raised his weapon. Too late. The metal was arcing through the air, a comet in the quad's light. He grunted as the Spetsnaz fling knife ended its flight, piercing his throat, severing his left carotid artery, and effectively nailing him to the door. His gun clattered to the cement of the porch as a fountain of blood painted the stone a dark black in the artificial light.

Judith saw him for the first time and gave a mousy squeak of horror. "He's pinned to the door!"

"The eight a.m. tort class is in for a surprise. C'mon, time to go."

She reached out, feeling the throat. "He's still alive. I might be able to help."

"Why would you?"

"Hippocratic Oath."

"Nobody tried to kill Hippocrates."

He took the Glock still in her hand, returning it to the holster in the small of his back. "We need to leave before we wind up explaining this mess to the cops."

"We haven't done anything wrong. We were just defending ourselves."

For the first time, Jason noted the sole survivor, the man he had wounded, had disappeared. "Not only 'defended,' but defended well. You're a better shot than I could have hoped."

He had her hand now, leading her away.

"I killed a man," she murmured. "I've never done that before."

Jason started to say she would never completely recover from it, that the act was a chasm between civilization and barbarity that could not be re-crossed. But that would provoke a lot of questions he would prefer not to answer.

Hours later, he rolled over in Judith's bed. Lovemaking had been furious, urgent. It almost always was after a violent death. Perhaps he and Judith, or anyone who had witnessed bloodshed, felt a need to go through the motions of procreation to replace the life snuffed out. All Jason knew was that with Judith, as with Maria, he enjoyed the clamant need and the magnified release.

Maria.

He was staring at the ceiling, where shadows cast by the streetlights outside created abstract patterns.

What the hell would he tell Maria?

Are you nuts? The inner voice asked. *You'll tell Maria nothing. By the time she comes back from whatever she's doing in Iceland with whatshisname . . .*

Sevensen.

Yeah, him. By the time she gets back to wherever you choose to live next, this Major Ferris, J., MD won't even remember your name.

Whaddaya mean, won't remember my name? After—

After what? After you nearly got her killed? Well, she may remember you for that. But a one-night stand? Get real!

In one way, Jason suspected the voice might be right. He certainly didn't have room for two women in his life. But not remember his name?

38

142 Hemphill Avenue
Atlanta, Georgia
The Next Day

The area abutting the western edge of Georgia Tech's campus consisted of student-friendly eating establishments, low-end retail, and a few of the original bungalows and Craftsman cottages of the blue-collar neighborhood now largely swallowed up by the school. Many of the latter housed student organizations or displayed ROOM TO RENT signs as did the gray shingle cottage into whose driveway Jason pulled the rented Ford. The dirt yard behind the house served as a parking lot for a pair of motorcycles, a scooter, and a pickup truck whose tires showed more cord than rubber.

Jason locked the car and walked along the edge of the building past a laboring air-conditioning compressor. Three steps led him up to a porch across the front, facing the street. A gray cat jumped from an old-fashioned glider, giving Jason a disapproving look. The animal seemed to be trying to decide whether to flee or stick around as it watched Jason ring the doorbell. He was not surprised the chimes played the first couple of bars of "(I'm a) Ramblin' Wreck." Neither was the cat. It sat statue still except for its tail, which waved as if to a rhythm only it heard.

The door behind the screen door opened, revealing a stocky woman with closely cropped hair. She wore a Georgia Tech T-shirt, shorts, and flip-flops. A black-and-white cat circled her left ankle, a tabby her right.

She stooped to shoo them away at the same time she unlatched the screen door. "Well, hello, Mr. Peters! Long time no see. I was surprised when I got your call."

Mind appearing to be made up, the gray cat dashed inside the open door.

"Good to see you, too, Sybil. Still keeping your feline menagerie, I see."

She opened the door wider. "About sixteen at last count. But that was a week ago. Could be more by now. Critters multiply faster than I can have them neutered or spayed. C'mon in."

Jason followed her down a corridor dark in spite of sunlight pouring through a window at the end. He imagined dozens of pairs of cat eyes peering out of the gloom. There was a smell of one or more litter boxes somewhere near.

Sybil stood aside, ushering Jason into the room at the end of the hall. A large and very comfortable-looking chair sat behind a dining-room table from which the faux mahogany veneer was peeling. On the floor underneath it were what looked to Jason like multiple computers. And cats—three of four of them. There were several more on the couch, the only other piece of furniture visible. The wall to his right was floor-to-ceiling bookshelves, most of the titles relating to computers, as far as Jason could tell. The other wall displayed diplomas, certificates, and photographs of Sybil shaking hands or draping arms around people Jason did not recognize. There were also a number of pictures of Sybil in her Tech softball uniform, several trophies, and, not surprisingly, a cat that was staring down curiously from its perch on the top shelf.

Sybil had come to Tech on a softball scholarship, majored in computer science, and excelled at both. If Jason remembered correctly, the Lady Jackets had won a national championship behind her pitching, and her grades had been good enough to warrant a graduate scholarship to Stanford. She returned to her alma mater to teach advanced computer science, a curriculum Jason gathered was designed for students who simply outpaced existing courses and that Sybil made up as she went along. In his few visits and conversations with her, there had been no hint of a boyfriend, partner, or companion of any description. As far as he knew, she rented out rooms, sought only the company of her cats, and designed computer programs for several governments and organizations including the United States and Narcom. Momma swore she was the best hacker that had ever been.

Sybil indicated the couch as she slid into the chair. "Have a seat."

Jason eyed the streaks of cat fur that would attach to his summer-weight wool Italian slacks and the light jacket he had worn against the chill of the airplane's air-conditioning. "I'll stand if it's all the same."

That served as the niceties that precede most business conversations in the South.

A cat vaulted effortlessly into Sybil's lap. "What can I do for you today, Mr. Peters?"

Jason handed her the matchbook cover. "I want to see their guest list for the last, say, three months."

She was scratching the cat's ears to accompanying purrs. "Looking for anyone in particular?"

"I'm not certain. I'd be interested in anyone named Uri, Urinov, or something like that."

Not much chance the man he'd left in the trunk would sign into a hotel under his real name, but worth a shot.

"You're aware that hacking into private records is illegal."

Jason cocked an eyebrow, "No doubt the first time you've crossed that threshold."

The ghost of a smile flirted with her face before disappearing. "Well said. I'll see what I can do. You could have just sent this matchbook to me. I'm flattered you came in person."

"Getting out of DC at the time seemed like a good idea."

Besides, he'd gotten a flight that was *not* Delta.

"Should I come back?"

She shook her head, already concentrating of the screen in front of her. "Not unless you're in a hurry. I can't imagine a hotel's firewall that can't be cracked in less than an hour."

Actually, it took seventeen minutes.

She motioned him over. "Come have a look."

Jason saw a list of names and numbers he guessed indicated dates and room numbers.

He watched her scroll down for several minutes. "Not a Uri in the lot."

The cat leapt down from her lap to be replaced by another. "Lot of Latino names, though."

"No wonder. The place is in San Juan."

She looked up at him. "And just when was the last time you stayed at the Ritz or Willard's in DC?"

It took a split second for her point to register.

"You're saying that locals wouldn't be staying in a hotel."

"And look at the place." The screen flashed a virtual tour of swimming pool, spa, and other amenities before going back to the lists. "How many couples do you see on the list of guests? I'd guess if those are legitimate businessmen, they would have chosen something a little less luxurious than a what looks like a beautifully restored old building. If they are tourists, why wouldn't they want to stay at the Caribe Hilton, the El San Juan, or someplace else on the beach? I'm saying there is something odd here."

"Can you get the home addresses of the guests?"

She gave him a real grin this time. "Mr. Peters, if it exists on a computer, I can get it."

A few strokes of the keyboard later, she exclaimed. "Wow! Talk about peculiar!"

Jason had been distracted by a pair of cats that seemed to be disputing possession of a toy mouse. At least he *hoped* it was a toy. "What?"

She pointed to the screen. "Not only have a number of the hotel guests paid multiple visits in three months, the ones that have give a local address"—she pointed—"see? Same zip code as the El Convento, Calle Luna 23. How weird is that, checking into a hotel in the same zip code as your home address?"

"Maybe they weren't alone. Maybe . . ."

He could have sworn Sybil blushed. "I wouldn't think four hundred dollars a night and up would cater to the hot-pillow trade."

Jason thought a moment. "Can you call up their bills? I mean, did they have their meals at the hotel?"

Keys clicked.

"I'd say these gentlemen have a strong preference for vodka. Not a piña colada or daiquiri between them. And they must have taken meals out of the hotel. Any other questions?"

Jason patted her shoulder. "Only how much do I owe you?"

"As always, depends. If you're paying by check or want a written bill, my fee is six-fifty. Five hundred in cash will do as well."

Like so many small businesses, Sybil operated below the IRS's radar.

Jason was already going for his wallet. "I remember. Tax evasion is also illegal."

She was reaching for five crisp bills. "It is also the American pastime."

As Jason left the house, the heat of a Southern summer hit him like a slap across the face. He slipped off his jacket. The back was covered in cat hair. How had that happened?

39

1201 Connecticut Avenue #1
Washington, DC
4:30 p.m. the Same Day

Jason had returned to Washington and gone from the airport to Brooks Brothers' Connecticut Avenue store, the one at which Monica Lewinsky purchased a tie for the president whom she would soon bring into national ridicule, if not disgrace. Jason was here not to revisit history but to supplement the meager wardrobe he had brought from Ischia. A half dozen polo shirts (Golden Fleece Performance in varying hues of pastel), a couple pair of Bermuda shorts (plaid), pre-hemmed khakis (with retro pleats), two swimsuits, and a pair of canvas shoes with rubber soles, the sort of things seen in resort areas and on Ivy League campuses.

"Headed to the beach?" the oversolicitous clerk wanted to know as he slid the credit card.

"Something like that," Jason said noncommittally.

But not the Hamptons, Newport, Martha's Vineyard, or any of the other places where the people who wore that stuff were likely to go.

Jason's attention then focused on a homeless man who had staked out his territory across the street. Between Dupont Circle and the

Cathedral of St. Matthew the Apostle, this section of Connecticut Avenue had heavy vehicular traffic and relatively few pedestrians to panhandle. The begging would be far more lucrative at, say, the National Mall, Capitol Hill, or the hotels clustered around Pennsylvania Avenue, Lafayette Park, and the White House.

The guy wore a long-sleeved, worn flannel shirt, soiled and wrinkled denims belted with a length of rope, and a pair of sneakers. He seemed determined, stopping the occasional few passersby. Most ignored him, a few made a show of detouring around him, and even fewer reached into their pockets. No matter what the result, though, the man seemed to always be in a position to observe the store's entrance.

The fact he had chosen this specific spot had first attracted Jason's attention, the long-sleeved shirt despite the day's heat his suspicion, and his interest in the comings and goings of this particular store his anxiety.

The sales clerk was folding the purchases into paper bags when Jason asked, "Is there a back entrance?"

The young man looked puzzled that a patron of such a high-end store would ask the question. Few if any of his customers would want to sneak out.

"Why, yes, there is. But it's there because of fire code. An alarm goes off if you open it. Why?"

What do you say? That the bum out there is not really a street person but someone who followed me here and wants to kill me? That he's part of a group that seems so dedicated to that purpose that I, personally, killed two of them and seriously wounded a third last night?

"Thought I saw my ex on the street. I make it a practice to avoid her whenever possible."

The clerk's face registered understanding. "If you'd describe her for me, Mr. Peters, I'd be happy to take a peek outside."

"Better yet, could you call a cab?"

As the taxi pulled away from the entrance to the store a few minutes later, Jason thought, but could not be sure, the homeless man's lips were moving as though speaking into the mouthpiece of a concealed cell phone.

Imagination, or was Jason being overly cautious? For certain, he had never known anyone who died from an overdose of paranoia. Four men had been either killed or disabled last night. The force arrayed against him must be substantial if it numbered enough to mount a surveillance operation so quickly.

Good thing Jason wasn't sticking around.

The cab stopped at the guard shack at the gate of Joint Base Anacostia-Bolling. Jason flashed his credentials and temporary visitor pass a second before the armed guard waved them through. The security here certainly wasn't what it would be in a war zone or even on foreign soil, but being adjacent to one of the nation's most crime-ridden urban areas assured the fence's electric charges were constant, the perimeter patrols vigilant, and the gate guards armed. It was, Jason supposed, ironic that here in the nation's capital, guards were necessary to ensure the safety of the lives and property of a military against the very citizens they had sworn to protect.

They also protected Jason against GrünWelt.

It was close to eighteen hundred hours, six p.m., when, in front of the BOQ, Jason paid the cabbie, took the packages, and went to his quarters. At the door, he stooped, checking the knob. The telltale he had left was gone; someone had entered his suite in his absence.

Leaving the packages on the floor, Jason put his ear against the door. Nothing.

Either the intruder had come and gone or was silently waiting to spring his trap. Whoever might be in there could well have seen Jason get out of the cab, since the windows faced the front of the building. So much for the security provided by a military base.

Leaving the packages in the hallway, he retraced his steps to the elevator and returned to the lobby. Behind the front desk, an Airman First Class looked up from his *Washington Post*.

"Help you, sir?"

"I think there's someone in my quarters."

The young man stared at him blankly for what felt like a full minute. "That would be Major Ferris, Captain."

"The doctor? In my quarters?"

"She made it quite clear you were expecting her. She had a number of grocery bags. In fact, I helped her with some of them. Said she was fixing dinner for the two of you."

A look at Jason's face made him ask, "Anything wrong, sir?"

"Quite frankly, I'm not sure."

Not remember my name, indeed!

Back upstairs, Jason used his key to open the door. Instantly, an aroma swirled around him that made his mouth water. He dumped his parcels on the couch and followed his nose.

The kitchen was small and full. Full of pots, pans, containers, and Major Ferris, wearing blue-jean cut-offs under an apron that nearly reached her ankles. Jason couldn't help but think she looked even sexier now than in last night's red dress.

"Oh! Hello!" she said as though surprised to see Jason in his own rented suite. "I do hope you don't mind! I've been trying to call you all day. The switchboard said you were out."

"I was out of town on business."

He lifted the top of a pot. In it, a small chicken was boiling amid strips of carrots, slices of onions, specks of herbs, and material he did not recognize. "What's this?"

"The broth for Brodo di Carne."

"You mean the soup with the noodles stiffened with ground meat?"

"The same." She pointed to a flour-covered cutting board. "You can see them there."

He lifted another top. "And this?"

"The yeast batter for the stuffed squash flowers. I had to look all over the District to find zucchini blossoms."

She took his hand away from the top of the pot. "Now, be a sweetheart and pour me a Martini."

"I'm afraid I don't have any gin."

She tossed her head toward the suite's diminutive refrigerator. "Standard medical supplies. In the freezer."

Using one of the wine stems in the cabinet, he made a makeshift shaker, handing her a frosting glass.

She took it, kissing him on the nose. "Now, be a sweetheart again and go amuse yourself for an hour or so while I finish here."

Jason was unsure he had ever been kissed on the tip of his nose before, and relatively certain no woman had ever told him to go amuse himself while she finished preparing dinner.

The meal was a pastiche of regional and seasonal Italian culinary art: the Brodo di Carne a wintertime Tuscan favorite; spring's squash flowers from Rome's ancient ghetto, batter-fried and stuffed with cheese and anchovies; and Piccata di Vitello, veal in lemon sauce, a Milanese specialty. She had even found a bottle of Gaja.

The after-dinner cheese selection consisted of an Asiago d'Allevo, a firm but creamy-tasting product from the Dolomite Mountain region northwest of Venice; Lombardy's buttery, semisoft Bel Paese; and a Sicilian Caciocavallo.

Jason sliced a bit of the latter onto a toast point. "I understand the 'cavallo' part of the name comes from the fact the Romans made it from mares' milk."

Judith's face scrunched into an expression of disapproval. "I don't know why, but I find that mildly disgusting. I understood the name came from the fact it was delivered by horseback."

"I think I like your explanation better. Where'd you learn all the Italian dishes?"

"I was married to an Italian—at least, a first-generation American one."

"An Italian in Iowa? I didn't know there was anything but corn and cattle out there."

She gave him a playful shove on the shoulder. "Silly! I met him when I was stationed at Lackland in Texas. Like me, he owed the service five years."

"Obviously it didn't work out."

She shook her head, stood and began clearing dishes. "No, he was a *mammone*."

Jason understood the word describing a uniquely Italian phenomenon that gave new meaning to the term "mama's boy." It was not uncommon for some men well into their thirties to still live with their mother. Once married, they would insist their unfortunate wives duplicate Mama's cooking, even the way she did his laundry. The woman would exist under the tyranny of her mother-in-law.

Judith stopped halfway to the kitchen, a stack of plates in her hands. "He even had his mother take an apartment in San Antonio. Every week, he'd bring seven days' worth of her cooking home. I should have known better when I had to put my foot down on the subject of her coming along on our honeymoon.'"

What were the odds of that, of having the two women presently in his life, Maria and Judith, both with Italian exes? Coincidence, or a commentary on Italian men?

"From the information I could get," Judith continued, "the Army's correspondence with you after retirement went to Italy, so I figured a Italian dinner might be appropriate."

"That information isn't in a service jacket. You must have done some digging. I'm flattered you went to the trouble."

Her eyebrows knitted in thought. "You have no idea. That was about all I could find out, that and you were based at Fort Bragg before being posted to the Pentagon. Your service record had more redactions than a CIA agent's diary."

She took the few steps needed to deposit the dishes in the kitchen sink. "With the First Special Forces Operational Detachment Delta based at Bragg, it doesn't take a lot of imagination to guess what you did. That, plus your performance last night."

Jason's raised eyebrows asked a question.

Judith giggled. "I mean what you did *before* you came home with me. I've never seen anyone handle a knife like that." She grinned. "Of course, what you did afterward was pretty spectacular too."

"You weren't exactly a slouch on either count."

She was wiping her hands on the apron as she grew serious. "I've given a lot of thought to that, too. I mean, like I said, I'd never killed anyone before."

"Not even a patient? Not many docs can say that."

Her hand brushed away the attempt at levity. "I'm serious. I thought I'd feel terrible about it. Now, I feel terrible that I don't."

Jason's experience with first kills was as varied as the individuals making them. Usually, if the event occurred at long range and in the confusion of unit combat, there was as little remorse as there was elation. Close-quarters, individual combat was another matter. It was up-close, messy, and personal. Near enough, and the victor was more often than not splattered with his enemy's blood, sometimes his entrails as well. Some had lingering guilt that ultimately impaired their usefulness to the service. Some felt godlike with the realization it was in their power to end a human life, an unmatchable high. Others simply saw the act as an unpleasant necessity of service to their country and went on with their lives. Jason was definitely not in the guilt category and refused to speculate as to the other two.

Jason moved from the small dining table to the couch and picked up the watery remnants of his pre-dinner scotch as he sat. "You did what had to be done. If you hadn't . . . well, I doubt I'd be here right now."

She tugged off her apron and sat beside him. "I'm not sure doing what you have to do is adequate justification. I mean, those people who tape bombs to themselves and blow up innocent women and children use that rationalization."

"There's a difference in killing in defense of yourself or someone else and blowing up people you don't even know. Where's the scotch?"

"You left the bottle by the fridge. I'll get it." She took the glass from his hand and stood. "Not to put too fine a point on it, but my understanding is killing people you don't even know is part of what Delta Force does."

"But I *do* know them. They're my enemy, the people you were talking about: the bombers, the people who want to take us back to the Dark Ages, to force their religion down our throats. Fanatical Muslims."

She was spooning ice into his glass. "I'm sure there are some Muslims who're not like that. Some are peaceful."

"Sure. The ones who've run out of ammunition."

She topped off the glass. "Those men last night didn't look like Arabs."

"They weren't."

"Then who . . . ?"

He stood to step beside her and take the glass from her hand. "Believe me, you don't want to know."

"Yes, I do. You just said I saved your ass. In doing so, I killed a man, remember? Whatever you're into, I'm in it too. I have a right to know."

"First, what I'm into is confidential, my employer's business. I can tell you the guy you shot was most likely former Spetsnaz, the Red Army's assassination and special-ops boys. OK?"

"What would former Russian special ops be doing here in Washington?"

"Trying to make sure I never leave here."

She poured the last of the Gaja into her wineglass. "And you're leaving here when? Or is that off-limits too?"

Her tone had an edge to it.

"Tomorrow."

"So, let me get this straight: You waltz into my life, I literally kill for you, and now you doff your helmet or campaign cap or whatever you Delta Force boys wear and say good-bye? The old love 'em and leave 'em?"

Jason would not have phrased it quite that way. In fact, it had been his guess that he'd be the one to be loved and left. Dinner last night had not been his idea. The woman had learned more than cooking from her former Italian mother-in-law; she learned the art of the guilt trip.

"I can't very well expect to get paid staying here. What do you suggest?"

"That I come with you."

For an instant, Jason was certain he had not heard correctly. "Come with . . . You're kidding, right?"

Her face said she wasn't. "Why not?"

Jason sat back down on the sofa, his drink forgotten. "First, you have no idea what you'd be getting yourself into. . . ."

"If it involves violence, I think I've demonstrated I can take care of myself."

That answered any question about how Judith felt about killing someone. She wanted more, a thrill seeker. Do assassins have groupies?

"I can't take care of the both of us. . . ."

"I'm not asking you to. I'm asking you to let me come along. Promise I won't get in the way. I'll have your back. Who knows, medical skill may come in handy."

"Judith, I'm dealing with some seriously bad-ass dudes, here."

"I know. I killed one of them."

Not a trace of remorse. She would have had him mounted as a trophy and hung on her wall if she could have.

Jason started to say they really didn't know each other well enough, realized that wouldn't fly, and tried, "But you've got your job here."

"And almost three weeks' annual leave coming. I'm sure as hell not going to take it in Iowa. Look, Jason, I've served my time, done my duty to the Air Force and my country. I'm not complaining, but I can't say it's been a thrill, either. Someone like you would have no idea of what tedium is like. Then, all of a sudden, you come into my life, big and handsome. First man I've looked at twice in longer than I want to admit. I'm not inclined to just turn my back and walk away. I want to do something besides treating venereal disease and dispensing flu shots. I may never have a chance to do something exciting again."

"Judith, this isn't Disney World. You can't just get off the ride and be finished. People get killed."

"I think I learned that last night. What do you want, that I sign something relieving you of all responsibility?

Jason knew a truly bad idea when he heard one, at least one pertaining to operations. Taking a brief acquaintance into danger, a woman with no combat experience, would be like . . . like having Maria present. At least Judith wasn't harping about the evil of violence. And Maria also, once upon a time, had saved his life.

A plan was beginning its birth process. Maybe Major Ferris, J., could be of use after all.

"Let's talk about it," he said.

40

Final Approach: Luis Muñoz Marín International Airport
San Juan
6:32 p.m. Local Time
The Next Day

The 777 popped out of the low-level clouds that were the detritus of Puerto Rico's daily afternoon thundershowers. Jason's window streaked with moisture that gave a distorted view of monolithic mega-hotels marching along the island's north shore. It reminded him of Miami Beach, a sanitized American monoculture. In contrast, the walls of the historic fort and of Old San Juan cast dark shadows on the verdant green of the national park that memorialized Puerto Rico's colorful past.

The tinny announcement of the necessity of seat belts and restoration of trays and seats to their original position elicited squalls from a leather-lunged child somewhere behind in the plane's coach section.

Happily, Jason had secured a first-class seat earlier that day. Even so, commercial air meant he was flying unarmed rather than trusting a disassembled weapon to the vagaries of the airline's baggage system. Having to explain to the local police why he had brought the Glock or learning it had been mishandled to Bangkok would be little help.

Tires shrieked on cement. Jason was shoved forward against his seat belt by the aircraft's howling reverse thrust. As the big jet cleared the runway, he noted, not for the first time, that the Caribbean was the elephant graveyard of aviation. Half a dozen DC-3s were lined up in front of one freight carrier. The newest had rolled off the wartime assembly line in 1942, and, quite likely, dropped troops over Normandy or braved Burma's Hump to bring supplies to a beleaguered Chiang Kai-shek, arms and equipment that would see action against Mao's communist rebels rather than the intended foe, the Japanese. There were equally elderly C-56 Lockheed Lodestars and newer—but still ancient—blunt-nosed Beech-18s. Anything that could still fly and manage to skirt the edges of the FAA's low profile was here.

The puddles on the taxiway were further evidence the afternoon thundershowers had already departed, retreating up the slopes of the rain forest, which Jason could see through the windows on the opposite side of the aisle. But the humidity, he knew, would linger like a wet blanket, smothering everything it touched in warm dampness.

That was one reason Jason took his time deplaning. He was in no hurry to enter the steam bath that awaited him outside. The other was to let as many passengers as possible clear the terminal before he passed through it, perhaps making it easier to spot anyone showing an interest in his arrival. He removed his single bag from the overhead bin and slung it over his shoulder by the strap. He sauntered past the Delta gates, past the T-shirt and fast food shops. He followed the stained blue carpet into the main terminal, where a combination of salsa music from portable radios and shouted Spanish filled the air. San Juan's airport was the Naples of the New World. Passengers pushed carts stacked six or seven suitcases high. Small children, often four or five to a family, gaped with wide brown eyes from behind their mothers' skirts, or, more often, pants tight as the skin on a drumstick. Puerto Rican women had an affinity for spike heels, low-cut blouses, and pants a size or two too small.

Jason stood still for a full minute, observing a crowd that swirled like the confluence of multiple rivers. No one seemed to show any particular interest in him. But in this organized confusion, he could not be sure. Deliberately, he made his way to the nearest men's room, taking care not to look over his shoulder or give any other sign that he suspected he might be watched.

Inside the restroom, he walked down a line of stalls, choosing the unoccupied one most distant from the entrance. Inside, he replaced his shirt with a pastel-blue one from Brooks Brothers from his shoulder bag. The wrinkled one in which he had traveled went into the luggage, then he removed a faded baseball cap, which he pulled low over his forehead. The change wasn't going to fool a careful observer, but it might divert an unwary watcher. Finally, he removed the shoulder strap of his bag to carry it by the handle, suitcase-style.

He had just cracked the stall's door open in preparation to leave the restroom when two men came through the door, one behind the other. Despite the tropical heat outside the airport, both wore light khaki windbreakers, just the thing to conceal a shoulder holster. Large, with muscular jaws. High cheekbones and barely perceptible angled eyes gave them an appearance Jason associated with Russians, particularly the Russians he had seen on the tube platform in London, although the absence of a facial scar told him these were not the same men. They could have been employees of a local fitness club. Or professional wrestlers. Jason doubted either. Particularly since one had a bandage covering half his face. As if, maybe, he'd had an unfortunate encounter with a tire iron.

It had been too dark in the parking lot in Durham to observe facial features, but what were the odds of two perfectly innocent Slavic-faced men of approximately the same build, both of whom had injuries to the right side, being here in San Juan at the same time as Jason's arrival? Not good. Not good at all.

He watched the pair wash their hands, using the mirror above the basins to survey the room. The one with the bandage fussed with his hair. The other examined his reflection's skin, running a hand across his cheeks. Both of these activities allowed them to keep the room under surveillance without being obvious. What was obvious was that the pair had not come to the men's room in response to nature's call.

More likely, they were waiting for Jason to come out of one of several stalls with closed doors. Or for all the others to change occupants. Either way, they seemed to have all the time in the world, time in which Jason was going to have to figure out an escape.

Wait a minute, he thought.

Jason had the means of his own salvation. Reaching into a pocket, he took out his BlackBerry. Previously, since its inception in 1994, the island-wide 911 emergency service had suffered the same ills as so many other American cities: too many non-emergency calls and a thirty-five-minute average response time, plus language complications with operators whose English was less than perfect. Unlike, say, Washington, the response time here had been cut to an average of seven minutes by an effort at public awareness and elimination of non-emergency calls. And an idea novel to government: firing the incompetent.

The answer was 911. A call to the local number and the restroom would be flooded with police. Jason could simply walk out.

There was only one problem: The BlackBerry didn't respond. Jason glared at the screen. He had a worldwide chip; the device should work. But it didn't. The San Juan airport, or at least this part of it, was an electronic dead zone.

41

Calle Luna 23
San Juan
At the Same Time

Carlos read the text message aloud before observing, "Peters has landed. It appears he is alone. He is by himself in the men's room near the airport's baggage-claim area."

The older man, Pedro, held his frosty glass up in mock toast. "Uri's team has an incentive to leave this man dead after the *polnyi pizdets—* er, fuck-up—in England." He noticed his companion was empty-handed. "Have a drink to celebrate, my young friend!"

"Perhaps when we have news Peters has been dealt with. But you are right: not only Uri but Maksim. They say he may never recover full use of his right eye."

Pedro tossed off the contents of his glass. "Once burned by milk, you will blow on cold water. Both Uri and Maksim will use more care this time."

"And if they fail again?"

The older man was refilling his glass. "Then we have but to wait. Peters did not come to San Juan on vacation. He will be seeking us out."

"And if he finds us?"

"He will, he will. We will make certain of that."

"We want him to find us?"

"Would not the wolf prefer the lamb came to him?"

Pedro lurched toward the bathroom, leaving Carlos to gauge how much his friend had drunk by the frequency of Russian proverbs.

42

Luis Muñoz Marín International Airport
San Juan

Jason questioned his wisdom in insisting Judith arrive on a separate flight. It would have been nice to have backup, someone who would come looking when he didn't return from the men's room. But what made him think Judith would have? She was hardly a trained operative, and he had no intention of utilizing her as one. Her role would be . . .

Well, if he could get to working his plan. Instead, he was stuck in a lavatory stall while two thugs, most likely ex-Spetsnaz, waited like a pride of lions watching some African water hole for the appearance of an unwary antelope.

Once they were aware of which stall he occupied, would they shoot? The flimsy door provided scant protection against bullets, but risk so brazen an act? Unlikely. The knives Jason associated with the Russian military group would draw less attention but were equally deadly in professional hands.

Except knives couldn't kill at gunshot distances.

Jason undid his belt and coiled it around his right hand. He took a deep breath. He was only going to get this single chance.

What he had in mind would have had a better chance of success if the stall's door swung outward. But it didn't.

Opening the door as though preparing to exit, Jason feigned surprise when his eyes met those of the two men's reflections in the brightly lit mirror over the sinks. In the split second it took for Jason to be sure he had been recognized, he slammed the door shut again and shot the bolt.

Below the bottom of the door, a pair of feet appeared. Jason could hear the metal groan as whoever was outside tested the latch.

Jason stooped, at the same time releasing the bolt with his left hand. With his right, he swung his belt so that it looped around an ankle outside the stall and slid back the door's latch.

Not expecting either the release of the lock or the leather around his ankle, the man with the bandaged face stumbled forward. With his left hand now free, Jason grabbed the belt's loose end and pulled with all his strength.

The intruder's momentum forward was abruptly reversed, yanking his feet out from beneath him. He did a half gainer that would have scored a 10 by any panel of judges had he been in dive competition rather than a public restroom.

His head met the surface of the tile floor. The sickening thud of bone smashing into ceramic froze not only the man's partner but the lavatory's other patrons.

Jason was on the sprawling figure with the quickness of a striking viper. Plunging his hand inside the man's jacket, he snatched loose the GSh-18 automatic from the nylon, angle-draw shoulder holster.

Jason looked up just in time to see the second man's hand going for the inside of his windbreaker. Rolling violently to his left for momentum, Jason sprang to his feet, the front sight of the Russian automatic aligned with the spot where the man's eyebrows met at the bridge of his nose.

"OK, OK!" Realizing Jason could get off a shot before his own weapon cleared the holster, the man slowly raised both hands.

Jason stepped out of range of the arms and legs of the man on the floor. "OK, folks," he addressed the audience, "showtime's over. Walk, do not run, to the exit."

There is nothing like a gun in a man's hand to ensure prompt, unquestioning obedience. Their eyes never leaving Jason, the five or six men in the restroom edged toward the door. Jason guessed he had maybe fifteen to thirty seconds before one of them found a cop.

Edging sideways so he could keep both the man on the floor and the other in sight, Jason indicated the near wall. "OK, now you assume the position."

The man looked at him blankly.

"Don't make it easier for me to kill you than take your weapon. You heard me!"

When the man was spread against the wall, Jason approached cautiously. With his shoe, he kicked the man's feet a little farther away from the wall, ensuring that the man's balance was such that any sudden movement would land him on the floor. Keeping the GSh-18 level in his right hand, Jason found its mate in another shoulder holster. Using his thumb, he pushed the clip release and let the magazine clatter to the floor. Ejecting the round in the chamber, he tossed the gun into the paper-towel disposal. The man on the floor was struggling to his feet.

"So long, boys. It's been a real pleasure."

Jason was no more than a dozen steps outside the entrance to the restroom when four burly men in police uniform, weapons drawn, dashed past. Once they were out of sight, he dumped the remaining gun in a trash bin. If the airport went into lockdown, he didn't want to be caught with a firearm.

Outside, Jason was embraced by an envelope of humidity. Prickles of sweat tickled his back. He toyed with the idea of concealing himself in hopes of a chance to follow his assailants once they exited the airport. Too risky. There was too good a chance the local cops might be looking for the man with the gun in the men's room.

Besides, he had a plan.

Instead, he slid into the first cab he saw, thankful for the air-conditioning.

The coquí were in full song in the little plaza in front of the hotel. The tiny tree frogs had voices far disproportionate to their one-inch sizes.

Catty-corner to the hotel and small park, San Juan Cathedral's alabaster facade, bathed in spotlights, pierced the night sky.

As he paid the cabbie and retrieved his bag, Jason was reminded of the church's most celebrated occupant: Juan Ponce de León, entombed there since his death by an Indian arrow in 1521. The man had to be one of Spain's more confused conquistadors. Searching for the Fountain of Youth, rumored to be on the island of Bimini, he found Florida, perhaps the last man to see the state with more flowers than high-rise condos.

Believing he had found an island rather than the southern part of North America, he set sail back to Puerto Rico, landing instead on the Yucatán Peninsula, this time convinced he had found Bimini.

Jason entered the hotel's high-ceilinged reception area across an Andalusian floor of large black-and-white tiles. The walls around the lobby were hung with tapestries depicting medieval scenes of hunts and battles. Jason wondered how the fabric survived the mildew endemic to the tropical climate. Beyond the open lobby, he could see a three-tiered courtyard bordered on three sides by cloisters. It took little imagination for shadows to become nuns silently sliding by the three-hundred-year-old níspero fruit tree that dominated the center. At the rear, a pool shimmered an inviting cool blue. No doubt an addition since the nuns' departure. At the end near Jason, a bar was doing a brisk business serving those waiting for a seat at the alfresco restaurant.

Jason resisted the temptation to join them, ignoring a protesting stomach. He'd had nothing but a light snack of pressed and tasteless chicken between dry bread garnished with wilted lettuce and perhaps a dozen potato chips on the plane. Through some oversight of the airline, though, the slice of dill pickle had a trace of flavor.

But at least he had arrived, nearly on time, on the flight he had booked and in the seat he had purchased. Today's air traveler was learning to be thankful for things taken for granted a few years earlier.

He needed to get to his room. If the bully boys at the airport had learned of his arrival before he had even deplaned, there was a good chance they knew where he was staying, as well. The downside of modern computerized society was that there was little information not available to even a modestly talented hacker.

His third-floor accommodation, the one he had requested after a virtual tour before booking his reservations, was at the end of an open-air corridor looking down on the courtyard. Designed and furnished to remind the occupant of its origins, the room had a high, oak-beamed ceiling, making the space seem as tall as it was wide and long, the dimensions of a monastic cell. The floor was Spanish tile. Furnishings, though stark in appearance, were tasteful and certainly more comfortable than the sisters would have enjoyed. Floor-to-ceiling French doors opened onto a terrace looking onto the plaza and cathedral below. He guessed daylight would bring a view of the rain forest beyond.

Jason stepped into the steamy night and paced the terrace. Empty lounge chairs were his only company. Only two rooms, including his, had access other than by way of the hall outside his door. All as he had seen on the computer before leaving home.

Perfect.

43

Hotel El Convento
Four Hours Later

During the summer in San Juan, you can set your watch by the rain showers. Between four and four thirty a downpour of short duration sweeps the city streets clean but leaves the air saturated. Shortly after dark, the cooling temperature squeezes the afternoon's lingering moisture out of the air like wringing a wet rag. This shower passes quickly also, making alfresco dining on Old Town's myriad patios almost comfortable.

By late night, the evening's rain was only a steamy memory. The sound of the patrons of the bar in the courtyard was diminishing. Guests were retiring to their rooms and other customers were slowly leaving for a livelier scene, for a nighttime flirtation with chance at the casinos, or to simply go home. Either way, the comparative quiet allowed Balduino, the night clerk, to slip into that semi-somnambulistic state of near sleep that would last until he was relieved at the hotel's front desk in the morning.

The sound of high heels on tile followed by the tinkle of the bell on the desk snatched him from a half slumber and sent him scurrying from the comfort of the lounge chair in the hotel's office to the front desk. For an instant, he thought he might still be dreaming. A blond woman fidgeted impatiently in front of the registration desk. Although she was dressed in simple jeans and a shirt, it was obvious she would more than adequately fill a bikini.

He suddenly wished he had taken the time to brush his hair and rinse his mouth before dashing out. "Yes, ma'am?"

Long fingers drummed on the desktop. "My name is Ferris. I believe I have a reservation."

Normal procedure, if there were anything normal about a check-in at this hour, would have required an explanation that the guest would be charged for tonight even though it was tomorrow. But Balduino was having too hard a time just trying to keep his eyes away from her blouse's top button at the beginning valley between her breasts. The button looked as though it might give way with the next breath. The anticipation was distracting to say the least.

"You *do* have my room?"

With no small effort, he tore his gaze away and sat down in front of the computer. For reasons he could not have explained, he had the impression that if an error had been made, if her reservation wasn't in the computer, he was going to be extremely sorry.

His breath whistled through his teeth as he let out a long sigh. "Yes, Ms. Ferris, right here. I see it's prepaid. I'm sorry that we have no staff at this hour to carry your bag and I'm not allowed . . ."

She extended a hand. "The key?"

"The key?"

If she was amused by the confusion she seemed to induce, she didn't show it. "I assume entry to the room is by key."

"Of course! The room key."

Hand inexplicably shaking, he reached to the rack over the computer, where a number of oversized keys hung, each attached to a decorative weight heavy enough to encourage guests to leave their room keys at the front desk when they went out rather than carrying—and possibly losing—them. It was a concept common in Europe.

"Third floor," he said, almost apologetically. "The elevator is around the corner there on your left."

Without another word, she swooped up her single bag and was gone, leaving Balduino leaning over the desk for a last look.

He remembered now: the guest, Peters, had made her reservation by phone the same time he had made his own. He had been very specific: two end-of-hall rooms, each letting out onto the terrace. Why a man would provide a separate room for someone like the Ferris woman was beyond Balduino's imagination. Ah well, the proclivities of the hotel's guests were not his to question.

With a little luck, when he returned to his dreams, Ms. Ferris would be in them.

Exiting the single slow elevator on the third floor, Judith turned left down an open, arcaded gallery of a cloister. The lights of the pool in the patio below made shimmering blue designs on the ceiling above her head as she stopped in front of the room at the end of the hall. Inserting the key, she pushed the door open, letting the light from outside probe the dark room before she entered and flipped on the wall switch.

Satisfied she was alone, she dropped her single bag on the bed and stepped over to the drawn curtains. She pulled them aside, revealing French doors opening onto a terrace. She gave the door to the bathroom a longing gaze. A hot shower would strip away the coat of sweaty grime with which she imagined the cloying humidity had covered her body.

No time.

Making certain the door to the hallway was securely locked and latched from the inside, she stepped out onto the terrace. For an instant she was blinded by the contrast between the brightly lit room and the indirect light outside. The coquí in the surrounding potted palms went silent.

A hoarse whisper came from her right. "Here!"

As her eyes adjusted, she moved toward the sound. "Jason?"

A figure materialized out of nowhere. "You were expecting someone else?"

They embraced briefly before she gently pushed back. "So far, nothing?"

He took her hand, leading into deeper shadow. "So far, nothing. But the night is young, to employ a rather trite phrase. Best get to your post."

"Think I have time to clean up?"

Jason shrugged. "The schedule isn't ours."

In seconds, Judith was gone, back to her room. She turned out the lights before crouching behind the curtains she had closed over the open French doors.

Jason was good at waiting. Long ago Delta Force training had inculcated patience by employing an indifference to time and applying the mind elsewhere while remaining alert to surroundings. He could only hope Judith was naturally patient. How long they waited at their separate positions, neither could have said. An hour, two, or only fifteen minutes.

Judith heard him before she saw him. Or, rather, the tree frogs in the terrace's foliage did. Their song went silent as suddenly as if some amphibian maestro had waved his conductor's wand. Alerted by the sudden silence, she risked a peek between widened curtains.

A wraith of a shadow, a specter without substance, glided across the terrace toward the French doors to Jason's room. It was only at the last moment the apparition gained substance, the shape of a man, a large man, climbing inside from the terrace.

Jason had also been brought to full alert by the termination of the tree frogs' serenade, and the vibration of his BlackBerry, his and Judith's prearranged signal. The closest thing he had been able to find to serve as a weapon was a lamp, two feet high, made of what he supposed was meant to look like forged Toledo steel. Hardly a defense of choice against a pistol or knife; but when combined with surprise, it should serve. Concealed behind curtains that barely moved in the fitful night breeze, he waited, the lamp raised in both hands above his head.

Leaving the French doors open had been a calculated risk. Any job made too easy aroused suspicions but a slip in prying the doors open, any undue noise was likely to frighten away the would-be intruder. The last thing Jason wanted was for his enemies to change plans, to strike at a less predictable time.

The curtains jiggled with a motion not induced by wind. With the advantage of having his target outlined by the slight illumination from the terrace, Jason could see a form, as yet indistinct except for an extended arm holding something long. Jason guessed an automatic with sound suppressor.

He waited until the shape seemed to float past him, intent on the mound of pillows Jason had carefully arranged in the bed. The arm extended.

There were two quick spitting, puffing sounds before the form moved closer to the bed. It was reaching for a light when Jason moved.

With a single step, he used his full weight to bring the lamp down on the back of the head. The neck would have been a better target, but the chances were too good that a blow there would fatally snap the spinal cord. Dead, the guy would be useless.

With a grunt, the figure stumbled forward, falling against the far wall. Jason took a second swing with the lamp, this time sideways, splintering the knuckles of the man's gun hand. The weapon thumped once on the bed and bounced to the tile floor with a metallic clank that was almost drowned out by a scream of pain.

The assailant was still groggy and gave no resistance as Jason grabbed him by the collar and threw him across the bed. He switched on the overhead light and was not surprised to see one of the men from the airport, the one without the bandage.

"You guys don't give up easily."

The man didn't answer. His eyes flitted around the room, no doubt searching for his weapon.

"I kicked it under the bed," Jason said calmly. "Afraid somebody might get hurt, playing with guns." He watched the man's reaction to the fact he was now unarmed. "And if you're thinking about going for one of those Spetsnaz pig stickers . . ."

He waved the iron lamp threateningly.

"Now, we are going to have that little conversation that seems to keep getting delayed." Jason had intentionally placed himself within range of the prone man's legs. "You're going to tell me . . ."

Jason's BlackBerry rang.

In the split instant of startled indecision, the man on the bed lashed out with a scissorslike kick that took Jason's legs out from beneath him and crumpled him on the floor. The intruder made a quick judgment:

instead of attacking, he bolted for the open French doors, his injured hand held in the other.

Jason watched him go, gratified that, so far, his plan had worked. Then he realized the cell phone in his pocket was still ringing.

Who . . . ?

"Hello?"

"Jason?" It was Judith, of course. "You OK? I was worried."

Oh, swell!

Jason had to clench his jaws not to say what was on his mind. "How thoughtful of you. Perhaps it might have served us better had you waited until I could have called you. I was, emphasis on the *was*, sort of busy."

"Guess I fucked up."

No, *I* fucked up by bringing an untrained, unqualified person along on a mission where professionalism is required, he thought.

But he said, "If that's your only mistake, everything will be fine."

"You didn't tell me *not* to call," Judith said, miffed. "I was worried about you."

"I'm fine."

"You sure?"

"I'm sure. Now do your part."

Jason pressed the Disconnect key. With him momentarily off his guard, if that guy had attacked instead of fled . . .

He shoved the BlackBerry back into his pocket. At least the first part of the plan had worked.

44

Judith watched the blur of a shadow bolt from Jason's room onto the terrace. The man was hunched over as though he had been hurt. Her impulse was to go to Jason to make sure he was all right, but there was no time and she could tell he was already angry with her.

All she had wanted to do was make sure Jason was all right. Some people, apparently including Jason, were just prickly by nature.

Stepping over to the door of her room that opened onto the corridor, she pressed an ear against it, waiting for the soft sound of footsteps on Spanish tile as the man leaving Jason's room entered the side of the cloister. As he passed, she kicked off her high heels, slipping her feet into a pair of sneakers that would make no noise on the cobblestone streets. Snatching up her purse, the one with the shoulder strap, she waited.

She waited until she heard the faint whir of the elevator before she bolted from her room and took the stairs two at a time. The elevator was leisurely passing the second floor as she dashed through the lobby and outside to seek shelter in the shadows of the plaza across the street.

Backing into the darkness under a towering ficus tree, she was certain she could not be seen from the hotel.

A sound, a flicker of movement, some sixth sense made her suddenly aware she was not alone. The man sent to kill Jason had backup.

The streets were brightly lit but she could make out little within the penumbra of shade cast by the tree. She could not see who shared the darkness, but she was certain he meant her no goodwill. Warily, she moved backward toward the line that demarcated a puddle of light from a streetlamp and the ficus tree's thick foliage.

Then, like a comet out of the night, a streak of silver sliced at her midsection. More from reflex than thought, she bent and recoiled like a batter avoiding an inside fastball.

Either her sight was adjusting to the night or she was getting closer to the streetlights, for she could make him out now. Or at least part of him. Tall, shaved, polished scalp. And the right side of his face, including the eye, were covered by a bandage. The latter possibly explained why his first strike missed: the loss of depth perception. She could see his teeth, exposed in a smile that said he did not anticipate his next assault would fail.

Jason stepped into the hallway, noting that Judith's door was ajar. She had left in a hurry, as would be the case if she were to get outside and into a position to follow the would-be assassin. Or at least get a license-plate number of a getaway car.

He knew he should stay in the room rather than chance spooking the man Judith was to tail. Instead, he took the stairs down to the empty lobby, arriving just in time to see the fleeing back of his attacker. Jason flattened himself against the wall next to the elevator, hoping Judith had made it into position across the street.

When he was certain the man had cleared the lobby, Jason followed to the hotel's entrance to see the back of his attacker disappear around the corner to his left.

Where was Judith?

A flash of movement caught the corner of his eye. Judith, barely visible in the shadows of a huge tree, seemed to be engaged in some sort of motion, twisting, swaying to no music Jason could hear. As he moved closer to the street, Jason saw she was not alone. His throat caught as he recognized the man with the bandaged face. Though he couldn't see the blade from where he stood, Judith's movement told him she was dodging a knife. As a rank amateur, she would be easy prey. The bastard was toying with her.

With a final glance at the point at which the intruder to his room had disappeared, Jason ran down the steps and across the narrow street. Careful to move as quietly as quickly, he kept the ficus tree between him and the man he was certain had a knife.

Judith looked directly at Jason as she dodged another swipe of the blade. If she saw him, as was all but certain, she gave no indication, only giving ground as she slowly backed away.

On the balls of his feet, the man made a balanced thrust. No doubt he had been trained in the use of the weapon.

With the grace of a matador avoiding the bull's horns, Judith stepped aside, using an open palm to knock the arm wide of the mark.

An amateur, perhaps, but not bad.

Jason was at the tree now. The time for stealth was past. "Freeze, fucker!"

The man with the knife did just that if only for a split second, an instant in which Judith landed a kick in his groin. "Shit-ass!"

With a muffled grunt, he bent double just in time to meet her knee squarely with his nose. The sound was like that of a ripe melon hitting concrete.

As he stumbled forward, his one good eye masked in blood from his flattened nose, Jason grabbed the wrist of the hand that still held the knife. A downward snatch and the blade spun into darkness as the man pitched forward, face-first, onto the ground.

Jason barely noticed Judith slip away.

For one of the few times in his life, training, common decency, and a sense of mercy deserted him simultaneously. In their place was the memory of the death of Boris and attempts on his own life. He waited for the man to struggle to his knees before delivering a running kick to the ribs. Jason imagined he heard bones crack.

"That's for Boris," he growled.

Impatient for the prone figure to attempt to rise again, Jason bent over and grabbed the shirt collar, twisting it tight against the Adam's apple until his victim gagged for breath.

"And this is for fucking with me and an unarmed woman!"

Later, Jason would be thankful someone had overheard the noise and called the police. Had not the approaching wail of sirens gotten his attention, he had little doubt he would have killed the man in his rage. He had killed enough in his life, but this bastard and his shadowy organization had pierced the wall of cool professionalism that had allowed Jason to go about his work without any qualms.

As the plaza filled with pulsating blue light, he slipped into the shadows.

Judith was gone.

There seemed little else to do but merge into a crowd of the curious that gathered with surprising alacrity considering the hour. Minutes later, he was back in his hotel room.

Judith wasted no time as soon as the man with the knife was no longer a threat. If she hurried, she might yet catch up to the man she had intended to follow. As she rounded the corner of the hotel, the streetlights caught a figure turning into an intersection two blocks away. She forced herself to move far slower than she wished. Anyone on the street at this hour would attract attention, and someone in a hurry even more so.

Moving from one pool of darkness to another between lights, she edged up the cobblestones' slight incline. She stopped at the first intersection, peering around the corner. She could well have been in a graveyard. Other than a pair of rangy cats exploring street-side garbage bins, there was no sign of life.

She hurried to the next crossing a little higher up the gentle slope. Her back absorbing the cool stucco surface of a building, she risked sticking her head around the corner. She almost missed it, a figure darting into a house. She counted. Five, no, six, doors down.

Though tempted to follow, she knew better. If that was the place to which Jason's assailant had retreated, someone would watch the street to make sure he had not been followed. Better to check it out in daylight when neighborhood activity would make her and Jason less conspicuous.

Looking up, she squinted at the street sign to make it out: Calle Luna.

45

Hotel El Convento
8:25 the Next Morning

Sitting at a table at the hotel's patio alfresco restaurant, Jason and Judith listened to the buzz of conversation around them, all on the same topic: the attack and near murder of a man in the plaza just in front of the hotel last night. There seemed to be two versions. The first held that the event was simply a brutal mugging.

A chubby woman with a distinct New York accent at the next table stated her anxieties at venturing forth from the sanctuary of the hotel at night, tossing curls that possibly could have been that blond twenty years ago. Her companion, a young man who might have been her son were it not for his dark Latino complexion, told her that one of the guests, unable to sleep, looked out of a window and saw a woman. Perhaps a lovers' quarrel turned near deadly?

Judith used her fork to spear the last pineapple section of her fruit plate. "If everyone here speaks the truth, we had an audience as big as the Super Bowl."

Jason nodded before popping the final bit of omelet into his mouth.

"Something exciting happens, everybody is a witness. Until subpoenas start getting handed out, that is." He wiped his mouth with the napkin. "Then nobody saw anything, nobody remembers anything, nobody wants to get involved. By the way, that was some fancy footwork on your part last night. And slapping the knife aside . . . Sure you never had Special Forces training?"

"May as well have. Had three brothers, all older. And I was ticklish. You learn quick."

"Any of them survive?"

She smiled. "All of them, but they learned early on that their baby sister could take care of herself."

Jason held up the coffeepot. She shook her head. He drained it into his cup, lowering his voice. "I'd like to take a look at this house. Calle Luna, is it?"

Judith nodded. "I doubt they are giving tours."

Sarcasm along with agile feet.

Jason ignored it. "'Tour' sounds like an idea. Maybe we should take a walking tour of Old San Juan."

Judith glanced at her watch. "He will be in the Parque de las Palomas in ten minutes."

"Who?"

"The tour guide from the service I called this morning. They give walking tours, mostly for cruise-boat passengers, but they can fit us in."

Maybe bringing Judith along was not as bad an idea as Jason had thought last night.

Park of the Pigeons was aptly named. At the lower end of Calle Cristo, it was located on top of the old city wall with a view of the cruise boats in the harbor below. Beyond, a curtain of clouds was already devouring the green slopes of the El Yunque rain forest. Like the Piazza San Marco in Venice, pigeons and their droppings were everywhere: coating the old stone wall, the few benches, tree limbs, and anything else that was still for more than a few minutes, including the occasional unfortunate tourist. Like their Italian counterparts, the birds feared no man, as if well aware of their protected status.

An old woman, occupying a lime-drenched bench, tossed pieces of bread into a seething mass of feathers.

Judith wrinkled her nose. "Pigeon fecal matter causes fungal infections," she announced disgustedly. "Filthy!"

"'Fecal matter'?"

"'Pigeon shit' to you."

"Sky rats," Jason agreed.

A minivan with a cruise line's logo on its side stopped at the entrance to the small park. Ten or so people were climbing out. None was under fifty. All had varying degrees of sunburn. Each wore white sneakers, white socks, white shorts, and T-shirts from various Caribbean Islands. Only the types and sizes of hats and cameras differed.

"This must be our group," Judith said.

"What was your first clue?"

By this time a man in a polo shirt and khaki shorts was herding his charges into a group. Jason and Judith went over and introduced themselves.

An hour later, the tourists had seen the crafts market, the old jail (now the tourist bureau, but with a few cells sanitized and preserved for viewing), the one remaining old city gate, and several museums, including one of primitive Caribbean art, with emphasis on *primitive*.

As the day got warmer, the tourists moved at a slower pace uphill toward the old fort.

Just as they drew abreast of the intersection with Calle Luna, Jason suggested, "There's a place down the street there. I'll bet they have cold drinks."

A number of his companions held up nearly empty water bottles.

"Yeah, let's take a break."

"I could use something cold. My water is warm as bathwater."

Their guide impatiently checked his watch. "OK, but no more than ten minutes. I've got another group on the hour."

The small bodega, little more than an open storefront with two tables on the sidewalk, did indeed have cold drinks, in addition to a surprisingly lengthy menu. Better yet, from Jason's point of view, it sat across the street from Number 23, the house into which Judith had seen last night's assailant retreat. Other than its pale-blue exterior, a cursory glance did not distinguish it from its neighbors. Standing in what little shade was available, Jason studied the building. Unlike most of the others on the street, the windows were shuttered tightly.

Cap pulled low over his forehead and swigging from a rapidly warming can of Coke, Jason crossed the cobblestones to feign interest in an elaborate brass door knocker on the adjacent building. The ornament was barely five feet from the common wall with Number 23. This close, Jason could see minor nicks in the paint on shutters, window frames, and door. Instead of the dark wood exposed by cracks and chips in adjoining woodwork, there was gray steel. He stepped back, seeming to admire the knocker. Was that a trace of wiring along the top of both windows and door? Certainly that reflection of glass in the shadows of the entrance bespoke some sort of camera.

The residents of Number 23 Calle Luna had a great deal more interest in security than the rest of the street, and Jason intended to find out why.

46

Isla Grande Airport
San Juan
Two Hours Later

Jason was uneasy enough in fixed-wing aircraft; flying in helicopters downright frightened him. In the first place, rising into the air without wings seemed an unnatural act, against the laws of nature. Like the American League's DH rule. Next, he had apprehensions about the safety of choppers: If the engine quit, he would be aboard an airborne crowbar. Finally, the things flitted back and forth beneath the tops of buildings at altitudes only the heartiest of birds would chance.

All his qualms had been explained away quite logically by persons far more knowledgeable on the subject than he, but he was just as nervous as ever. Fear, he told himself, is an illogical emotion.

He felt it just the same.

The Bell 47J Ranger on the tarmac of the general aviation airport offered little comfort. With a single pilot seat up front and a three-passenger bench behind, the aircraft was almost as old as the DC-3s at San Juan's commercial field. The tropical sun had bleached its paint into chalk and the Plexiglas had cracked in a number of spots.

It was, however, the only helicopter immediately available for rental.

The only comfort Jason felt was the weight of his Glock in the small of his back. The weapon had been delivered in parts in multiple packages by UPS that morning, within fifteen minutes of the time given to Judith when she had shipped them and a couple of other items before departing from Washington. His National Security Agency permit would have satisfied the TSA people, but producing it would have surely attracted unwanted attention. The pistol would not make the helicopter flight less harrowing; but, should he survive it, he would feel a great deal more secure.

The pilot, every bit as old as his ship, helped Judith into the rear seat. "Any particular part of the city you want to see?"

She gave the preplanned spiel. "Just a general view. The beach, the fort, the old town."

What they really wanted to see was Calle Luna 23, but prolonged hovering over a specific building was likely to alert its occupants.

Jason climbed aboard, strapped himself in, and pulled a newly purchased pair of binoculars from its case. "I'd like a long look at the old fort."

Only a few blocks from the subject of their attention.

The engine made grinding noises as twin blades rotated slowly overhead. Jason felt a momentary and irrational hope the thing would not start, hope that evaporated in a cloud of blue smoke and the roar of a piston engine. Suddenly, sickeningly, the ground dropped away, along with Jason's stomach.

After "taxiing" a few feet above the airport's single runway, Jason heard the tower's permission for departure through the ill-fitting headset, the sole means of communication because of the racket created by the turning blades.

Another reason to despise whirlybirds.

At no more than a few hundred feet, the aircraft's shadow was soon skimming along the golden crescent of Condado. With no small feeling of consternation, Jason noted the upper floors of a number of mega-hotels were looking down on him. The pilot called out names of the various structures, the El San Juan, the Caribe Hilton, Conrad San Juan. Jason tried to concentrate on orienting himself. The updrafts that bounced the chopper like a small boat in a rough sea did not make the task any easier.

Leaving the beach, the helicopter headed for Felipe del Morro, the fortress brooding on its promontory above the mouth of the harbor. Through the headset, Judith gave instructions to the pilot, who maneuvered while she took pictures. On the other side of the aircraft, Jason used the binoculars to study the houses whose flat roofs were the top of the old town's wall. Counting from the intersection, he quickly located Number 23. Chairs, lounges, even a small inflatable wading pool or two demonstrated that the inhabitants of adjacent dwellings used their roofs as an extra room. Number 23 was bereft of amenities. Most houses boasted an array of potted plants, no small number of which appeared to be marijuana, discreetly pulled back from the edge and prying eyes from the street. The local residents, it seemed, were ardent agriculturists.

No living thing graced the roof of Number 23.

There was, however, a forest of antennae, dishes, and devices whose purposes Jason could only guess at. More than enough electronics to satisfy the most avid ham radio operator or satellite-TV fan.

The air-conditioning units for many of the houses were also on the roofs, in addition to small structures housing the head of the stairs leading up from below.

The supposition strengthened when the helicopter made a couple of passes over the old city, low enough for Jason to see that several of these little shacks had their doors open, exposing steps. A young woman wearing only the bottom of her bikini waved gaily as the chopper passed overhead.

Once on the ground, Jason and Judith took a cab back to the hotel. Both examined the doors to their respective rooms before entering. The telltales they had left showed no signs of tampering. They packed what little they had removed from their single bags, mostly toilet articles. They had defeated an assassination attempt the night before; to remain in the same place would be foolhardy.

Jason noted with some amusement the attention the desk clerk paid Judith as they checked out.

"You have paid for two nights, ma'am."

"I'm aware of that," Jason responded.

The man's eyes never quit feeding off Judith. "Was there something unsatisfactory?"

"No. A sudden emergency," Jason responded.

"We will credit your American Express."

"*My* American Express," Jason said. "The rooms were on my American Express, Not Dr. Ferris's."

For the first time, the man seemed to take note of Jason's existence. "That is what I said, Mr. Peters."

A short cab ride deposited them in one of Old San Juan's many plazas. Jason paid the driver and watched the taxi depart. Once it was out of sight, Jason and Judith rolled their bags over uneven sidewalks.

"How am I doing?" she asked.

Jason, his mind on the next phase of his plan was barely aware she had spoken to him. "Pardon?"

"How am I doing?"

He stopped, facing her. "Doing?"

She stopped, leaning on her roll-aboard. "*Doing*. You know, how am I doing as a spy, secret agent, or whatever you call yourself? What would you give me as a grade?"

"A-plus."

Her eyebrows went up in surprise. "Really? That good?"

Jason began walking again. "In this business, there are only two grades: A-plus and F. If you're alive, you get an A-plus."

What he didn't say was the final exam was still pending.

Without further conversation, they trudged uphill to a small hotel. On his arrival yesterday, Jason had seen it from the cab's window. Men and women in the uniforms of airline flight crew had been arriving. A layover base suggested the place was clean, cheap, and comparatively anonymous.

With a little luck, the guys from GrünWelt wouldn't know they had left the El Convento. In the meantime, he and Judith had some shopping to do.

47

Old San Juan
1:34 a.m.

The streets were still steaming from early evening rain showers and traffic was beginning to thin out. Judith and Jason, clad in black jeans and black long-sleeved jerseys, carefully picked their way from dark shadow to dark shadow along the old fortress's walls. The body of the citadel, now a national park, had been closed for hours but its outer defenses surrounded the old town, easily accessible to anyone who, for whatever reason, decided to take the same evening stroll along the ramparts as a Spanish sentry might have done nearly five centuries before.

Jason suspected such excursions might be prohibited, judging from the razor wire that was strung across the wall at regular intervals. Whether it was there to discourage impromptu exploration and possible injury, to prevent access to some of the roofs of the old city, or plain-and-simple bureaucratic desire to thwart any activity it did not control, Jason could not have said.

Whatever its purpose, the wire yielded to two pair of wire cutters and the black costumes blended with the darkness of a Caribbean night, a velvet that provided the backdrop for a million sparkling diamonds above. Once or twice, an unusually bright pair of headlamps passing on the adjacent road had sent Jason and Judith diving flat onto the broad surface of the wall's top. Generally, though, they were unmolested by light or other human contact.

They had been traveling along a section where the streets below seemed to sink farther and farther away, when Jason stopped.

"This is Calle Luna. The house should be the sixth one down."

"You're going to cross one roof to another?" Judith asked.

Although she couldn't see it in the dark, Jason gave her a nod. "Yeah. You got a better idea?"

She shook her head no, nonetheless pleased her opinion had been solicited. "Can't come up with one at the moment."

She ran the beam of a flashlight along the row of roofs. A wicked reflection of more razor wire blazed between each rooftop. Not exactly neighborhood-friendly.

"Shit!" Jason grumbled, "I couldn't see that from the air! We can't cut every strand; someone would notice tomorrow."

Judith switched off her light, using it as a pointer. "That is not the problem. I doubt anyone checks the wire regularly. The problem is we are not alone."

Jason saw them now. Two or three couples on two or three different roofs—roofs that provided a cool place away from kids, parents, or whomever someone wanted to leave behind for a few minutes—all taking in the damp night air.

"If we wait until there is no one here, we could be here when the sun comes up," Judith observed.

Judith, the optimist.

Jason had a plan. It was the reason he had allowed Judith to come. She might be untrained, but she could sure cause a diversion if one were needed.

Fifteen or twenty minutes later, excited voices rose from the street below. Jason, now alone, had no need to look. He knew what had happened. One of the city's opportunistic pickpockets/purse snatchers had no doubt made a poor choice. He had seen a woman alone, a *norteamericano*, possibly intoxicated and with her purse held loosely in her hand instead of slung from her shoulder by a strap.

Jason had no trouble visualizing the scene as he slunk across roofs where the occupants were enthralled by the activity below. The criminal had, Jason guessed, snatched at the seemingly carelessly held purse. Maybe he succeeded, maybe not. Either way, the ruckus would get the attention of the people on the roofs.

The sirens and flashing blue lights arrived as Jason reached the roof of Number 23 and stuffed the wire cutters into a pocket. He lay flat on the cool tiles for a full minute. In the reflected light of the city, he saw no security cameras or motion detectors. Of course, both could easily be obscured in the darkness that covered most of the roof.

Crawling on his belly to eliminate any silhouette an unseen camera might pick up, he made his way to the structure that housed the staircase. Placing an ear against the door, he listened closely for a full two minutes.

Nothing.

Standing, he gripped the Glock at the small of his back with his right hand and tapped gently on the door with his left.

Again, nothing.

He had to assume there was nobody in the space behind the door.

He took a penlight from a pocket and examined the lock, a standard deadbolt as far as he could tell.

Holding the light between his teeth, he reached into another pocket, producing an odd, remotely gun-shaped object. A screwdriver-like blade extended from what would have been the gun's barrel. Inserted into a lock, the blade vibrated, causing the pins to fall into the lock's preset pattern. The device had arrived from Washington via UPS along with his weapon.

SouthOrd electric lock-pick gun, available on the Internet to anyone who could come up with $49.95, no identification other than a credit card required. The thought had done little to increase Jason's sense of security, but he had gone right ahead and ordered it anyway.

The click of metal on metal told him the lock had yielded. Replacing the lock pick in his pocket, he squatted, reaching up to the knob. There was only one way of telling if the door was connected to an alarm system. He turned the knob and eased it open a mere crack. The absence of sound did not mean the system was not in place, just that the occupants of the building didn't want an intruder to know it had been set off.

When there was no reaction after a full five minutes, he guessed there was no alarm or it hadn't been armed. He opened the door wider and slid into darkness. He waited another moment, hoping his eyes would adjust. Too dark. Blind, he felt for the railing along the steel spiral staircase and slowly eased down to the next floor.

When he reached the bottom, he could see light squeezing under a door. There were muffled voices inside, although he could not tell if they came from this floor or the one below. The one sound definitely emanating from the other side was a muted hum that Jason associated with high-powered electronics.

He mentally discussed the pros and cons of breaching this door also. Too great a risk. If there were someone in this room, he not only would be in trouble but his penetration of the building discovered, bringing stronger security measures. No, better to try again when he could be relatively certain he would have the opportunity to look around.

The question was, when would that be?

Jason thought he had the answer.

48

Hotel Coral by the Sea
Calle Rosa 2
San Juan
The Next Afternoon

Hotel Coral by the Sea was not beside any sea Jason could ascertain. The fourth-floor room did, however, have a narrow view of the beach some three blocks distant. Other amenities were a remarkable similarity to a 1960s Holiday Inn, including, as Jason had insisted, a small kitchenette. Refrigerator, sink, and two-eyed electric range. That the place was neat, clean, and inexpensive was the most benign description Jason could think of. It was also probably not in the first tier of hotels whose registers would be hacked by someone trying to find him.

Jason and Judith were unpacking for the third time in as many days. "What makes you sure it will rain tonight?" she asked as she folded a pair of jeans and put them in a dresser drawer.

Jason had a pair of folded polo shirts in his hand. "The fact it has rained the last two. At almost exactly the same time. Say, can you save at least one drawer for me?"

She noted the bed where he had dumped the small number of clothes from his suitcase: two T-shirts, two polo shirts, two pair of underwear, one swimsuit, one pair of jeans, two pair of socks. Nothing that could not be washed in a bathroom sink. "You don't need a whole drawer. All you brought, you could store them in the medicine cabinet in the bath."

Jason nodded toward the closet, where she had hung up two dresses, rayon that easily dropped the wrinkles of being rolled up in a suitcase. "You didn't bring a whole lot more."

"You were pretty insistent on the point. 'If it doesn't go in the overhead, it doesn't go,' you said. 'We're not going to have time to spend packing and unpacking,' you said. 'Certainly no time to chase lost baggage.' Well, OK, I did as I was told."

"It's the military training for you."

"Maybe, *Captain*, you're forgetting your rank." She smiled as she brushed a strand of hair away from her eyes.

Jason put the two polo shirts in a bureau drawer. "My operation, my command. You're the one who wanted to come."

She sat down on the bed. "Truth is, I'd have invited myself along if you'd been going to the North Pole. Time for a break in the routine."

"I thought you liked the travel, the lack of hassle."

"The travel's OK as long as you like Air Force bases. But it's not thrilling, either. Then, along you come with your good looks, mysterious past, just reeking of excitement and adventure. No chance I was going to let all that slip away without a try."

Jason turned from the bureau. "Candor is among your more endearing traits."

"Candor gets what I want; feminine shyness doesn't. Look, I'm an MD, not some bimbo who flirts with every man she sees. I'm not getting any younger and I don't see much future with the career military types who, up until you came along, were pretty much all the men I met. I'm not looking to get married again anytime soon; I'm not even looking for a 'committed relationship,' whatever the hell that is. I didn't invite myself along to be Robin to your Batman or Wonder Woman on my own. All I want, when it's time to cash in my chips, when it's time to retire someplace, is to have done something besides treat the common cold."

"And VD."

"And VD," she echoed. "So much for what I want. What about you?"

"I want to accomplish what I came here to do, and for both of us to leave in at least as good a shape as when we arrived."

She shook her head. "There must be something in your life besides whatever mission you're on. What happens when it's over? Where do you go, what do you want?"

For the first time, Jason asked himself just that: Where would he go? Not back to Ischia, where Moustaph's men had found him. And what did he want, just to be left alone to paint? Obviously not, since he had accepted this job. And what about Maria? He realized he had intentionally, if unconsciously, postponed making some very hard decisions.

"What do I want? I haven't planned that far ahead. There'll be time for that when we're finished here."

Judith took a step back to allow Jason to toss the polo shirts into another open drawer. "And if it does not rain?"

It took a second for Jason to understand that she had switched back to the original conversation. "I guess we get a rain check."

She turned toward him, holding a pair of bras. "Suppose it doesn't?"

Jason finished putting away the last of his clothes. "I'd say we change hotels and wait for the next rainy night."

"Why is the rain so important?"

"Those people on the roofs of adjoining houses. What I have in mind doesn't play well before an audience."

"And exactly what is it you have in mind, blowing up the house? That's the sort of thing Delta Force does, isn't it?"

"No. We aren't going to get rid of this bunch by destroying bricks and mortar. Or, for that matter, the people in it. What will put a finish to them is exposure. But we will use a bomb of a sort, though."

He explained.

"And you want me to . . . ?"

He explained that, too.

"I'll need incentive," she said, unbuttoning her blouse.

An hour later, incentive provided, they were in a garden store. Jason was mesmerized by the varieties and colors of tropical flowers. Frangipani, hibiscus, and bougainvillea were among the few he recognized. Potted citrus, avocado, and mango waited to grace someone's yard and dining table. He wished he had both his art supplies and the time to use them. This garden of tropical delights would be beautiful in acrylic.

"We came for the fertilizer and some pots," Judith reminded him.

"Er, yeah." He was examining the lists of contents on several bags while a bemused salesman watched. "Potassium nitrate is what I need."

"We have a number of products that contain varying amounts," the salesman offered.

Jason shook his head. "Won't do. I mix my own fertilizer. Surely you have pure saltpeter."

A smile cracked the man's face, showing dazzling teeth. "Ah! Saltpeter! You should have said so. Yes, we have it. How much do you need?"

"A couple of pounds."

The man's face fell. "But it only comes in fifty-pound bags."

"I'll take one."

Back at the hotel, Judith watched Jason fill a dented frying pan with a combination of sugar and saltpeter. "It matters how they are mixed?"

Jason nodded as he added just enough water to give the blend a claylike substance before turning on the stove's eye. "About five parts to three." He stirred with a wooden spoon. "We want to caramelize the sugar, not melt it."

Fifteen minutes later, he was putting the frying pan into the small oven. Judith watched skeptically. "It won't ignite from the heat?"

Jason shook his head. "It will ignite only from direct contact with fire. The oven will only dry it out."

"Now what do we do?"

"We go shopping for the rest of what we'll need. By that time, the stuff in the oven should be ready."

"Incentivize me again."

Jason rolled his eyes. "I'm beginning to think it wasn't the chance of excitement that made you want to come along."

"Depends on how you define 'excitement.'"

On their backs an hour later, both stared at the featureless ceiling.

"And now?" she asked.

"We make fuses."

49

Old San Juan
8:32 the Same Night

It rained.

The anticipated downpour beat against shutters of the old buildings like a demon seeking entrance and sent torrents of water boiling down the streets' open gutters. Even the coquí were silenced by the intensity of the deluge Jason knew would last half an hour at best.

Covered by a recently purchased poncho, Jason reached the point where the old city's fortifications began a steep rise above the street. He was thankful to note that the cuts in the razor wire from the previous night had not been detected. He stopped in shadows to reach under his rain gear to make sure the three pots from the garden store were dry. Then he looked through the curtain of rain at the row of rooftops. The deluge had chased their nocturnal occupants inside, at least for the moment.

But they would be back shortly after the rain stopped.

On the street below, a blond in a black dress entered the bodega across from Calle Luna 23. Used to a familiar clientele, the chubby, white-haired proprietor, owner, sole waiter, and, most importantly, cashier was surprised to see her. Surprised and delighted. She was by far the most attractive customer he had enjoyed for some time. In fact, he thought she might have been with a tour group that had briefly visited his establishment yesterday. It was unlikely he would forget the blond hair, the full figure. And the eyes, pools of green that reminded him of the water just off the island's coast before the sandy bottom fell away. It was enough to make a man weep that he was not twenty years younger.

He wiped his hands on an apron, smiled, and indicated one of the two tables that had hastily been moved in from the street and now crowded the bistro's already-small space, which included a tiny kitchen visible in the rear. She had seemed interested by some feature of the house across the street, but she turned, sat, unslung her purse from her shoulder, and ordered a Caribe, sipping the local beer as she studied the menu.

Was she dining alone, the owner asked?

As a matter of fact, she was.

He tried not to show his surprise. Only an unromantic gringo would miss the opportunity to dine with such a magnificent creature.

An angry rattle of cookware from the rear told him his wife, the cook, was tuned in to the conversation.

Under the scowling eyes of his spouse, the owner apologized that most of his customers were locals and, therefore, he had not had the bill of fare printed in English. Perhaps she would allow him to translate some of the house's specialties?

He did so, leaning over her shoulder to point out each entree. His enthusiasm might have been attributed to the view down the front of her dress. He took the extra time to tell her the *cocina criolla*, the local cuisine, was a blend of Spanish, Taino Indian, and American cooking. Only an angry explosion of Spanish from the kitchen put an end to his explanation.

She ordered the chicken and rice soup, grilled fish with a *mojo isleño* sauce, and a side of plantains fried with rum. She deferred a choice of dessert but did order another Caribe.

As he turned to hand her order to the chef, he noted the customer was again looking intently at the building across the street. He was tempted to explain what strange neighbors lived there and their peculiar comings and goings, but an admonition from the kitchen to tend to his business dismissed the thought.

"*Cabra viejo!*" his wife snorted as he reluctantly turned his attention to arriving customers.

On the rooftop, Jason's BlackBerry vibrated. He removed it from a pocket. "Check" was the only word he spoke. Judith was in place.

Holding the penlight in his teeth, he fumbled with the front plate of the air-conditioning unit on the first house. It came free with a clatter Jason could only hope was covered by the drum of rain on the flat roof. Careful to shield the clay pot from the downpour, he inserted it into the mechanism's housing, making certain it was close to the fan that sucked fresh air into the unit.

Leaving the front plate leaning against the unit, he moved to the next two roofs, Number 23 and the one beyond, and repeated the procedure. At the last, he produced a cheap cigarette lighter and touched the flame to his improvised fuse. He made sure it was lit before moving back to Number 23, setting that fuse alight and then the next.

Then he returned to Number 23 and waited in the shadows cast by the housing of the stairwell to wait.

50

Calle Luna
Seven Minutes Later

Judith had taken only two spoonfuls of her soup when her Black-Berry buzzed.

She placed it to her ear.

"Ignition," Jason's voice said, and the connection went dead.

She returned the device to her purse and continued to spoon the broth. It had a unique blend of coriander, garlic, and spices she could not quite identify. She leaned over her bowl, sampling the fragrance in hopes of recognizing more of the ingredients.

Concentration on matters culinary was interrupted by the sound of shouts and a banging door across the street. Two men and a woman stood coughing on the rain-slicked sidewalk as white smoke billowed from doors and windows. Judith had barely time to take this in when four or five people, the men in sleeveless undershirts, the women in old-fashioned slips, burst out of the house on the other side of Number 23 with a cloud of smoke following them into the street. They did not seem to notice they were instantly drenched by the rain.

Arms outstretched, one of the women was wailing in incoherent Spanish when Judith first heard sirens and the rumble of heavy engines. At the same time, four men stumbled out of Number 23, coughing into handkerchiefs. Judith noted one had a bandaged face. She was certain it was the man from in front of the El Convento who had tried to kill her.

She selected "Call Jason Mobile" on her BlackBerry. "Go!"

On the roof, Jason had already used his electrical lock pick, waiting for Judith's signal that the house had been evacuated. There was no way to know for sure that no one was left inside, but fear of a fire was the best way to make that possibility as remote as it could be.

He pulled goggles over his eyes and tied a wet bandana over his nose and mouth. A small oxygen tank would have been far better, but there was a limit as to how much he could carry given the swiftness the job required. Glock in his right hand, penlight in his left, he moved down the stairs to the door at the bottom. The beam of his light was diffused by the smoke, forcing him to hold the light in his mouth while he groped for the lock. It, too, yielded to his pick.

Inside, Jason swept the room with the Glock. The smoke bomb had done its job: total evacuation. A metal file cabinet sat against the far wall next to a generator. Puzzled for a moment, he wondered at its purpose. What he guessed was a shortwave radio was on a desk to his left. A table on which rested two computer monitors and a pair of keyboards was next to the door.

All the electronics, of course. That was what made the generator necessary. Dependable power supplies in the Caribbean were rare at best and nonexistent more often than not. The generator he had heard buzzing last night from the other side of the door made certain there was no interruption of communications.

Also on the table was a printer with a sheaf of paper hanging from its mechanical lips. Jason snatched up the papers.

Russian.

His command of the language had been limited to a few standard phrases ("Surrender! Hands High!" "What is your name?"), and even this had faded with disuse, but he recalled enough to know at a glance that these pages alone justified the risk he was taking. He rolled the papers and stuffed them into a back pocket.

One of the computers had been left on, deserted in a smoke-induced panic. An incredible bit of luck. Then his heart sank. The monitor showed a picture of a waterfall in a rain forest, a screen saver. There would be little time to try to penetrate what he was certain would be sophisticated firewalls.

Screen saver? There were no icons for program selection. Jason looked closer. Pretty picture, but hard to believe GrünWelt was using computers to exchange innocuous photographs. What was the word he had read recently? *Steganography*, that was it. The use of perfectly innocent images to hide messages. Prying eyes would see only a waterfall, mist, and a few orchids dripping from the trees that hosted the plants. Special software could coax text from the images.

Jason touched the Shift key and the screen filled with Cyrillic letters, five to a group. Double encryption, the image and now code. Some contemporary electronic version of the Enigma, the World War II machine where randomly selected wheels made deciphering possible only by a comparable device? No matter. Software was available that could accomplish in minutes what last century's code breakers had been unable to do in months.

Leaning over the keyboard, Jason made a few clicks that sent the screen's contents to Sybil. He'd call later with an explanation.

Right now, he wanted to steal as much information as he could in the time he had left.

In the bodega, Judith wondered how the hook and ladder had navigated the old city's narrow streets. But it had, as evidenced by the firemen hopping down from it. In the first moment, all seemed confusion as every firefighter was shouting at another. Order quickly emerged as a hose was connected to a nearby hydrant, a ladder slowly rose toward the roof of the first house, and two men dashed inside.

Judith keyed her BlackBerry. "Two on the roof, two inside."

"Which house?" came the reply.

"The one closest to the intersection."

Jason shoved the BlackBerry back in his pocket. Shit! The roof! When the fireman found what had been put into the air-conditioning housing . . .

No time to worry now. Just keep calling up files and forwarding them to Sybil.

Perhaps a minute later Judith watched a fireman scamper down the ladder. Her heart sank when she saw what he was carrying: A large flowerpot from which thick, white smoke poured. A part of the crowd drawn by all the excitement was already jostling for space at the bottom of the ladder before the man reached the last rung.

She noted the big man with the shaved scalp push his way to the front. The one with the bandaged face was close behind. Were there others? None she saw. With growing consternation, she saw each take a look at the smoking clay pot. She could imagine the cartoon lightbulbs above their heads.

The reaction was immediate. Shaved Head pointed to the roof of Number 23. Two men she had not noticed before broke from the spectators contained behind hastily erected barricades and shoved aside the fireman blocking the doorway of Number 23. The man with the shaved head and the one with the bandaged face also pushed firemen aside, this time to appropriate the ladder as they scrambled toward the roof, followed by Spanish invective from the firefighters. And orders in vain from the police.

Jason was somewhere between the two who had entered from the street and the pair on the ladder.

Judith threw a twenty onto the bodega's table, slung the purse strap over a shoulder, and lurched into the street past the concerned owner, who tried to slow her down long enough to enquire about any problem with the food. She slid by him impatiently and was already running down Calle Luna as she speed-dialed Jason.

51

Calle Luna 23

Jason returned the BlackBerry to his pocket with the hand that wasn't on the computer's keyboard. He'd never have time to copy and send all these files, let alone check out the filing cabinets. He hadn't expected to have all night but he had hoped for a few more minutes before the origin of the "fire" was discovered.

He thought he heard footsteps pounding up the metal stairs. He picked up the Glock he had set beside the keyboard and stuck it in its holster in the small of his back. Sending the monitor crashing to the floor, he dragged the table to and through the door. It took effort to stand it on end, but he was gratified to note it neatly filled the landing outside the room he had occupied. He shoved harder, wedging it fast. Though the two men who, according to Judith, were on their way up, would not be impeded for long, he very well might need any delay he could get.

Now he was certain he heard feet clanging on the metal stairs. Pulling the Glock from its holster, he fired two shots into the generator. The crash of gunfire reverberated in the narrow stairwell as sparks flew and the smell of cordite mixed with the acrid odor of fried circuitry. The electrical hum became a whine and then was silent. The lights, already dim, flickered and died.

It took seconds to reach the top of the stairs. Behind him, Jason could hear the scrape of the blockading table being wrestled aside. On hands and knees, he crept out onto the roof. The rain had stopped but the moisture clung to the air like a living embrace. Keeping low so that the roofline was limned against the glow from the fire trucks and police cars below, he edged slowly toward the adjacent building, moving sideways like a crab so he could keep both the roofline and the staircase entry in view.

The rain had provided secrecy to get Jason in and now its remnants saved his life. He heard a splash, the sound of something striking the surface of one of the numerous puddles the earlier shower had created.

He flattened himself against the tiles of the roof just as there was a coughing sound and something nasty whined by where his head had been an instant before.

The muzzle flash had come from the adjacent building. His opponents had apparently discovered the breach in the razor wire he had cut. He was caught between the men trying to come up the stairs and the shooter.

On the street below, Judith was hurrying to the place where she and Jason had gotten up onto the old city's defenses. She had no idea what she could do, only a sense of urgency to get there. Twice she nearly slipped on the sidewalk still wet from the evening's rain.

Her concentration on keeping her balance was the most probable reason she didn't see him: another man with a shaved head. Well over six feet, she guessed he weighed two hundred pounds or more as he materialized out of the darkness of a doorway to block her path.

"Excuse me," she said, sidestepping in a fruitless hope the man meant her no harm.

That prospect disappeared with the whisper of a knife being drawn from its sheath. She cursed her carelessness in not spotting him sooner.

He moved forward, streetlights reflecting on what looked like an eight-inch blade. The space between them was not enough to give Judith any chance of slipping by him. She could only watch the blade move side to side. No stabbing or slicing movement, just the sure and certain advance of a man who knew what he was doing. At some point he would lunge with practiced precision, but at the moment he seemed to enjoy toying with her, feeding on the fear he sensed.

She knew she had two chances of survival. First, if she could delay his assault long enough, there was a good chance someone would see her plight and summon the police.

Secondly, her assailant was confident, perhaps overly so. She was unsure how this might help her; she could only hope.

Not far away, Jason lay belly-down, soaked by the roof's wet tiles. He had crawled fifteen or so feet from where he had been when someone had taken the shot at him. He turned his head slowly, aware the corner of the eye was more likely to catch movement than a direct stare was. Nothing moved other than a breeze, swaying leaves of several potted marijuana plants on the adjacent roof. Even if he could see his enemies, taking a shot would betray his position as clearly as a beacon. Staying put was not an attractive option either. Sooner or later, someone would risk making themselves a target by using a flashlight.

He had no sooner considered the possibility than it happened.

Judith's back was all too literally against a wall. Her antagonist had backed her up step by step until she was pressed against the side of a house, one of the few on the street that was dark and shuttered. She considered making a desperate effort to escape, maybe find a house with doors open to catch the rain-cooled breeze before her assailant could drive the knife into a fatal spot.

The old adage of watching your opponent's eyes to predict a move is just that: an old adage. Any skilled street fighter feints with his eyes as well as any other part of his body. Judith's attention was on the blade he held.

She faked a move to her left, instantly trying to come right. He easily anticipated her. It was an amateurish ploy, one he would expect of one untrained in close-combat tactics. But it gave her a reason to extend her arms from her sides as though trying to keep her balance.

She repeated the move to the other side, provoking a grin from the man with the knife; she was too dumb to know she had no chance.

This time, though, she swung her purse at his head, a clumsy effort easily deflected.

But grabbing the purse strap required him to watch the intended blow, not her.

Only an instant, but enough.

Pushing off the wall, the top of her head struck his chin with an audible crunch while her spread arms kept the blade at a distance. He lost his grip on the purse strap and staggered back half a step. Trying to clear his head, he brought the knife up as though to fend off further attack by the purse.

Too late he realized his mistake.

Being a physician, Judith was aware of the more tender parts of the anatomy. As a woman she chose the obvious. With all the force she could muster, she delivered a fifty-yard field-goal kick to the groin. Her assailant turned to try to take the blow with his hip rather than his crotch but was only partially successful. She got enough of the testicles. He folded like a jackknife. Then he knelt slowly, his hands clutching his groin.

Judith had no idea what happened next other than the fact she was running as fast as she could.

Jason's immediate problem was avoiding being targeted by the seemingly random sweep of flashlights. There were three of them now, painting the roof with erratic movement. There was also enough light both from the flashes and from the emergency vehicles on the street to see that the lights were held by firemen.

So far, the men in the fire-retardant suits and unique rear-billed fireman's helmets hadn't noticed they were not alone up there. Because each house's roof was separated by razor wire, they had been forced to use the ladder to ascend to the top of each of the three smoking homes.

Jason had an idea as he watched the three firemen remove the still-smoking pot from the air-conditioning housing. Perhaps not the best idea, but the only one he had at the moment.

Still on his stomach, he crawled commando-style to a position that put him on the side of the air-conditioning unit opposite from the fire-fighters. He was close enough to hear a conversation in Spanish even if he could not understand it. The man holding the remnants of the smoke bomb carried it to the edge of the roof, holding it aloft so those on the street below could see. A second man gave the roof a cursory sweep with the beam of his flashlight before he, too, headed for his turn to descend the ladder. Somehow the men who had come up the stairs remained unseen, although Jason knew they were around somewhere.

Now came the tricky part.

As the third man turned to leave, Jason reached out and grabbed his foot, sending him sprawling. Before the guy had a clue what had happened, Jason was holding his head in one hand, the Glock pressed against it with the other.

Jason had always thought the old description of eyes big as saucers was an exaggeration. Even in the dim reflected light, he had living proof it wasn't.

"Nobody's gonna get hurt," Jason told him with little effect. "I just want your hat there and maybe that jacket."

He would have liked to have the big turn-down-top boots, too, but he hadn't the time required to pull them off the fireman and put them on. Sooner or later, the men on this roof and the one next door were going to come looking for him. The fact there had not been another shot made him fairly certain they didn't know exactly where he was and that they had no night-vision equipment.

Clad in the fireman's attire, Jason stood, leaned over, and took the strap from around the man's shoulder and the small radio attached to it. "If I hear a peep out of you, you are dead," he said to the trembling fireman, who was still prone. "*Comprende?*"

A violent nod was his answer.

Jason forced himself to walk slowly to the place the ladder jutted above the roofline, praying the lights from below would only silhouette a figure in a fireman's helmet and bulky jacket. If not, he made a perfect target.

Just as he reached the ladder, the radio he had confiscated crackled with words he didn't understand. He could only hope that, if someone were calling the fireman left on the roof, they wouldn't come looking for him for a few seconds yet. He swung a leg over the roof's edge and looked down into a maelstrom of flashing lights and upturned faces.

At the bottom, he was greeted by relieved firemen, slapping him on the back and chattering in Spanish. Until one got a look at his face.

For an instant, there was a shocked silence punctuated by the idling of big engines.

Jason didn't wait to see what happened next.

He ran without looking back.

If there was pursuit, he never heard it. Instead, he shed the hat and jacket as he alternated turning corners of the narrow streets. Finally, he glanced over a shoulder. The street was deserted. The chase, if there had been one, was over.

He called Judith's BlackBerry.

"Where are you?" were her first words.

He looked across the street into a small plaza. In the center was a bronze statue of what looked like a conquistador. He told her as much.

"Plaza de San José," she informed him. "The statue is of Ponce de León and was cast from English cannon captured in the late eighteenth century. You are panting like a dog."

"Did a little roadwork. Good for the heart. You know how to get to this Plaza . . ."

"Plaza de San José. I can be there in a few minutes."

"Best come in a cab if you can. I have a feeling we may have worn out our welcome."

How the hell had she known the name of the plaza? Or the history of the statue?

52

Five Minutes Later

"You want to go *where*?" Even with the heavy Latino accent, the cabbie's disbelief was quite clear.

"Mercedita Airport, Ponce," Jason said. "You know, the city on the south side of the island."

"It will cost you a hundred fifty."

Jason managed both shock and indignation. "For an hour-and-a-half ride?"

The driver shrugged. "It is late, *Señor*."

Jason knew what the man meant: They had been lucky to flag this cab down. After dark, tourists tended to move between the casinos at the big beach resorts, not the old city.

Guessing GrünWelt would immediately put the San Juan airport under surveillance, Jason had opted for the other Puerto Rico airport with flights to the States, Ponce. The problem, as revealed by using the BlackBerry's Internet app, was that the next plane to the continental US was a JetBlue flight to Charlotte at one o'clock tomorrow afternoon. By that time, Ponce would likely be watched as well.

"You have a hundred fifty dollars, *Señor*?"

The taxi driver was getting nervous, not wanting to miss other fares if these gringos did not have the money.

Jason waved a wad of bills in front of him. "And a tip if you get us there in a hurry."

"You have your passport?" Judith asked.

"Of course. You?"

Jason knew well the wisdom of carrying cash, credit cards, and travel documents at all times in case an expedited departure became necessary. Although passports were not required of US citizens or legal residents traveling to or from Puerto Rico, the precaution was fortunate. The first flight from Ponce was to St. Maarten, an island half Dutch, half French. From there almost hourly flights departed for the mainland United States.

By seven o'clock that evening, the weary travelers were in another cab, this one from Dulles International.

"You have no idea what you sent to your computer expert?" Judith asked.

"Nope." Jason was staring out the window. "But if any of it was half as incriminating as the papers I swiped, I'd say GrünWelt is finished."

"You don't think there will be reprisals?"

He shook his head. "No point. The organization will already be exposed for what it is. I think everyone connected to GrünWelt will be scattering for cover like cockroaches when you turn on a light."

She leaned back into her seat with a sigh. "I hope so. I've had about as much excitement as I can stand."

"That's why you insisted on coming along."

"If I do that again, you have my permission to slap my face until I return to reality."

The cab pulled up to Judith's contemporary-styled town house.

"No point in your going all the way back to the base tonight," she observed as she climbed out of the car.

"No point," he agreed as he paid the driver.

The inside of her home was as modernistic as its exterior. Chrome and glass was far more in evidence than wood tone, if the blond Danish modern pieces could be described as having any tone at all. Canvases paraded as contemporary "art"—blank, single-colored earth tones hung above a pair of acrylic cases housing blobs of metal in no ascertainable shape. One corner was occupied by a bust only vaguely human. It might have been life-sized, had any such creature existed.

In short, the place was hideous, a physical assault on his artist's eye. Even worse than he remembered from his first visit. It did, however, awaken a question he had about so-called metal sculptors: did they have any form in mind when they began, or did they simply let the laws of physics determine the end product?

But then, the decor was not the reason he was there.

He was headed to the kitchen, where Judith kept the liquor. "Make you a Martini?"

She was standing in front of one of the cases, staring at one of the metal slugs as if she had never seen it before. She didn't answer.

Jason walked up behind her, putting hands on her shoulders, "Tired?"

Reaching behind her, she ran a hand along the back of his neck, her touch tingling like electricity. "A little. And I think I feel a head-ache coming on."

Jason turned to look at her. "That old excuse?"

"Not that kind of headache. But I do have bottle of aspirin in the glove box of my car. Would you be a good boy and go down to the garage and fetch it? I'll start drawing a nice, hot bath for both of us."

Jason stepped away. "An offer I can't refuse. I didn't even know you had a car, thought you used the Metro."

"I almost always do going to and from the base, but it's nice to have your own wheels on weekends when . . ."

"When what?"

She shook her head. "The keys, that's it, the keys."

"The keys?"

"The keys to the car. I used to lose them every other day, so I started putting them right here."

She pointed to a roundish lump of metal that might have begun life as a compressor for a household appliance. "Right here, next to *Complaint*. That's the name of the sculpture."

Full title *Complaint: The Fridge's Compressor Has Gone Belly-Up?* he wondered.

But he said, pointing, "That looks like car keys to me."

She was staring. "It is. But I didn't put them there. I left them next to *Complaint* when I took the cab to the airport."

"You're sure?"

"I'm sure."

Jason scooped them up. "Take a quick look around. See if anything else is not where you left it."

Her eyes widened. "What are you saying, that those . . . those people have been in my house?"

"I'm not saying anything. Just take a look around. If everything else is in its place, then the odds are you simply put your keys in a different spot."

A few minutes later, she returned from an inspection tour. "Everything looks normal. Guess I was mistaken."

Jason tossed the keys up and caught them. "Then get on that hot bath. I'll get the aspirin. By the way, why do you lock your car when it's in the garage?"

"Man at the service department where I bought it said to, something about cutting down on the drain of the battery."

Jason chose not to admit he had never heard of an electrical system that went into slumber mode when the car was locked. A few years ago, he'd never heard a GPS that spoke to you either.

Two flights down, Jason entered the garage. A flip of the wall switch illuminated stacks of cardboard boxes on the far side of a concrete pad, the River Styx of unused but not-yet-unwanted items. Between them and Jason a red Mazda MX-5 Miata gleamed under the fluorescent lights.

Jason took a step forward and stopped. The driver's window was not flush with the convertible top. Moving to the side, he could see the door wasn't shut tight.

Locked?

Not with the door not completely closed.

An unlocked car that should have been locked.

A key not where it was supposed to be.

Absurd.

Rather absurd than dead.

Kneeling, Jason looked under the car. At first, he saw nothing unusual. Only when he lay on his back and inched underneath the automobile did he find what he suspected was there: a bundle duct-taped to the frame. Two wires, undoubtedly a negative and positive, ran up into the engine compartment, most likely attached to the ignition. That was why the keys had been needed: to get to the hood lock inside the car.

Jason knew only two things about homemade explosive devices: he was not qualified to do anything but call on the experts, and that they were often unstable. The device might be set to explode when the ignition was turned on, but that didn't mean it wouldn't go off on its own.

Judith was in a flimsy bathrobe when he returned upstairs. Under any other circumstances, the bathwater would have long cooled before they got into it.

"What do you mean, 'Get dressed and get out'?" she demanded.

"I mean there's something attached to your car, most likely an explosive device." He was reaching for the phone. "I'm calling 911."

She stared at him as though he had announced the landing of space aliens. "An explosive . . . A bomb? But who, how . . . ?"

"I think we can guess who."

"But you said you didn't expect reprisals. Besides, how did they know . . . ?"

Jason had the phone next to his ear. "I said I didn't expect any reprisals *after* GrünWelt was exposed. It'll take a day or two for the info on that computer to be circulated. As for the how? Who knows? Anyone who can use a computer can find out pretty much anything they want. Your registration at the El Convento, the fact we were both on the same flight out of Ponce. GrünWelt may be a criminal organization, but no one said they were stupid."

"But where I live . . . ?"

"My bet is they not only know where you live but your birth date, where you've traveled in the last few years, your favorite restaurant, anything they want to know. Like it or not, privacy died with the World Wide Web. Now, we can stand here and lament the fact, hoping that bomb beneath our feet doesn't go off or . . ."

She turned toward the bedroom. "I hear you five by five."

53

The flashing red, blue, and white lights gave an otherworldly pall to the residents of the condominium complex who had piled out into the street at the sounds of sirens and large diesel engines. Two fire trucks, half a dozen police cars, and an ominous, boxy-shaped truck with BOMB DISPOSAL UNIT stenciled on the side blocked the street already closed by yellow crime-scene tape. Four men in heavily padded uniforms had entered Judith's garage as the crowd murmured and waited.

A burly black cop in uniform made his way through the assemblage to where Jason and Judith stood. "You Ms. Judith Ferris, the owner of that condo?"

Without taking her eyes off the place where the four bomb-squad members had gone, Judith nodded. "That's *Dr.* Judith Ferris and yes, I am.'"

The policeman produced a notepad, turning to Jason. "And you are?"

"Jason Peters, a friend of the doctor's."

The officer seemed to struggle to get this down on his notepad. "You the one who called 911?"

"Yes."

The policeman nodded to a pair of men in cheap, off-the-rack suits who were making their way through the spectators as he shoved the pad back into his pocket. "I'll have some more questions when they finish."

The two were like Laurel and Hardy. The thin one, Laurel, was black and appeared to be in his forties. Hardy, white and losing his hair, was wheezing from the exertion. As though on cue, they both flashed their creds.

Hardy announced, "Franklin. Firearms, Alcohol, Tobacco, and Explosives."

Laurel said, "Johnson. Firearms, Alcohol, Tobacco, and Explosives."

Jason said nothing.

Hardy asked, "You got ID?"

Both Judith and Jason produced driver's licenses.

Franklin handed Judith's back. "Mr. Peters, your license shows an address in Chevy Chase. That your residence?"

Jason shook his head. "That's my US address. I reside outside of the US."

Franklin and Johnson exchanged glances.

"And just where might that be?"

"Most recently, Italy. My employer requires I live abroad."

"And just who might that be?"

Jason handed them a business card with his name on it. Below that was "Contract Defense, Inc." If anyone checked, they would find the company in good standing with the State of Maryland. A closer inspection would reveal a lawyer in Baltimore was the sole agent named in public documents, all that was required for a corporation whose stock was not publicly traded. The attorney-client privilege would block further inquiry.

Johnson put the card in his wallet. "Any idea how that bomb, if it is a bomb, came to be in Dr. Ferris's condo?"

"None whatsoever."

Johnson's eyes narrowed. "But you did recognize it as an explosive device, did you not, Mr. Peters?"

"People don't usually leave gifts wired to other people's cars."

A sharp elbow from Judith dug into his ribs. "And I spent some time in the military. I have a good idea what a potentially explosive device might look like."

Franklin opened his mouth just as the bomb squad emerged from the garage, signaling for their truck to move up. Both Johnson and Franklin turned away.

"Stay put," Johnson said in what could be construed as a command. "We'll want to talk later."

Judith watched them go. "Do you always smart-ass federal agents?"

"Only when they ask stupid questions."

She took a step back, looking him up and down. "Just who are you, Jason Peters?"

"You know who I am."

She shook her head. "I thought I did. Oh, I know what your service jacket says and that you work for a 'private contractor' who does jobs for the government. But what kind of work? I had to kill a man to save your ass and I almost got killed myself in San Juan. Now people are putting bombs under my car. What next, I get machine-gunned down on the street? I like you, Jason Peters, maybe even a little more than that. And I appreciate the excitement you've brought into my life. Oh, man, that scene on the George Washington campus was a total rush. But enough is enough. Whoever you are, I'm not willing to die for you."

Jason had the distinct feeling he was being told good-bye in much the same manner he had departed from a dozen or so women. He didn't like the feeling of being dumped.

"Meaning?"

"Meaning I don't like the odds of my reaching retirement while I'm around you. Looking over my shoulder the rest of my life isn't what I intend to do."

"I told you, once GrünWelt is exposed as a criminal organization, you have nothing to fear."

"And in the meantime? And what about whatever is involved in your next 'contract'? I'm getting nothing but negative vibes here. Either I'm with you, risking my neck or I'm sitting home wondering if you're coming back. Not very attractive options."

Jason started to say something but she put up a hand and continued. "It would be all too easy to fall in love with you, Jason. Then I'm hooked, really hooked. Let's say I'm cutting my losses here."

"I understand."

The hell of it was that he really did.

He backed away slowly. "Tell our two federal friends whatever you want when they come back. In the meantime, I'm outta here."

"Leaving me holding the bag to explain everything?"

"Your idea, not mine."

"But they have your business card; they'll track you down."

"Better men have tried. It's been great."

By this time, Jason was at the periphery of light from the condos and the emergency vehicles. Another step and he disappeared like a phantom, leaving Judith to wonder if she had done the right thing.

54

Chevy Chase, Maryland
Two Days Later
6:42 a.m. Local Time

Phineas Simpson rarely came to work this early but a client needed a current balance sheet in a hurry to satisfy a potential purchaser. So, here he was, pulling his Prius into one of the dozen empty parking places in front of the three-story, black-glass office building that was the twin of a dozen such structures, each on its own eighth of an acre of manicured lawn, grass now shining in the early morning light with the rainbow colors of water supplied by a sprinkler system.

At the moment, Phineas's interest was not in the grass, the sprinkler system, or even the day's work ahead. He was watching as a huge black Lincoln Town Car slid silently into a parking place in front of the building next door. In the three years he had worked here, that building, or rather, its occupants, had been the subject of speculation. There was no flow of workers, only an occasional visitor, most of whom arrived in that same car, or one just like it, visitors who uniformly had coat collars turned up or hats pulled low and who inevitably looked around before walking swiftly inside as if fearful of being recognized.

This morning's arrival was different.

The driver, a black man in a black suit, opened the passenger door. Out climbed the largest woman Phineas had ever seen. A brightly patterned cloth was wrapped around her in a manner that matched the turbanlike headgear she wore. Phineas had never seen her before, although several of his coworkers had reported sighting such a creature. She had, of course, been the subject of wildly divergent speculation. An African ruler of some sort in exile? An extension of an African embassy?

The small plaque beside the front door was no help. It only bore the street number and a single word: "Narcom."

Whoever she was, she exhibited none of the furtiveness of her infrequent visitors. Instead, she waved a cheery good morning to Phineas as he sat in his car and walked in no particular hurry to the building's front door, leaned over presumably to insert a key, and let herself in.

Phineas's curiosity would have taken a quantum leap had he known a little more about what he was looking at but could not see. First, the golf-course quality of the lawn concealed dozens of buried weight sensors. The step of anything larger than an average dog would set off an alarm as well as show up on an electronic map. The smoked glass standard in the office park was absent here, replaced by darkened glass reinforced to withstand any projectile smaller than an artillery round. She had used no key. She had exposed her right eye to an iris-recognition system that automatically opened a locking mechanism that would have done credit to Fort Knox. Once she was inside, it locked itself again.

Momma passed through the indirectly lit lobby, treating the man behind the 24/7 reception desk to a smile. The desk itself served to conceal both a small armory of automatic weapons and an elaborate silent alarm that could be activated by a single button.

In her office on the third floor, a timer-activated pot yielded a single cup of black Haitian coffee. She took the cup to the sofa opposite a fruitwood-inlaid French desk from which she took several newspapers. She sipped as she read, nodding her approval.

The New York Times
August 3

BERN — In a surprise move, Swiss authorities have frozen bank accounts of GrünWelt, the international Green and anti–global warming organization, under international treaties waiving Swiss bank secrecy laws where international criminal activity is suspected.

The Swiss police, Interpol and unnamed law enforcement agencies have so far declined comment but a source who spoke on the condition of anonymity speculated the action was taken as the result of the discovery of an arms cache in the headquarters of a heretofore unknown branch of GrünWelt in San Juan, Puerto Rico, along with seizure of both written and computer records that implicate the organization in a number of violent acts directed against institutions and persons not subscribing to the concept of man-caused global warming.

Ivor Klingov, CEO of GrünWelt, denied any connection with the San Juan group and was quoted as saying . . .

Momma folded the paper, placed it back on the desk, and exchanged it for another.

The Washington Post
August 5

SAN JUAN, PR — Heime Norriaga, spokesperson for the Puerto Rico office of the Federal Bureau of Investigation, announced today that records of an alleged branch of the international conservation and anti–global warming organization GrünWelt seized in a raid days ago reveal a course of extreme and violent action against those with whom the organization disagreed as to the source of global warming or the fact of warming itself, as well as possible worldwide industrial sabotage and possible ties to a Chinese-owned company.

Although declining to make public the names of those arrested,

Mr. Norriaga stated the charges included weapons possession and possession of false identification, including forged passports. He also stated six of the men had international criminal records, as well as connections to the former Soviet special service.

It is unclear what other charges . . .

"Go gettum, Jason," Momma said to no one in particular, again swapping papers.

Chicago Tribune
August 6

LYON — At its headquarters here today, Interpol announced that records seized in Bern earlier this week definitely demonstrate the international anti–global warming and conservationist organization GrünWelt subsidized a secret branch in San Juan, Puerto Rico, and was, in turn, owned by a company suspected of having ties to the Chinese government. The duties of the San Juan "office" were not the slogans and peaceful advocacy of ecological "green" causes for which GrünWelt is known but intimidation, violence and, in at least one instance, murder.

Additionally, Interpol claims to be decoding special computer programs that may link the organization to a number of unexplained mine disasters, oil leaks and spills, gas explosions and other catastrophes of which GrünWelt seemed to have knowledge before the events occurred.

Interpol has posted names and photographs of suspects not in custody in all 29 participating nations. A spokesperson for Greenpeace and other "green" organizations denounced Grün-Welt as . . .

Momma drained the last drops of coffee as she dropped all three papers into a magazine rack. Sitting behind the desk, she picked up the phone, the only object other than a computer monitor on the leather-inlay surface.

A response was almost instant. "Yes, ma'am?"

"Our man Jason Peters, find him."

"How soon do you need that information?"

"No rush," Momma replied. "But somewhere down the line we gonna need him again an' I 'spect he don' wanna be found."

EPILOGUE

**Sark, British Channel Islands
November**

Painting the placid blues and greens of the Tyrrhenian Sea upon which Ischia floated so placidly was very different from portraying the gray violence of the English Channel. The wind was as native here as the rock outcroppings, the fields of yellow sea oats, and the universally unpaved lanes from which almost all motorized traffic was banned. The wind hummed, sang, or howled. It was rarely silent.

And it changed the seascape from second to second. As Jason set up his easel—he had learned the hard way to make sure it was secured lest it take flight—the dove-colored waves were frothing against the rocks below in rhythmic surges. By the time he had mixed his pigments, the water had become a darker gray, spitting angry foam.

It had all been very frustrating until he had learned how to approximate the shades of dun color and premix them.

Standing on a naked cliff, Jason paused long enough to watch Pangloss in his perpetual exploring expedition, although the dog had covered almost all the tiny island's three by one and a half miles, including the unfortunate excavation of a neighbor's flower garden.

The smallest of the inhabited Channel Islands, Sark bore the footprints of stone-age men, Roman conquerors, Vikings, Normans, and invading Germans during World War II. Since the grant of a fiefdom by Queen Elizabeth I and the lord's right of first night with the island's brides, all unobserved since long before living memory, were finally abolished, no one was certain if the feudal lord was still required to keep a musket at hand for defense of the island. That was the major change of the century. Or the last several centuries, for that matter. Under elected council or feudal lord, horses and cows still outnumbered the five hundred or so hardy souls who called the hilly, rocky island home. Except for the advent of the bicycle, transportation along the dusty lanes was the same as it had been in the days of Good Queen Bess, lanes that became quagmires with the winter rains. Transportation to and from the island was pretty much the same, too. The Isle of Sark Shipping Company's vessels were now turbo-powered and steel-hulled rather than wooden sailing ships, making two or three trips a day, but Guernsey was still Sark's only destination. People still greeted both friend and stranger with cheery hellos.

Here, Jason felt relatively safe. Anyone approaching his house would be on a bicycle, in one of the island's two-wheeled horse carts, on the back of one of the shaggy ponies, or on foot. True, they would be concealed by the lane being sunken between two rock outcroppings, but it was a good hundred yards from the road to the house, ample time to mount a defense when warned by the sophisticated system of weight and motion detectors.

He had kept this in mind when he had leased the three-hundred-year-old Norman stone cottage on the edge of an apple orchard. The relentless wind had shortened and bent the trees like the rank and file of arthritic old men. Behind the house was the promontory from which Jason was painting today. He had wanted to buy the building, but the Channel Islands' peculiar real estate laws made purchases by those not living there year-round difficult, in addition to the fact that only about twenty percent of land for sale was on the "open" market—that is, available to nonresidents.

So, he had leased it, moving his entire household from the sun of the southern Italian coast in summer to the gloom and chill of the English Channel in fall. The furniture had survived largely intact, due to Gianna's close supervision of the packers and movers, all related to her in some fashion no doubt.

Gianna had not fared as well. After ten days of English cuisine and weather, she had begged Jason to forgive her but she needed to leave this place where the fish was salted, meat was cremated, and vegetables were reduced to tasteless mush. And it rained for days on end. Nowhere, she wailed, could one find oregano, cumin, bay, or the other seasonings of her native land. The single store's selection of wine was a meager and seemingly random selection of French bottles most probably rejected by the better shops in Le Havre, an hour's airfoil ride from Guernsey. Besides, the grass-fed meat was too stringy to be considered fit for human consumption and the sole butcher had never heard of veal. Admittedly, tomatoes were plentiful, but somehow they were inadequate when compared to those of Italy. Besides, the perpetual damp aggravated her rheumatism, a malaise of which Jason had never before heard her complain.

Jason had summoned one of the island's two-wheeled horse-drawn carts, onto which he had loaded Gianna along with such possessions as she had wished, including a generous severance check. He followed behind on his newly acquired bicycle until they reached La Maseline Jetty from which all island departures took place. Tears running down her cheeks, she had waved farewell from the deck as the boat pulled out into the Channel, rounded a huge jutting rock, and disappeared.

But not before selecting her successor, Abigail Prince. Mrs. Prince was a grandmotherly type with a Wagnerian bosom, a smile missing a few teeth, and a lineage stretching back to the days the island was governed by the dukes of Normandy. Even though she was a relentless cleaner, she had the English love of animals, managing to overlook Robespierre's peccadillos and Pangloss's fondness for sneaking a nap on Jason's bed when he thought no one was looking.

It had taken her a couple of weeks to abandon her machinations to introduce Jason to the few single women on the island, mostly sorrowful widows or women who for one reason or another had been passed over as the first rounds of marriage rampaged among their contemporaries.

Jason put his brush down on the tray under the canvas and scowled. The damn wind had shifted again, sending spray up from the opposite side of the rocks below. In the past, he would tune out such annoyances by simply turning up whatever he was listening to on his iPod and letting the music sweep him along. Lately he had left his earphones inside, preferring to let the wind's music play a part in reproducing the slashing waves below.

But that wasn't the wind.

It was the dog barking.

For reasons known only to Pangloss, he had begun barking at anything that moved: a meandering cow, the postman on his bicycle, even the occasional tractor going to or from the field—the only motorized vehicles permitted on the island. Yelling at him to hush did no more good than howling at the moon might have.

At first, Jason thought the mutt had unearthed another mole, though how the tiny animals survived in Sark's rocky soil was still a mystery. But no, it was something in the lane hidden by the rocks.

Jason's right hand reflexively went to the Glock in its holster at his back. Slipping from rock to rock, he quickly made his way back to the cottage. The angle of the sunken road gave him a clear advantage and he reached the back door before anyone could have made it from the road to the house.

He dashed through the kitchen, catching Mrs. Prince red-handed in pouring a bowl of cream for Robespierre from the morning's milk delivery, a luxury she admitted only enhanced the cat's sense of entitlement. Surprised at his sudden appearance, she watched him take giant strides across the single room that served as dining and living room toward the rough wooden staircase leading to his bedroom, the only room on the second story.

Oblivious to anything but his own comfort, Robespierre continued his dainty sipping of his treat.

Reaching his bedroom, Jason pulled aside the curtains that covered the one window facing the road. The added height enabled him to partially see into the sunken pathway. He was looking at a horse in the harness used to pull one of the island's two-wheeled wagons, a vehicle that served to haul freight or people.

A wagon would be hard pressed to carry more than three adults, including a driver with the local knowledge to find Jason's house. There could be no more than two intruders unless others were infiltrating his property by the orchard. A quick glance showed naked tree limbs supplicating an unheeding sky. No sign of human life.

Good. Two he could handle if need be.

He knelt, rolling up a woven hearth rug, a local product the former occupant didn't think worth the effort to take with him. It was perfect to conceal a modification Jason had made. Underneath the rug, a rectangle had been cut into the wooden floor. Lifting the specially modified boards, Jason was looking at a small arsenal.

A Heckler & Koch PS61 with scope, identical to the sniper's rifle he had used in Africa; a Striker Street Sweeper shotgun, whose stubby barrel and rotary cylinder gave it the appearance of a hand-held Gatling gun; and a Mac 10, a banana clip already fully loaded and inserted into the machine pistol. Besides extra ammunition, the cache was supplemented with a half dozen grenades, both fragmentation and flash-bang; a vest of Kevlar body armor; and his killing knife. Since access to the Channel Islands was only from France and the UK, both Common Market countries, no customs or immigration controls existed. The weaponry had been shipped from La Havre.

He chose the Street Sweeper, checked to make sure there was a full complement of twelve-gauge shells in the cylinder, and dropped the boards back into place.

Before descending the stairs, he took another look out the window and stopped, dumbstruck.

Shit!

He reversed his course to furiously replace what he had removed and cover the hiding place with the rug. He was just smoothing it out when the front door opened downstairs.

He heard voices, feminine voices, but could not make out the words. He went downstairs.

Maria stood just inside the door. Behind her was a white-haired older man Jason didn't know. The rough tweed trousers stuffed into rubber wellies suggested he was local. He had a suitcase in each hand.

"Well, Mr. Peters," Mrs. Prince asked, "will you be extending a proper greeting to the young lady who's come all this way or not?" She nodded toward the man in knee boots. "And Mr. Frache there is getting no younger while he waits."

Jason momentarily wondered who employed whom. Maria correctly interpreted his expression and let a smile at his confusion creep across her face. Pangloss, suffering no uncertainty, bounced back and forth from Maria, barking joyfully. Finished with licking an empty bowl, Robespierre demonstrated the aloof disinterest only a cat can display.

Jason stepped around the dog, whose exultant glee belied the fact this woman had been out of his and his master's life for nearly half a year. Ingrate that he was, Pangloss seemed to become increasingly delirious in his happiness with every second.

Reaching for the two suitcases, Jason said, "I'll take those."

Mr. Frache set them down and stood, looking at Jason expectantly. "That'll be eight quid, six."

Maria shrugged, doing a poor imitation of being embarrassed. "I barely made the connection at Heathrow, didn't have a chance to change currency from euros to pounds before catching the flight to Guernsey."

"I assume you paid the ferry," Jason said sourly.

"They took a credit card. Mr. Frache here wants cash."

"And what if I hadn't been here?"

"But you are. Jason, don't be like that. I thought you'd be glad to see me."

He was.

But he would be damned if he was going to admit it this easily. Other than an occasional text, he had not heard from her for months. She had not even acknowledged receipt of his new location, much less acknowledged that she cared. Now she appeared unannounced, certain he would take her in. Let her suffer a few minutes.

"If you want me to go away, just say so."

"If I do, who'll pay Mr. Frache to take you back to the ferry?"

She stared at him, he at her. Later both would swear the other broke into laughter first. Whoever it was, an instant later, they were embracing.

Jason never remembered Mrs. Prince making some excuse to visit the small local market as she joined Mr. Frache, closing the door softly behind her. In fact, Jason remembered little other than the wild, joyous, noisy lovemaking that occupied the rest of the afternoon.

Tomorrow there would be ample time for accusations and explanations, justifications and excuses. Home is not always a geographic location. It is, as Pliny the Elder observed nearly two millennia ago, where the heart is. Maria was home.

AUTHOR'S NOTES

I'm unaware of any evidence of grapes growing in Iceland, today or during the Medieval Warm Period (c. 800–1300), but there is no doubt that wine grapes were (and are again) grown in improbably northern latitudes. Iceland does have a local "wine," however. It is made from berries, not grapes.

The fact that some ice caps, or glaciers, are melting is true. But then, some, as noted in the story, are growing. As far as I know, no one has come up with a plausible explanation for the inconsistency.

The hockey stick and the Climatic Research Unit have, in fact, been pretty well discredited. Dr. Kench's study of the growth/diminution of Pacific islands is accurately, if briefly, described. That does not mean, however, that there is no real global warming or that it isn't caused by CO_2 emissions. Doesn't mean that it is, either. Reputable scientists on both sides are still unable to convince either one another or those who stand to politically or economically profit from either side of the controversy.

The only thing that is certain is that the statement that "there is no disputing global warming or its cause" is grossly inaccurate. The debate is likely to continue for years. Perhaps into the next ice age.

I plead the excuse of literary license for rearranging the geography of part of Old San Juan. Although there are houses built into the old wall, Calle Luna 23 is not one of them, nor are there residences along the fortifications of the three-story town house variety.

Likewise as to the carbon-credit scam participated in by the Chinese company. The research required to adequately understand the market in carbon credits is not justified by the brief mention of it here and neither is the long and boring explanation necessary to explain it.

Although I haven't tried it, I'm told the sugar-saltpeter combination makes a safe and workable smoke bomb.

G. L.
2013

Copyright © 2013 by Gregg Loomis

Cover design by Mauricio Díaz

ISBN 978-1-4804-0552-3

Published in 2013 by MysteriousPress.com/Open Road Integrated Media
345 Hudson Street
New York, NY 10014
www.mysteriouspress.com
www.openroadmedia.com

OPEN ROAD

INTEGRATED MEDIA

Open Road Integrated Media is a digital publisher and multimedia content company. Open Road creates connections between authors and their audiences by marketing its ebooks through a new proprietary online platform, which uses premium video content and social media.

Videos, Archival Documents, and New Releases

Sign up for the Open Road Media newsletter and get news delivered straight to your inbox.

Sign up now at
www.openroadmedia.com/newsletters

FIND OUT MORE AT
WWW.OPENROADMEDIA.COM

FOLLOW US:
@openroadmedia and
Facebook.com/OpenRoadMedia

CPSIA information can be obtained at www.ICGtesting.com
Printed in the USA
BVOW070105080513

320153BV00002B/6/P